UNEXPECTED DESIRES

Silence crept between them, this time soft and comfortable, measured by the tick of a wall clock Sean hadn't even noticed until now, the stir of branches against the cottage wall as the wind lifted them, the rhythm of Grace's breathing.

For the life of him, he couldn't have pinpointed when it changed. Became more. But change it did, and suddenly he found himself aware of more than just Grace's warmth against him. He knew without looking exactly what part of her anatomy pressed against his ribcage. Felt the warmth of her breath through his t-shirt. Inhaled the headiness of her strawberry scent.

And knew by her stillness that something had shifted for her, too.

His throat went dry.

Damn.

This was so not supposed to happen. He'd already had this conversation with himself. Multiple times. He didn't get involved with women like Grace. Didn't do commitment. And sure as hell wasn't about to take on fatherhood...in *any* guise.

"Grace..."

Her breathing stopped.

He closed his eyes and gritted his teeth, trying to find the words to explain why he couldn't do this. Hell, trying to *remember* why. He sucked in a steadying breath and pulled back to look down at her, at the liquid heat of dark-chocolate eyes, the flush of heightened color across her cheeks. A low, heavy ache spread through him. Grace's lips parted. Reason crumbled.

Praise for **Gwynneth Ever After,**
First in the *Ever After* Series

"Sweet, real, and sensual, Gwynneth Ever After is one of the most heart-warming romances I've read. A delicious hero and a sigh-worthy happily ever after--prepare to fall in love." - *Sharon Page, USA Today Bestselling Author*

"Gwynneth Ever After is double-chocolate cake" - *The Romance Reviews*

"I couldn't put it down, the characters became instant favorites, and the story was simply beautiful." - *Literal Addiction*

"Endlessly fun and charming! Gwynnth Ever After is the ultimate Cinderella tale complete with toddlers, single parenthood, and paparazzi." - *Carolyn Crane, author of The Disillusionists*

"…endearing characters, full of warmth and depth, in a beautifully compelling story so deftly told it made me feel like I was coming home to old friends." - *Romantic Reads and Such*

"I laughed, I cried, I cringed and by the end of the story, I definitely wanted more." - *Unconventional Book Reviews*

FOREVER GRACE

BY LINDA POITEVIN

FOREVER GRACE

Published by Michem Publishing

Cover art by Designs by Lynsey

ISBN: 9780991995837

In loving memory of René Poitevin

ACKNOWLEDGMENTS

As much as the responsibility for writing a story ultimately rests with its author, there are usually many people involved in its creation. Such is certainly the case with **Forever Grace**, and I'd like to extend my heartfelt gratitude to two in particular: Pat, my unflaggingly patient husband, for putting up with me through the rollercoaster of emotions I tend to experience during the writing process; and Marie Bilodeau, my writing buddy, for her support, encouragement, and the many, many laughs over our weekly coffee. I really couldn't have done this without both of you!

Special thanks also go out to Laura Paquet for her fabulous copy edits (and for not complaining when I missed my deadline with her not once but three times); Lynsey, my amazing cover designer who gave me exactly what I wanted even when I didn't know myself; Jen Desmarais for what has to have been the speediest beta read ever; and Ottawa family lawyer Jennifer Reynolds, for making the time to answer my questions about custody issues.

And finally, thank you to the many readers who enjoyed the first book in the *Ever After* series so much that they wanted a second. I hope you love reading **Forever Grace** as much as I loved writing it!

Chapter 1

Grace Daniels grabbed the smoking skillet on the stove, only to drop it again with a gasp of pain. Would she ever learn that the damned handle got as hot as the pan? Four weeks of burning herself, along with the food, and still the lesson hadn't sunk in. She snatched up a tea towel and dragged the pan off the burner, then thrust her hand under the tap. Turning on the cold water, she grimaced at the crisp, smoking black mess on the stove. So much for tonight's fried potatoes with sausage dinner. She sighed. Canned ravioli it was. Again. If the kids didn't mutiny.

Glancing out the window overlooking the deck of the borrowed cottage, she did a quick head count. Joshua was still curled up in the chair hammock with his book. Lilliane and Sage were at the picnic table, practicing their letters in the late afternoon sun that filtered through the brilliant autumn leaves. That was three present and accounted for, and the fourth was due to wake up from her nap at any—

"Maaa-ma!" came a faint call from the rear of the cottage. "Mama mama mama maaa-ma!"

The thin knife that had taken up residence in Grace's heart twisted. She blinked back a prickle behind her eyes. An entire month of repeated encouragement, and Annabelle still hadn't grasped the auntie concept. While Grace understood the two-year-old's insistence on calling her "mama," every utterance of the word seemed to add to the pall hanging over them all.

"Maaa-ma!"

Dabbing her hand dry with the tea towel, Grace dug deep to find a smile. Then she dropped the towel onto the counter and turned to answer the summons. "Coming, punkin!" she called.

Seconds later, she opened the door to the bedroom she shared with Annabelle, and the toddler squealed in delight.

"Mama!" Annabelle held out the soiled diaper she had removed and announced, "Poop."

Grace swallowed a gag. "I see that."

She relieved Annabelle of the soiled cloth and wrapped it up so the mess was hidden. Then she regarded the beaming, curly-headed imp with a wry shake of the head. "So. Diaper pins just made it onto tomorrow's grocery list, did they?"

"Poop!" said Annabelle. "Peee-yew!"

"Peee-yew," Grace agreed. She dropped the diaper into a covered soaking pail, then returned to lift the toddler from the portable crib. With what she considered admirable expertise, considering the scant month she'd been on the job, she plopped Annabelle onto the vinyl-topped dresser that served as a change table, washed and re-diapered her, then set the little girl on the floor. Annabelle wobbled for a moment, then found her balance and toddled back to the crib.

"Bankie?"

Grace lifted the bunny-decorated blanket, mercifully unscathed by the poop incident—she still hadn't recovered from the baby's trauma the last time she'd had to launder the treasure—and passed it to the little girl. Annabelle grabbed it in a hug, nuzzling her face into its folds. She pointed a chubby finger at the crib again.

"Sussie?"

Grace followed her niece's point to the pacifier wedged in the corner. She shook her head. "No way, munchkin. Sussie stays in your bed, remember?"

Annabelle peered through the mesh side of her bed and waved. "Night-night, Sussie."

Then, still clutching her blanket, she headed for the hall. She paused in the doorway to look back at Grace.

"Fine Jossa?"

"Yes, you may find Joshua, but you leave your diaper on this time." Grace put on a stern face and repeated, "Diaper on."

"Dipe on," agreed Annabelle. She turned and headed down the hallway at an unsteady run. "Jossa! Jossa! I up, Jossa!"

Grace waited, listening for the sliding door and the voice of the big brother Annabelle so adored. At only ten years old, Joshua had proved mature beyond his years. Grace didn't know how she would have managed without his help and guidance as she'd taken over the little family. Hell, with the exception of Annabelle, who was too young to be affected, all of them were mature beyond their years. Far too much so, but that's what happened when—

The knife in her heart twisted again, cutting off the thought. No. No dwelling. She had things to do. Little people to look after, dinner to remake...

Her gaze dropped to the sheets in the portable crib and she wrinkled her nose.

And more laundry to do. Again.

She sighed, thinking wistfully of her other life. A life where she'd been a successful thirty-two-year-old business analyst who wore smart pantsuits and wholly impractical shoes instead of blue jeans and sneakers. Where she'd traveled all over the globe and had hotel laundry services instead of being tucked into the backwoods of Perth, Ontario, with a crotchety old washing machine that needed its rinse cycle reset three times before all the soap was gone.

Out in the living room, the sliding glass door to the deck opened.

"Jossa!" squealed Annabelle.

"Annabelly with the big round belly!" Joshua replied.

The little girl shrieked with laughter, and Grace smiled, picturing her nephew poking a finger at the toddler's belly button and grinning one of his rare, lopsided grins.

More giggles followed, and then Joshua called out, "Aunt Grace? I'm taking Annabelle onto the deck with me. Don't worry, it's warm enough, and I'll keep an eye on her."

"Thank you, Josh," Grace called back. "I'll have dinner ready soon."

The sliding door opened again, but this time it stayed open and Grace heard the screen pulled shut instead. Josh knew she liked to be able to hear them when Annabelle was outside. He was careful never to forget. None of them ever forgot. Not their manners, not their chores, not anything that was asked of them. Ever.

For the third time, the knife twisted in Grace's heart. Also for the third time, she pushed away the melancholy and turned to practicalities, because time for dwelling was a luxury she didn't have these days. Not while Julianne's children needed her. Leaning down, she moved Sussie out of the way, gathered up Annabelle's sheets, then trudged down the hallway to the mudroom off the kitchen, where the ancient washing machine resided. No dryer, but it was enough for now. As long as the kids stayed safe, that was all that mattered. All that Julianne had wanted.

Grace lifted the lid on the washer and stuffed the sheets in. Laundry, then dinner, then a movie, she decided, and tomorrow, a coveted trip into town with a stop for ice cream.

And a call to the hospital.

Sean McKittrick moved the driver's seat as far back as it would go and then, using both hands, maneuvered his plaster-encased leg past the car doorjamb. His foot landed with a thud in the gravel of the driveway, sending a jolt through the limb that traveled all the way up to his gritted teeth. He squeezed his eyes closed and waited for the breath to return to his lungs. Damn, he'd be glad when it stopped doing that at every little bump.

Three more weeks, he reminded himself. *Just three more weeks.*

Followed by a leg brace and months of physiotherapy, but hey, one hurdle at a time, right?

With the pain reduced again to its usual aching throb, he set his right foot beside the first and twisted around to reach the crutches he'd stowed in the back seat. A grunt and an almighty heave brought him to his feet, where he teetered for a precarious few seconds before finding his balance. Then, glumly, he regarded the sloping, uneven stretch of path between him and the cottage porch. Huh. Maybe it was as bad as he'd remembered. He sighed. Well, he was here now, and he couldn't very well sleep in the SUV. Nor could he manage the trip back to Ottawa today. He'd already skipped the last two doses of pain meds so he could drive up here in the first place. If he didn't get something more than ibuprofen into him soon, he'd be tempted to rip the damned leg off altogether and be done with it.

Besides, the peace and quiet of autumn here was exactly what he needed. No one dropping in to see how he was doing, and no noisy neighbors. Hell, no neighbors at all at this time of year. He surveyed the cottage with satisfaction, letting the stillness penetrate. Set about ten feet lower than the driveway and tucked beneath massive maples and pines, the little cedar-clad box wasn't much to look at, but it was watertight and comfortable.

He slammed the driver's door and crutched his way around to the rear hatch, his travels made more awkward than usual by the crutches sinking into the driveway's gravel. Just as he reached in for his duffel bag, the cell phone hanging from his belt rang. He unclipped it, glanced at the display, and grimaced. Yep. Right on time, as expected. He thumbed the button to answer.

"Hey," he said. "How's the happy honeymooner?"

"A little stunned to find his cousin has up and left town three weeks after being shot and having his leg put back together like a bloody jigsaw puzzle," a familiar and famous Welsh-accented voice retorted. "I thought we agreed you'd come and stay with us when we got back."

Sean snorted. "You and Gwyn agreed. I don't remember having any more say in that than I did the nurse idea."

"The nurse idea was the only way they would release you from hospital," Gareth Connor reminded him. "*And* the only way Gwyn agreed to leave you here alone in the first place."

"Yeah, well, I decided I'd recover faster at the cottage than I would at your place. No offense, cuz, but watching the two of you make post-honeymoon cow's eyes at one another for the next three weeks wasn't my idea of fun. And as cute as

Gwyn's kids are…" Sean shuddered. "Not my idea of a peaceful convalescence."

"And being on your own out in the middle of nowhere seemed like a better idea how? You're in a full leg cast and on crutches, Sean. What happens if you fall?"

"Then I imagine I'll figure out a way to get up. Look, I'm not planning to go on any hikes, Gareth. I'm just going to read and nap and hang out in the hammock on the back deck. I'll be fine."

"You could have at least taken the nurse with you."

"Are you nuts? Have Perky Pam at the cottage for three weeks with me? God, no." Sean shuddered again, remembering the cheerfully efficient private nurse Gareth had insisted on hiring for him. Nice enough. Cute, even. But the woman had never stopped talking. Ever. He shook his head. "I'd have had to kill her, and that's kind of frowned upon in my line of work."

"So is stupidity, I would think."

Sean eyed the path to the cottage once more, inclined to agree with Gareth but not about to tell him so. Especially when his gaze settled on what looked like awfully fresh bear scat just off the driveway. Great. Just freaking great.

"Gareth. I'm thirty-eight years old, I have my cell phone, and I'm a cop. If anything goes wrong, I'm pretty sure I can figure out what to do. Now, I know you're used to getting your own way, being a Hollywood star and all —"

"Screw off."

Sean grinned and continued as if he hadn't heard, "But if you don't mind, I'd like to get settled sometime before dark."

"You really are annoying sometimes."

"Back atcha, Connor."

Gareth's annoyed sigh echoed down the line. "Fine. Have it your way. But keep your cell phone on you at all times, and call me every couple of days so I at least know you're still alive."

"Anything else, *dad?*"

"Damn it, Sean—"

"I'm sorry," Sean interrupted. He needed to get off this damned leg before it collapsed under him. Time to stop needling his cousin. "I know you're worried, but I really am all right. They put the cast on yesterday, the incision has healed beautifully, and they said I handle the crutches like a pro. And yes, I'll call every few days. You have my word. In the meantime, say hi to Gwyn and the kids for me, all right?"

"I still don't like this," Gareth muttered. "But fine. Just look after yourself."

The connection went dead, and Sean slid the cell phone back into its clip on his belt. Then, the sweat of exertion already turning his shirt clammy, he took the duffel bag from beside the four bulging grocery sacks in the trunk, slung it across his back, and settled his crutches into his armpits for the first of several trips down the slope to the cottage.

Chapter 2

With Sage keeping Annabelle out from under foot, and Lilliane and Joshua helping to carry groceries, Grace had the minivan emptied in short order after their jaunt into Perth. Spirits and energies had remained high all the way back to the cottage, possibly due to the sugar rush of their final stop. The ice cream had been an enormous hit all around, especially with Annabelle, who had delighted in smearing the cold confection over most of her body.

Grace glanced into the living room and grinned at the sight of quiet little Sage patiently trying to wipe the toddler's sticky face as she sang, "This is the way we wash our face, wash our face, wash our face..."

"Aunt Grace?"

She looked down at Lilliane, whose arms strained under the bag of potatoes she carried. She shoved the cans of stew and ravioli she was holding onto the shelf, and relieved the eight-year-old of her load.

"Thank you, sweetie," she said, smoothing her free hand over her niece's dark hair. "You're an amazing helper. You, too, Josh."

Her nephew shrugged. "We're a family," he said, his voice quiet. "It's what we're supposed to do."

Grace forced a smile and reached past him to flick on the kitchen light switch. The early evening gloom retreated. "You're right. It is what we're supposed to do. And now I'm supposed to make dinner, which is already late, and you are supposed to go and find something fun to do until it's ready."

Josh and Lilliane exchanged a glance.

"Ravioli again?" Lilliane asked with studied casualness.

Grace laughed. "How about I take another shot at the sausages and fried potatoes? I promise not to burn them this time."

Another glance was exchanged.

"If you're sure..." said Josh.

She ruffled his hair playfully. "I'm sure, smarty pants. Now go, before I change my mind and put you to work peeling potatoes."

"Do you want me to do that for you? I can."

Grace held back a sigh. "I was only kidding. You've done enough today, Josh. Now go find something you want to do."

"Can I go next door to read?"

"Do you think you'll have enough light?"

"Sunset isn't for another half hour."

"All right. Just make sure you're listening for me when I call, and use the side door so Annabelle doesn't see you leave."

Joshua nodded agreement, picked up the book he'd left on the counter earlier, and slipped into the mudroom behind the kitchen. A few seconds later, Grace watched through the kitchen window as he disappeared along the path leading to the neighboring cottage, where he liked to go when he needed a break from all-female company.

Luc, her friend and lawyer who owned their cottage, had said his neighbor only put in an appearance during the summer months, so letting Josh hang out and read on the deck would be fine. She'd been a mess of nerves the first few times, hating that he was out of sight and reach, but now that their little family was settling into a routine, she'd begun to relax. It did Josh good to have the independence, and he was still near enough that he could hear her call to him.

And she could hear him if anything went wrong.

She opened the window a few inches, then turned and smiled at Lilliane. "You, too, kiddo. Go find something fun to do. You're officially off duty."

Too-serious brown eyes regarded her. "What about you, Aunt Grace? Are you ever off duty?"

Grace shrugged off thoughts of how bone-weary she was these days. She gave her niece a wink. "Didn't you know? That's what kids' bedtimes are for. And cartoons. In fact, why don't you put a cartoon on now? Something Annabelle likes, so she'll leave you alone for a while."

Lilliane rewarded her suggestion with a smile. "I'll put on *Snow White*. It's her favorite."

"Lovely," said Grace. Then, as her niece joined Annabelle and Sage in the next room, she took a paring knife from the drawer, slit open the bag of potatoes, and gritted her teeth in preparation for yet another onslaught of *Some Day My Prince Will Come*.

Sean came awake to the screech of a blue jay outside his bedroom window. He listened to its scolding for a few minutes, a grin on his face. Noisy, yes. But it still beat the hell out of being roused from a nap by Perky Pam's, "*Wakey, wakey! If you keep sleeping now, you'll never sleep tonight, you know!*"

And Gareth had wanted him to bring her along to the cottage? Ha. Not in a million years.

Sean stretched leisurely. By the time he'd finished hauling the groceries in from the SUV, turned himself into a pretzel in order to get the cottage's water supply back on, and finally been able to take the long-overdue painkillers, his leg had felt like someone had run it through a grinder. He was much relieved to find that sleep and medication had worked a small miracle to ease the discomfort.

First, because he really needed time to recuperate away from the well-meaning questions and concerns of so many. And second, having to admit to his cousin he'd made a mistake in coming here—or even worse, ask for a rescue—would so not have been cool. Gareth would have never let him live it down.

Flexing the foot of his injured leg, Sean gauged the pain level. Definitely better. Tolerable, even. And, judging by the deepening shadows in the bedroom, he'd slept a good three hours, which meant he could take another painkiller soon. He grinned again, feeling quite vindicated in his decision to make the trip out here. A couple of weeks of tranquility were exactly what he needed.

He levered himself upright, swung the cast off the bed, and reached for the crutches. In short order, he visited the facilities, took another capsule, and made himself a cup of tea in a spill-proof travel mug that he tucked into a pocket for transportation. He eyed the bottle of Scotch sitting on the counter as he passed by.

Soon, he promised himself. As soon as he was off the pills. Two days, maybe three, and he'd start cutting back. See if he couldn't wean himself off them by the end of next weekend, so he could at least enjoy a good, stiff drink—his first since the weekend before getting in the way of that damned bullet.

For now, however, tea, his hammock—if he could manage to get into the thing without killing himself—and a lakeside evening would do quite nicely.

He flicked off the kitchen light switch, then traveled across the living room to the sliding glass door onto the wooden deck. Thud, swing. Thud, swing. He grimaced. Damned if he wasn't getting the hang of this crutch thing. He flipped the lock on the door and slid it open, then maneuvered awkwardly through the gap—in time for a child's angry wail to shatter the early evening silence.

Sean's head shot up. He stared through the shadowed woods at the cottage next door, its partial outline visible through the leaves and gathering shadows. A *kid?* What in—

The scrape of a shoe against the deck caught his ear. He swiveled, teetered, regained his balance. He gaped at the boy who had frozen, half out of Sean's hammock, eyes wide and terrified behind wire-framed glasses. For a long few seconds, neither of them moved. Sean recovered first, just as another screech echoed through the trees.

"Who the *hell* are you?" he snarled, thudding toward the boy. "And what in God's name is that racket?"

The boy bolted from the hammock and dived past him, headed for the stairs. Sean threw out an arm to stop him. His fingers brushed against a nylon jacket but closed on air. One crutch fell away to land with a hollow thump on the wooden deck. Sean struggled for balance as the boy's footsteps thundered down the stairs and onto the dirt path through the trees dividing the cottages. Sean's free arm pinwheeled madly. He tipped forward. Back. Further forward. Then, losing the battle, he pitched full length onto the deck floor, white-hot agony tearing through his thigh.

"Son of a goddamn *bitch*," he bellowed.

CHAPTER 3

Grace met Joshua at the cottage door, heart lodged in her throat. She grabbed his shoulders, stopping him in mid-flight, the roar of a man's voice still echoing in her brain. "Josh? What happened? Who is that? Is it—?"

She broke off, glancing over her shoulder at the girls, clustered in the kitchen behind her. Pale, wide-eyed, silent. Even Annabelle had given up her tantrum, seeming to sense the sudden change in atmosphere. Grace swallowed hard and made an effort to pull her shredded nerves back together. She mustered a smile.

"It's all right, girls," she said. "I'm sure it's nothing. Right, Josh?"

It had to be nothing, because the alternative was unthinkable. If Barry had found them, if he was out here with them in those woods, in the middle of nowhere—

"It's not him," Josh panted. "It's someone else. I think he must own the other cottage. He startled me and I got scared. I ran."

Relief turned Grace's entire body to liquid, but somehow she managed to stay upright and pull her nephew into a fierce hug. "Of course you got scared," she said. "I'd have been terrified if someone yelled at me that way. And you were right to run."

Joshua shook his head against her, his nose scraping her collarbone. When had he grown so tall?

"No. He yelled after I left. His leg was hurt and he was on

crutches. I think he fell."

Grace pulled back, her gaze searching his. "Seriously?"

Guilt and lingering fear stared back at her from behind Josh's glasses. He nodded. "I think so."

"Shi—" Grace caught back the curse halfway through. She released her hold on her nephew and braced one hand on her hip, running the other through her hair. She forced herself to think past the instinct to pack up and flee. It wasn't Barry, she reminded herself. And if Josh was right and it was the cottage owner, Luc had said he was a decent guy. Or seemed to be. Or—

She drew a steadying breath. Whatever. The bottom line was that she had no reason to panic. Yet. Not until she'd at least assessed the situation. She reached past Joshua for her jacket, hanging on one of the hooks by the door.

"All right. I'll go over and make sure he's all right. Josh, you can serve dinner for everyone. It's on the stove keeping warm." She flashed him a grin. "And no, I didn't burn it."

She shrugged into the jacket and lifted her hair free. Instructions poured from her mouth. "Lilliane, you set the table for Josh, and Sage, you keep Annabelle out of trouble until dinner is ready. Josh, make sure you cut Annabelle's food up for her, all right? Do you think you can get her into her booster seat?"

Josh nodded, already stripping off his coat. "Aunt Grace, should I have gone back to help him?"

"No, sweetie, you were right to come and get me." She ruffled his hair. "I'll be back as quick as I can, but don't worry if I'm gone for a little while. If you need me, just call and I'll come running."

"Even if you're helping the man?" Lilliane asked.

"Or if you meet a bear?" Sage added.

"I'll drop the man on his head if I need to. Or throw him at any bear that comes along." Grace gave her nieces a wink that earned her a giggle in return. Then she turned to Josh and lowered her voice so the others wouldn't hear. "You lock the door behind me, and if anyone comes but me, you know where my cell phone is. Luc's number is in it. He'll know what to do. Got it?"

"Got it." Josh's too-serious gaze met hers. He held out a flashlight. "It's cloudy out there. It'll be dark by the time you come back."

Grace dropped a kiss on his forehead, took the flashlight, and smiled over her shoulder at the others before she stepped out the door into evening's rapidly fading light.

From his prone position, Sean stared up through the canopy of trees at the cloudy, darkening sky, deck planks digging into his shoulder blades. Out on the lake, a loon called, its haunting voice echoing across the water. A leaf drifted down from one of the maples and landed on his chest. He lifted it, peering at it through the gloom. Wondered how many more would cover him by morning. Or by the time someone came looking for him and found him dead of exposure, lying on his back just feet away from the protection of his cottage.

He considered making another attempt to rise, but the pain still thrumming along his bolted-and-wired-together thighbone was a serious deterrent. Best to give it a little longer to recover from the last effort. Passing out right now was definitely not in his best interests. He dropped the leaf back onto his chest and returned to staring at the sky.

The situation would have been funny if it wasn't so goddamn unnerving. His cell phone still lying beside the bed. The faulty lock on the sliding door barring him re-entry. One of his crutches shooting off between the rails and disappearing into the brush beside the deck. All the deck furniture—which might have aided his efforts to regain his feet—long since stored in the shed because he hadn't planned on returning to the cottage before spring. The encroaching dark, the rapidly cooling temperature, and the presence of that damned bear scat beside the driveway.

And the distinct possibility he'd dislodged at least one of the pins holding together his shattered leg.

A fine mess you've gotten yourself into this time, McKittrick. A fine, fine mess.

From the woods beyond the deck came the snap of a breaking twig, the sound of something pushing through the undergrowth. Something big. Sean tensed. What now? A freaking bear?

A flashlight beam wavered across the leafy bower above him.

"Hello?" a woman's voice called, its tone cautious. Guarded. "Is anyone there?"

Sean levered himself up onto his elbows. "Here! On the deck at the back."

"How badly are you hurt?"

"Apart from my pride?"

A pause. "Um, yes. Apart from that."

"No worse than I was before I fell off my crutches, I don't think. But I've lost one of the damned things over the side of the deck, and I can't get up."

More crashing of brush ensued. "Which side?"

"Opposite where you are now. And watch out for poison ivy. I cleared it out this summer, but I'm not sure I got it all."

The flashlight beam grew brighter and traveled around the deck. Branches and foliage rustled. A muttered "Hell!" came from the dark, followed by an exasperated "Seriously?"

"Problem?" Sean asked.

"You want the good news or the bad first?" The woman sighed and continued without waiting for his answer. "The good news is, I found your crutch. The bad news is that your poison ivy problem is back—and the crutch is in the middle of it. It will have plant oils all over it, so I'm going to have to wash it before you can use it."

Sean closed his eyes and lay back again. Wonderful. Just freaking wonderful. And all this because of some kid.

"I suppose he belongs to you, too," he growled.

"I beg your pardon?"

"The kid who caused this whole mess."

"How is this *his* fault?" The woman's voice went tart. "You're the one who yelled at him and took ten years off his life."

"He's the one who was trespassing."

"We didn't know anyone would be here."

"And that makes it okay to wander around my house?"

"He was sitting on your deck reading," she snapped. "It's not like he was doing any harm."

"Way to teach him about private property and laws, lady."

Silence. Then, "You know, for someone in your current predicament, you're being awfully snarky."

Sean opened his mouth to retort. He snapped it shut again. She had a point.

More silence.

A sigh.

"Do you have any gloves in the cottage?" she asked.

"No. I threw them out after dealing with the poison ivy this summer. I haven't replaced them. There's a bag of old cloths under the sink, but you'll have to go through the front door to get them. This one's locked."

"You locked yourself out?"

"The lock button is loose. I haven't gotten around to fixing it."

"I see. And is that Josh's fault, too?"

He ignored her. "Front door's unlocked. Light switch is on the wall beside it."

Her footsteps receded, and a few seconds later a light came on inside the cottage. Sean waited. And waited. And waited. He frowned. How long did it take to get a couple of rags? His mouth twisted. It would just figure if she was in there going through his stuff, robbing him blind. Maybe she and the kid had a scheme going. Son distracts a cottager, causing unknown injuries, and then mom steps in to "help" and cleans out the place.

Sean winced at the weirdness of his own thoughts.

Whoa. Put a cop on painkillers and stand back from the imagination.

Another light came on in the cottage, this one in the living room, and the door slid open. Sean looked over at the woman who stepped out, scanning her with a practiced eye. Caucasian. Five feet, five inches tall—maybe six—it was harder to estimate height from a ground position. Straight, long brown hair, average build, wearing black pants and a red, thigh-length jacket, cinched in at the waist. The woman turned to him, the light from inside falling across her face.

And damned good looking, too.

Kids, Sean. Even if she's not married, you don't do kids, remember?

His gaze dropped to the bundle she carried. He frowned. "Blankets?"

"And a pillow." She crossed the deck to kneel beside him. "This is going to take longer than I thought, so I need to go home and check on the kids before I rescue your crutch and give it a bath. Then we'll get you upright and back inside."

He lifted his head from the planks so she could tuck the pillow beneath him. "Kids, plural? How many?"

"Four." She unfolded a blanket and spread it over him.

Four? He reappraised her as she unfolded a second cover.

"That's a lot of kids."

"They're not—" She broke off. "Maybe to some. To me, it's just the right number."

"And your husband agrees?"

"I'm not married." A third blanket followed the first two, and the woman pushed to her feet. "I'll be back as soon as I can. Don't run off anywhere."

"Funny."

"I try."

"One last thing before you go. In my bedroom, behind the door, there's a shotgun. The shells are in the bedside table drawer."

She went still. "You keep a gun?"

"I bring one with me when I come out here, as a precaution. For bears. There was a sow and her cubs hanging around the area this summer, and fresh scat beside the driveway when I pulled in earlier. They'll be trying to fatten themselves up for the winter, and I'd rather not have to fight them off with my bare hands if they decide to come investigate."

The woman stayed quiet for few seconds, probably mulling over the bear idea. Good. Maybe she'd take her oversized brood and go home.

"I don't like guns," she said.

"You'd like cleaning up my remains a lot less," he pointed out. "I think."

Her gaze met his. In the faint light coming from the cottage, he couldn't make out the color of her eyes, but he could see the tilt of one eyebrow above them.

"You sure about that?" she asked. But she disappeared into the cottage again, and re-emerged a few minutes later with his 12-gauge in hand.

Sean raised an eyebrow of his own. She might not like guns, but the way she held it told him she'd handled them before. She crossed to his side a second time, leaning down to place the gun at his side and drop a handful of slugs into his hand.

"I'll be back soon," she said. Warm fingers curled over his. "Hang tight."

Sean watched the flashlight beam disappear into the night again.

CHAPTER 4

As soon as she reached the shelter of the trees, Grace paused to regroup. Leaning against a birch that flanked the path, she closed her eyes and sucked in the deep, steadying breath she'd needed since a man's bellow had reached her in her kitchen. Since she had pulled Josh into her arms, the specter of Barry looming in her brain. Since her entire world had teetered for a moment on the brink of implosion.

She took another breath, in through her nostrils, out through her mouth.

It wasn't Barry.

Breathe in. Breathe out.

Barry hadn't found them.

In. Out.

They were safe. At least for now.

Slowly, the rush of blood in Grace's eardrums subsided until other sounds could penetrate again. The rustle of the wind through the trees over her head, the scrabble of something small in the dry leaves to the side of the path. The faint who-whoo of an owl near the cottage she'd just left.

And the distinct snap of branches breaking beneath something substantially larger than a mouse.

Grace's heart did a back flip and crawled into her throat.

How many bears had he said were in the area?

She shone the flashlight beam into the trees. A pair of eyes—at about the height of a bear standing on its hind legs, she estimated—gleamed back at her. Her innards turned to water.

She turned to run, but instead sprawled headlong onto the leaf-covered path and watched in horror as the flashlight rolled out of reach. Behind her, more branches snapped as something pushed through them. That did it. Her fallen neighbor might not be able to shoot whatever hunted her, but maybe a shot would scare—

A trill reached her, and her throat clamped shut on a half-formed screech. She listened to an answering call and more rustling. Relief flooded her. Raccoons. She'd been running from raccoons. And she'd nearly shrieked her head off over them.

She dropped her head onto her forearm. Laughter born of sheer reaction burbled up in her. Dear Lord, imagine if he'd heard her. What would he have thought? And if he *had* fired a shot...what would the poor kids have thought?

Clamping her lips together, Grace pushed up from the ground and dusted off her knees. She peered through the trees at the cottage waiting for her. The porch light shining like a beacon, Josh's silhouette moving past the kitchen window. She took another breath and focused on the wire-tautness of nerves that had nothing to do with raccoons.

Barry hadn't found them. They were safe. They would stay safe. She could do this. She had to.

Squaring her shoulders, Grace walked over to retrieve the flashlight. Then she stepped back onto the path and finished her journey home.

Josh answered her knock and reassuring, "It's me, Josh," before the words were half out of her mouth.

"Is he all right?" he asked, guilt shadowing his brown eyes.

"He's fine." She stepped inside, stripping off her jacket and draping it onto a hook. "Just in a bit of an awkward position."

She explained their neighbor's predicament over her shoulder as she went through to the kitchen, ending with her intention to go back out as soon as she'd made sure everyone here was settled. Arriving at the table where the three girls still sat, she surveyed Annabelle's personal disaster area with a sigh.

"Did *any* of your dinner make it into your belly?" she inquired.

Annabelle lifted her shirt with one fried-potato-covered hand and patted her stomach with the other. She grinned. "Belly."

"She ate most of it," Josh said. "But she yelled whenever I tried to take the rest away. I guess I should have tried harder."

"You did a great job," Grace told him as she unbuckled the safety harness on Annabelle's booster seat and lifted the toddler free. "Seriously, Josh. Thank you for taking over for me. Now, if I get the munchkin bathed and into pajamas, will you be okay to read her a story and get her into bed?"

"Won't you need help getting the man up? He looked pretty big."

Josh had a point. In Grace's estimation, their neighbor was well over six feet tall and close to two hundred pounds, but she preferred not to dwell on the *how* just yet. Besides, he looked to be in decent enough shape, so surely once he had both crutches back, he could do most of the work himself. She hoped.

She settled Annabelle on one hip. "I'd love your help, to be honest, but I need you here more. Someone has to watch the girls for me."

Josh nodded, and she turned her attention to her nieces.

"Lilliane and Sage, can you get yourselves ready for bed tonight?"

Sage, never much of one for words, nodded solemnly.

"We'll clean the table and wash the dishes, too," said Lilliane. "Won't we, Sagey?"

Sage nodded again.

"That would be amazing, ladies. Thank you! And now, Miss Annabelle," Grace made a face as she picked a glob of potato out of the littlest one's hair, "it's off to the bath for you. Or maybe *two* baths."

It took half an hour to accomplish bath, pajamas, and general organization, and then Grace was back on the path to the other cottage, her hurried steps propelled by guilt and a serious chill in the air that had settled with the dark. She'd given him enough blankets, hadn't she? And she hadn't heard a gunshot, so she assumed there'd been no attempted bear attack.

Her fingers tightened on the flashlight as she emerged from the trees into the cottage clearing. A few minutes to wash the poison ivy oils off his crutch for him, a few more to help him back onto his feet and into his cottage, and then—

"If that's you and not a bear, you should probably say something," a deep baritone drawled from the deck. "Me being armed with a shotgun now and all."

"It's me. Are you holding up okay?"

"Apart from having to pee something fierce, just fine," he said. "I totally should not have had that tea I brought out with me."

Despite herself, Grace's lips twitched. "I'll be as quick as I can," she promised briskly. "Are you warm enough?"

"Snug as a bug, thanks."

"Good. I'm going to get the crutch and give it a bath, then I'll be out to help you. You do have hot water?"

"I do. I also have a tub in the bathroom, first door off the kitchen. That might be easier than using the sink. There's shampoo there you can use."

With her hand swaddled in one of the rags she'd stuffed into her coat pocket earlier, Grace extracted the crutch from its resting place and carried it into the cottage. Like the rest of the place, the bathroom was basic but clean, with plywood walls whose white paint looked relatively fresh, open shelves holding towels and facecloths, a mirrored cabinet over the sink, and as promised, a bathtub. She set the crutch in the bottom, turned on the hot water, and squirted a spicy-scented shampoo along its length. Then, kneeling at the side, she unwrapped her hand and set to scrubbing the crutch's wooden length, turning it over to do both sides, paying the closest attention to the pad at the top and the handgrip.

Several hot water rinses later, satisfied she'd erased all trace of toxic oils, she dried off the crutch with a hand towel and then carried it through the living room to the sliding doors. The man on the deck floor looked over as she stepped outside.

"All safe again?"

"All safe. Ready to be upright?"

"You have no idea." He pushed aside the blankets and reached for the crutch at his side.

Grace watched him roll onto his good hip and push up onto the knee, his casted leg extended awkwardly to the side. He wiggled his fingers for the other crutch. She frowned, foreseeing impending disaster if they continued with his plan. "Wait. I have a better idea."

She leaned the crutch beside the door and went back into the cottage. The kitchen table was flanked by two benches rather than the chairs she was looking for, but when she leaned her weight on one, she found it solid and sturdy. Far more so than a pair of wobbly crutches. She lifted the end of the bench and dragged it across the floor, over the doorsill, and onto the deck.

"Good thinking," he said.

She slid the glass door closed and picked up the bench end again. "Let's hope," she grunted, tugging it over the planks to his side.

Between them, they positioned it for maximum support, and then she took the crutch from him and set it aside with the other—along with the shotgun.

"Right. Let's give this a try."

It took two attempts and very nearly flattened both of them, but at last her neighbor was upright. Almost. Grace retrieved the crutches from beside the sliding door and handed them to him. Standing back, she watched him tuck one under each arm and then, at last, stand tall. A look of sheer pleasure settled over his face as he stretched out his spine.

"That," he said, "feels incredible."

Grace pulled her gaze away from shirt buttons straining across a muscled chest. Ignoring the inexplicable increase in ambient air temperature, she herself smile. "I'm just relieved we managed it. Now let's get you inside so I can get back to the kids."

She went back to the sliding doors, gripped the handle, and tugged.

Tugged again.

Oh, hell.

She rested her forehead against the air-chilled glass. Hell, hell, *hell*.

"Tomorrow," the man announced behind her, "I will fix that. You have my word."

She squeezed her eyes shut.

"Hey," he said. "It's not the end of the world. You can just go through the other..."

His voice trailed off. Grace squeezed harder.

"You locked it, didn't you?" he asked.

Had any voice ever sounded so carefully neutral?

"It's a habit." She lifted her head at last and turned to face him. "I wasn't thinking. I'm so sorry."

"Well," he said, his face half hidden and unreadable in the shadows. "Well."

"I'm guessing that means you don't have a spare key hidden outside."

"The one I used to let myself in because I forgot mine in Ottawa? Yeah, no."

"Ah. Window open that I can crawl through?"

"The bathroom one can be jimmied open with a bit of work, but I don't think you'll fit, and it's too dark to give it a try right now."

"Shit," she said.

"My sentiments exactly." He sighed. "Good thing you brought those blankets out earlier, I guess."

Grace realized his intent, and for a moment actually considered the idea. Then guilt—and reason—kicked in.

"You can smell the rain in the air as well as I can," she said. "There's no way you can spend the night out in that. Even if you didn't catch pneumonia, your cast would be mush by morning. You'll have to come back to my place."

He tipped back his head, and in the faint light reaching him from the interior lights, she saw his eyes close and his jawline go tight.

"That path will be hell on crutches," he said.

"I still have my flashlight." She pulled it from her pocket. Thank heaven she'd tucked it in there instead of setting it on a counter inside. "We'll go as slow as you need to."

More silence. More jaw tightening. A sigh.

"In that case..." He lifted his right hand from its grip on the crutch and extended it. "Sean McKittrick."

Grace's stomach did an uncomfortable flip-flop, and she bit the inside of her cheek. The idea of telling him her name raised every warning flag she could imagine. What if he mentioned it to someone? Ottawa wasn't that big a city. People knew people who knew people...what if Barry caught wind of a woman and four children camped out in a cottage?

Panic licked through her, kicking paranoia into overdrive. Maybe she should just leave him in the rain after all. Or maybe tomorrow, when she got into his cottage, she could take his cell phone...and his car keys. If he couldn't go anywhere or talk to anyone—

"Is something wrong?"

Sean McKittrick's voice shattered her wild imaginings. She met his narrowed gaze. Uncurled her fists. Set aside her wholly inappropriate plan to become another Annie Wilkes from *Misery*. She was being ridiculous—and probably raising all kinds of suspicions in her neighbor's head.

"No." She shook her head, forcing a smile. "No, nothing's wrong. And it's Grace. My name is Grace."

She switched on the flashlight and stepped around his outstretched hand to scoop up the shotgun from the deck.

"We should go," she added, shining the light onto the stairs. "Before the rain starts."

Her neighbor regarded her for a long, silent moment before he lowered his hand to the crutch again and swung himself around. "Of course," he agreed. "After you."

CHAPTER 5

The short traverse between the cottages seemed to take forever. Even with Grace walking backward, shining her flashlight on the trail to light the way, Sean had one hell of a time keeping both himself and his crutches aligned with the packed surface. Too many times to count, one crutch tip or the other sank into the soft earth at the sides, throwing him wildly off balance. Most times he steadied himself against a nearby tree. Twice, Grace had to dart forward to catch him and hold him upright until he regained his footing.

She smelled like strawberries.

Which he totally had no business noticing.

Kids, he reminded himself. *You don't do kids.*

Especially not four of them.

At last, his leg on fire and throbbing from the repeated jarring it had received, they emerged from the woods at Lucien Tremaine's cottage. Which reminded him...

"So how do you know Luc, anyway?" he asked, pausing to flex fingers aching from their death-grip on the crutches. "Are you family?"

Grace-with-no-last-name stopped a few feet away, a shadow among shadows, flashlight pointed at the ground near his feet.

"He's a friend."

Sean waited for more. An owl hooted in the trees behind them.

"You're not really the talkative type, are you?" he asked.

"Not really."

He tended to like that in a woman. Hell, he preferred the trait in most people. But something about Grace niggled at him, making him want to know more. He squinted at her through the dark, wishing he could see her face, judge her expression. Decide if this was normal reticence on her part, or—

The flashlight's beam flicked impatiently. "Are you ready yet?"

Well. He could figure that out tomorrow.

"Of course," he said. "Lead the way."

He negotiated the last stretch of path to the cottage—including the three steps up to the porch—without mishap. Ahead of him, Grace knocked at the door.

"Josh? It's me."

Footsteps sounded inside, the porch light came on, and the door opened. The boy who had triggered the entire evening's chain of events stood framed in the opening, his wire-framed gaze zeroing in on Sean. Brown eyes widened, and he stumbled back. Sean frowned. His bellow hadn't been that scary...had it? He cleared his throat, but Grace forestalled any words of greeting with a quick, fierce look over her shoulder. She stepped into the cottage and put an arm around the boy, pulling him in for a hug, resting her chin atop his head.

"Everything's fine, sweetie," Sean heard her murmur. "We got locked out of Mr. McKittrick's cottage, so I had to bring him back here with me. He's going to spend the night on the couch, and then we'll help him get back home in the morning, all right? It's all good, I promise."

Despite the reassurance, tension riddled the boy's body, pulling his shoulders taut, curling his hands into fists, sucking the color from his face. The kid looked like he'd either bolt or disintegrate on the spot if someone so much as sneezed. Sean wiped the frown from between his brows and swung himself into the cottage entrance on his crutches. Balancing there, he extended his right hand.

"You must be Josh," he said. "Your mom told me you like to read on my deck."

Damned if the kid's face didn't go even whiter—just before he buried it in Grace's shoulder.

Sean raised a perplexed eyebrow. "Something I said?"

Lips pressed tight, Grace shook her head. "He's talking about me, Josh. *I* told him you like to sit on his deck."

"Of course I was talking about —" Sean stopped. "You're not his mother."

"Aunt."

He blinked, adjusting to the information. The woman who smelled like strawberries *didn't* have kids? Well.

"Mommy isn't here," a new voice informed him. "She's in the hospital."

Sean looked sideways and down to meet the solemn brown gaze of a little girl with braided, dark hair and pajamas covered in purple penguins. A smaller girl peeked out from behind her with round, darkly fringed blue eyes.

"Are you the man who yelled at Josh?" the taller girl asked.

Once again Grace cut off his response.

"That's enough, Lilliane. Take Sage and go into your room. I'll be there in a minute to tuck you."

Without so much as an instant's hesitation, the two girls turned and departed. Sean blinked.

"You certainly have them well trained," he said to Grace, and damned if she didn't flinch and go pale, too. What the hell?

He shifted his weight on his crutches. His injured leg responded with an intense flash of pain that twisted through his gut. "Son of a bi—"

Grace's scowl cut him off mid-word. Right. Children on the premises. He swallowed a slow roll of nausea.

"Sorry," he muttered. "I moved the wrong way."

Her gaze dropped to his leg. "Is it bad?"

"Getting that way, yeah."

"Right, let's get you inside." With quick efficiency, she popped the shells out of the shotgun she still carried and slipped them into her jeans pocket. Stretching up on tiptoe, she placed the weapon on top of a cupboard over a washing machine, then stripped off her coat and draped it over a hook. "Josh, can you grab a couple of blankets out of the closet and one of the pillows from my bed?"

With a lingering, wide-eyed glance at the shotgun's resting place, Josh sidled out of the mudroom toward the kitchen, then disappeared around the corner.

"Do you need help getting your shoes off?" Grace asked.

"Um..."

Again her gaze dropped, then rose to meet his, shocked and more than a little horrified. "You're not wearing—you walked that entire way in bare feet?"

Brown, Sean realized. Her eyes were brown, like those of her niece and nephew, only darker. A rich, just-sweet-enough, dark-chocolate brown.

And they were scowling at him again.

His mouth twisted. "Only one bare foot, technically. My shoes were in the cottage, and there didn't seem much point in mentioning it when neither of us could do anything. Besides, we're here now."

He tacked the last bit on hastily, when she flicked her hair back over her shoulder and planted both hands on her hips, looking as if she might launch into a full-blown lecture. She favored him with tight-lipped silence in return and lifted one hand to point toward the kitchen.

Sean took hold of the crutch's handgrips again, trying not to think about how bruised his palms had become or how little sleep his leg would likely give him without painkillers available. Once he reached the kitchen, Grace went ahead of him to the couch in the living room, clearing a path through the toys and books scattered across the floor.

She didn't apologize for the mess, a fact that bumped her up a notch in his estimation. After spending a great part of his own childhood being apologized for and feeling in the way, he liked families who embraced the chaos rather than trying to hide it. It was how he would have raised his own kids, if he'd ever been inclined to have them.

Grace swept a final pile of books up from the couch and waved to Sean to take a seat. He eased himself down, crutches in one hand, other hand braced against the couch's arm. Then, teeth on edge, he struggled to lift his casted leg up onto the coffee table. Grace plopped the books she held onto a nearby shelf.

"Here," she said. "Let me help."

She lifted his injured leg gently, seeming to know any quick movement would exacerbate matters, and settled his foot where he'd been aiming for. "Is that all right?"

"Better. Thanks."

"Let me guess. Your painkillers are in the cottage, too."

"I just need a few minutes with it up." He laid his head back against the cushions and put his other foot up to join the first. "I'll be fine."

"Sure you will," she said. "All right. Give me five minutes to tuck the girls in, then I'll be back."

"You don't have to—"

She cut him off with a raised eyebrow and pointed look at his pine needle- and dirt-encrusted foot. "Unless you have a way of washing that foot before you put it on any more of my furniture, yes, I do have to."

Without a word, Sean lowered the offending foot and placed it on the floor as she disappeared down the hallway behind him. Then he rested his head against the couch again.

Strawberry-scented, chocolate-eyed Aunt Grace might not be Mommy, but she sure played the role well.

Getting the kids settled required a great deal more than the five minutes she'd promised, but at last Grace headed back toward the living room and their guest, bedding in her arms, pill bottle clutched in one hand, towel and dampened washcloth in the other. Sean McKittrick hadn't moved in her absence except to close his eyes, and she hesitated at the edge of the room.

Had he gone to sleep? Should she wake him just to get him—?

Bottle-green eyes snapped open to meet hers, turning unexpectedly warm, stealing her breath for an instant. Then they shuttered again.

"I thought you might have changed your mind," he said.

Grace loosened her grip on the pill bottle and made herself hand it over. "I was looking for these. They're the strongest thing I have."

Sean glanced at the label. "Codeine. Pretty heavy-duty."

"I get migraines sometimes. I'd put them away where the kids couldn't find them, then forgot where that was. I'm sharing my room with Annabelle, so I had to be quiet while I searched."

"I'd like to say you shouldn't have bothered, but I'm glad you did." He grimaced and tipped three of the tablets into his palm. "Things are starting to get a little dicey pain-wise."

"Are you sure you should take that many at a time?"

The green eyes met hers again. "I'm sure."

"I'll get you some wat—" She paused as he put the tablets in his mouth, tipped his head back, and swallowed. "Or not."

"Maybe just a cloth so I can clean up my foot?"

Grace set the blankets and pillow on the couch beside him, and held up the cleaning supplies she'd brought. She sat on the coffee table beside his casted leg. "Can you lift it up by yourself, or do you need help?"

Silence. She looked up to find Sean staring at her.

"I'm not letting you wash my foot," he said. "That's just..."

"Logical?" she suggested dryly. She reached down, grabbed his pant leg, and hauled up his leg to rest in her lap. Many of the pine needles that had decorated it had already fallen to the floor, so she brushed the others off to join them and made a mental note to sweep in the morning. Preferably before Annabelle got around to tasting them.

She glanced up at Sean. He wore a perplexed, somewhat horrified expression that made her smile. "Relax, would you? It's not like I'm giving you a sponge bath."

Though she'd admit there was an odd level of intimacy in bathing the man's foot that came awfully close to being a parallel. Her smile departed in a sudden flush of awareness, and she lowered her head again, concentrating on her task, hiding behind a curtain of hair. Where the heck had that thought come from?

Refusing to dwell on it—after all, said man would be out of her life first thing in the morning—she dried off his foot and lowered it to the floor again.

"There," she said, her voice brisk. "Now, you must be hungry. Josh said there were leftovers from dinner, if you're interested. Sausage and fried potatoes. And maybe some tea?"

"That sounds wonderful. Thank you. And may I use your washroom?"

"Door at the end of the hall."

She watched to make sure he could get up without incident and listened to him make his way down the hall, the steady thump of crutches marking his progress. Then she rose from the coffee table, put all thought of any sort of intimacy firmly from her mind, and went into the kitchen.

By the time Sean returned ten minutes later, she'd started the fire in the woodstove that would heat the cottage overnight, and she had tea and dinner ready for both of them. She looked up at his entrance, taking in his freshly scrubbed appearance and the damp, spiky hair standing up around his forehead, lending him a boyish look. Sean raised an eyebrow, and she blushed, realizing she stared. She indicated the table and covered her discomfort with words.

"I thought you'd like to use the bench so you can put your leg up. Unless you're more comfortable in a chair with a back.

I'm happy to swap places with you. It's no trouble at—"

"I'm fine with the bench," he said, a thread of amusement running through his voice that singed her cheeks a second time.

She scowled in return, as much at herself as at him. He had no business getting any ideas, and she even less business giving them to him. She turned away as he seated himself awkwardly at the table, and in tight-lipped silence, collected the filled plates from the counter. She would have continued not speaking if she hadn't felt obliged to apologize for the lumpy, pale heap of food she placed before him.

"I'm not much of a cook, but Josh assured me it tastes better than it looks."

Her guest poked experimentally at the mush with his fork. A glob of it stuck to the utensil, resisting efforts to dislodge it again. Sean gave up and shoveled the food into his mouth instead. He chewed, swallowed, and didn't quite meet Grace's gaze as he looked up.

"It's delicious," he said.

They ate in silence, and Grace discovered that the food was far from palatable, never mind delicious. It was, in fact, awful. Undercooked in places, overcooked in others, and far too salty throughout. Sean ate it anyway, though he declined an offer of seconds. She ate hers as well, as much out of a sense of guilt as anything. Those poor kids. How Josh had convinced his sisters to eat their dinner was beyond her.

Unless they were just getting used to her cooking.

She swallowed another mouthful and reached again for her glass of water. That was probably it. After two months, they'd become immune. Or perhaps they'd just given up any hope of a decent meal. She finished the last bite and met Sean's thoughtful green eyes across the table. Hell. Here it came. She braced herself.

"What?"

"Just wondering what your story is," he said. "You and four kids, camped out in the woods on your own like this during the school year. I would've thought you'd want to keep them closer to the hospital."

"The hospital?" Grace's stomach did a twist that threatened to dislodge her meal. How did he know about the hospital?

"One of your nieces—Lilliane, I think you called her—said her mom was in the hospital."

Grace pictured her sister lying in the bed, pale and silent, tubes and wires sprouting everywhere. She stood. Expecting his questions didn't make answering them any easier. She stacked their plates and gathered the cutlery.

"She was in an accident," she said. "I'm looking after them until she recovers."

"I'm sorry to hear that. Was it serious?"

"Are you done with your water?"

He handed her the glass and watched her carry the dishes to the sink. She knew, because she felt his gaze following her, watching her every movement, from taking out the dish soap, to turning on the tap, to nearly dropping a glass on the floor because her fingers no longer seemed to have any nerves. So much for calm.

"You haven't answered," he said at last.

"And considering that it's none of your business, I'm not going to." She abandoned the dishes in the soapy water and wiped her hands on a tea towel. "I need to get to bed."

Sean folded his arms on the table before him. "Something I

said?"

"Of course not. I just have a busy day ahead with the kids, that's all."

"You really aren't very forthcoming, are you?"

"Mr. McKittrick—"

"Sean," he interrupted.

"Mr. McKittrick, I suspect you came out here for the peace and quiet as much as we did, am I right?"

"Today's events to the contrary, yes. I did."

"Then I suggest we agree to accommodate one another. You'll be back in your cottage tomorrow, I'll keep the kids away from you, and we'll both be happy. This" —she indicated the couch in the living room with a wave— "can be the sum total of our neighborliness. Agreed?"

Sean drummed the fingers of one hand against the table, curiosity at war with acceptance in his expression. At last he nodded. "Agreed."

Relief making her knees wobbly, Grace wrapped both hands over the sink edge and held tight. "You can have the washroom first. There's a new toothbrush on the top shelf that you can have. I'll make up your bed while you're brushing."

"I can make do without brushing until tomorrow."

"And live with the taste of those potatoes all night?" she asked wryly.

The corner of Sean's mouth quirked. "Good point. I'll brush."

CHAPTER 6

Sean lowered himself to the sheet-wrapped couch and let out a long, heartfelt sigh. He was tired—no, beyond tired—and in more pain than he'd been since they'd put on the cast. He shook his head, leaned back, and let the simple act of sitting wash over him. This cottage plan of his had so not turned out the way it was supposed to. He'd known he was pushing his limits when he'd wedged himself in behind the wheel of his SUV after the painkillers had worn off, but he'd been so determined—

Stubborn, McKittrick. Call it like it is, you pigheaded idiot.

He scowled at his internal voice, which sounded remarkably similar to his cousin's.

But to whomever the voice belonged, it was right. He'd been so fixated on the idea of being at the cottage, he hadn't thought ahead to how he'd manage once he got here. Had conveniently forgotten he'd have to make multiple treks on crutches down a sloped path to the cottage, carrying heavy bags. Forgotten he'd have to do his own cooking and cleaning. Forgotten he'd have to find a way to bring in firewood now that the nights were cooling off.

And sure as shit had forgotten the broken door lock that had gotten him into this current predicament.

In all honesty, he owed young Josh a debt of gratitude, because if it hadn't been for the boy's presence on his deck...if that lock had slipped into place when Sean had been alone...if he'd somehow fallen even without Josh's help, and no one had known...

Sean listened to the steady drum of rain on the roof overhead. His mouth twisting, he glanced at the makeshift bed beneath him, barely wide enough to accommodate his frame. He might have a long night ahead of him, but at least he'd be spending it indoors.

Down the hallway, a door opened and footsteps sounded. His most reluctant hostess had finished her nighttime preparations and was no doubt coming to check on him. Time to pretend he'd be able to sleep. Sean reached up to undo the buttons of his shirt. He shrugged out of it as Grace came into the living room, balling it up and tossing it onto the table. To his amusement, Grace stopped dead in her tracks for an instant and turned the same color as the strawberries of which her scent reminded him. He raised an eyebrow.

"I hope you don't mind." He indicated the shirt. "It's not very comfortable for sleeping in."

Her gaze left his bare chest and flicked down to the tearaway athletic pants he wore—the only garment he'd found that would accommodate his cast. Sean grinned.

"Those stay on," he promised.

"I wasn't—I didn't—" Grace's blush deepened, and she crossed her arms and favored him with a sour look. "I just wanted to make sure you have everything you need."

"I do, thanks."

"I'll leave the light on in the bathroom in case you need to get up. Do you still have the painkillers?"

He patted the pocket of his pants.

Grace nodded her satisfaction. She crossed the room to the wood stove, opened the glass door, and bent down to feed two sizeable chunks of wood into the flames. Sean's gaze skimmed her silhouette against the firelight, lingering on the line of her—

Grace straightened again and turned to him, and he yarded his attention back up to her face.

"I should warn you that Annabelle is an early riser," she said. "I'll try to keep her quiet, but I can't promise anything."

"Don't worry about it," he replied. "I'm not likely to get much sleep as it is, so an early wake-up won't be much of a hardship."

Her gaze traveled to the couch. "I'm sorry I can't offer you something more comfortable..."

"Don't be. Given the sound of that"—he tipped his chin toward the roof and the rain that drummed against it—"I'm just glad to be inside."

"I suppose."

"I'll be fine. Seriously." He watched her begin to turn away. "And, Grace?"

Chocolate eyes met his.

"Thank you," he said. "For everything."

She raised a finely arched brow. "If I remember correctly, it was my nephew who initiated your predicament. Giving you my couch is the least I can do."

"And if I'd somehow gotten myself locked out without your nephew knowing I was even at the cottage?"

Grace considered the idea, then smiled faintly. "You're right. You definitely owe me—and him. You can begin by apologizing to him in the morning for yelling. Good night, Mr. McKittrick."

She disappeared back down the hallway, and a moment later Sean heard the soft closing of a door. With a rueful shake of his head, he plumped up the pillow she'd left him, got himself arranged full length and covered on the couch, and reached to switch off the table lamp near his head. The room plunged into dark, the pitch-black kind that came from having no street or city lights, and silence settled, leaving him with nothing to focus on but the grim, angry throb of the leg he had so abused that day. Sean drew a long, deep breath through his nostrils. Then he paused, sniffing at the scent rising from the pillow beneath his head.

Strawberries.

He smiled faintly.

"Sweet dreams, Grace," he murmured.

Grace slid under the duvet, shivering at the chill of its cotton cover. Annabelle's soft, even breathing drifted from the cot on the other side of the room, muffled by the utter silence that came with living in a cottage in the middle of nowhere.

It had taken Grace a full week to adjust to the lack of familiar, everyday sounds here. No sirens, no traffic, no neighbors. Not even so much as a dog barking. The absence of sound had felt deafening. And that had only been half the equation.

The dark had been the other half. Once she turned out the lights on her way to bed, a blackness descended over their little haven that seemed absolute. Impenetrable. Eerily isolating. She shivered again. On the other side of the wall, the couch springs creaked beneath shifting weight. She froze, but heard nothing else.

Her unexpected guest had only turned over. He hadn't gotten up.

Grace released a breath she hadn't realized she held. Quiet

settled over the cottage again.

It was weird, having another person here.

Another adult.

A man.

Hell, she didn't remember the last time a man had stayed overnight at her place. She snorted into the dark. Whenever it was, she guaranteed he hadn't slept on the couch. Way back then, things had still been normal in her life. Travel, work, friends around the globe who had become like family to her; she'd had everything she wanted. *Been* everything she wanted...

Until a single phone call had changed everything.

"I don't know what to do," Julianne's taut, quivering voice echoed in Grace's memory, tearing down the one corner of her world that had been her constant. Her anchor. "Barry's so terribly harsh with the kids. They're scared of their own shadows around him, and every time I try to intervene, it just gets worse. I don't think I can stay with him anymore, Grace. We can't stay."

"He hasn't hurt them, has he?" Grace demanded. On the other side of the world, she was already tossing her belongings into a suitcase, planning what she would tell her Singapore client in the morning when she called to say she wouldn't be coming in to the office. What she would tell her boss. Who she could recommend sending in her place.

"No! No, he hasn't raised a finger to them. I would never have stayed if he had. It's only verbal, but it's getting worse, and—" Julianne's voice broke, and she took a shaky breath. "Josh's grades have dropped, he's sick all the time with headaches and stomach aches, and—oh, Grace, you should have heard Barry tear into him over the baseball game last night. It was brutal. It seems the older Josh gets, the more he's after him."

Grace closed her eyes. Clenched her teeth. It wasn't hard to picture her slim, quiet, owl-eyed nephew as his father's verbal punching bag. She'd always known Barry had a temper. Hell, everyone knew Barry had a temper...

But she hadn't known about this.

Hadn't so much as suspected.

"I found him sitting in the car in the garage this morning when I got up," Julianne continued, her words almost inaudible. "With the keys in the ignition and the garage door closed. Just sitting there, staring out the windshield."

"Barry?"

"Josh."

Bile rose in Grace's chest, burning her throat. She felt behind her for the bed and sat down on its edge. "Are you serious? He's only ten years old! How does he even know...?"

"Television. Internet. He knows, Grace, and I may not find him next time."

Air shuddered into Grace's lungs. She strove for calm. Tried to ignore the vibration trembling through her. She could only imagine how much worse Julianne felt. "All right. First things first. You need a place to stay. You have the key to my townhouse—"

"Really?" Julianne's voice wobbled. "You'd let us stay with you?"

"Of course. That shouldn't even be a question. I'll call Sarah— she's the neighbor across the street—and let her know you'll be staying there. Let yourself in and make yourselves at home. If you don't know where something is, feel free to toss the place until you find it." Grace carried the cell phone into the hotel bathroom with her and pulled back the shower curtain on the tub. "I'll head to the airport as soon as I'm dressed. I'll catch the first flight out."

"God, no. Don't do that. You have a client—a job—"

"I have a sister," Grace interrupted, "who is far more important."

Julianne sniffled some more at her end.

"There's one more thing, Jules. My friend Lucien Tremaine's phone number is in my address book in the kitchen drawer. You met him at my Christmas party last year. He's the best family lawyer out there—a veritable bulldog. Call him. Tell him you're my sister, and tell him everything you've told me."

"It's too early for lawyers. I haven't even told Barry I'm leaving yet."

"That's why you need to call Luc. You're taking Barry's kids, Jules. He won't take this sitting down, and he's got a lot more clout than you have when it comes to the system. You need someone to walk you through this. Someone on your side."

"I hadn't thought of that." Julianne's voice cracked.

"That's why you have me, sweetie. Now promise me: straight to my place, and call Luc."

"I promise."

"Good girl. I'll see you tomorrow sometime, all right?"

"I don't know what I'd do without you, Grace."

"And you'll never have to find out, because I'm there for you. Together always, remember?"

A childhood pact made under the covers when their parents had died and they'd begun the endless shuffle from relative to relative, only just avoiding being thrown into the system.

"Together always," Julianne whispered back, and Grace's lips curved in response to the smile in her sister's voice.

In the dark of the bedroom, Grace wiped away the tears cooling her cheeks. She listened to the gentle breathing of her niece, letting the stillness seep into her. She and Julianne had managed to uphold their pact, and regardless of what happened to her sister now, Grace would move heaven and earth to make sure Julianne's kids had the same opportunity.

"Together always," she whispered to her sister.

Then she turned onto her side and closed her eyes.

CHAPTER 7

Sean's hands came down on Grace's shoulders, tugging her inexorably closer. Her heart thudded wildly, threatening to break out of her chest altogether. She knew she should object, knew she should pull away, but his bottle-green gaze had turned so intense. It seared into hers, holding her captive. His hands slid down her arms, spanned her waist, drove the last remaining oxygen from her lungs. His head descended. Desire licked through her veins. Need hollowed her belly.

"Oh, Grace," he whispered, burying his face in her hair, wrapping her against him.

A hand cupped the soft flesh of her breast, thumb circling the nipple, teasing, tormenting. Grace closed her eyes and arched against him.

"More," she gasped. "Please...more."

"Baa," Sean replied.

Grace's eyes shot open. *Baa?*

She stared up at the shadowed ceiling, struggling to regain her bearings and calm her breathing. Reality slowly filtered in. She was in bed. Alone. Her skin tingled with remembered sensation, but it wasn't real. She'd dreamed it. Dreamed it all.

She sat bolt upright, sweat-soaked sheets falling away from her. Dear God, she'd dreamed about Sean McKittrick? Heat flooded her—part mortification, part something she didn't want to think about.

And what the hell was *baa?*

"Mooo!" came a deep male voice from the other side of the wall behind her head. Grace froze. Her gaze darted to the portable crib in the corner of the room, then to the door standing partially ajar. Her heart dropped into her belly. Annabelle.

She scrambled from the bed, tripping over the covers wrapped around her feet and narrowly avoiding a flat-on-her-face fall. How on earth had the child gotten out of the crib? She'd never—

Utter horror stopped Grace dead in her tracks. Wait. Sean hadn't—he wouldn't—oh, Lord, please don't tell her he'd come in to get Annabelle and seen her all tangled up in the covers and dreaming of—

Her last functioning brain cell snorted at her. *Really, Grace? A man who can barely stand up on crutches, coming into the room and lifting a wriggly two-year-old out of her crib without you hearing a thing? Really?*

She put her hands to her overheated face and stood swaying in the middle of the floor, willing her lungs to draw air. Her pulse slowed. Reason returned. Mortification subsided.

It didn't quite disappear altogether, but it was enough.

She opened the door and tiptoed down the still-dark hallway toward the glow of lamplight and the first pale streaks of dawn. Reaching the living room, she found her niece comfortably tucked into the crook of Sean's arm, intent on the book he held. Annabelle removed the pacifier from her mouth with one hand and pointed to a page with the other, looking up at Sean. He'd put his shirt back on but only half buttoned it. From where Grace stood, the deep vee opening allowed a rather tantalizing glimpse of crisp, curling, sandy-colored hair and the muscles that had featured so prominently in...

She swallowed on a suddenly parched throat.

"Whassat?" Annabelle asked Sean.

"That's a dog," he responded. "Woof, woof!"

"Oof! Oof!" Annabelle repeated. "Whassat?"

"A goldfish. I don't think he makes any noise, though."

"Fiss!" Annabelle pursed her lips and made a little popping sound as she imitated the gaping mouth of a fish.

"I see." Sean chuckled. "I stand corrected."

As if suddenly aware of Grace's presence, he looked over his shoulder. "Ah. Good morning."

It took all of Grace's willpower not to put a hand up to smooth her uncombed hair. "And an early one, at that."

He grinned. "I can't say you didn't warn me."

"Mamaaa!" Annabelle squealed. She scrambled down from the couch and ran—as only sturdy two-year-olds can run—over to Grace to be picked up.

Grace swung her into her arms, and the little girl removed Sussie long enough to give her a wet kiss on the cheek. Pulling back after returning the favor, albeit a little less damply, Grace put on a mock stern face.

"And just what," she asked, "is Sussie doing out of bed?"

Annabelle giggled. "Sussie story."

"Sussie wanted a story, did it?"

"Man owie," Annabelle added, pointing to Sean. She struggled to get down. Grace set her on the floor and watched her run back to the couch.

"Owie," she said again, patting Sean's cast. "Kiss better."

Grace scooped her up after the tenth wet lip-print marked the white surface covering Sean's knee. "That's quite enough, Miss Annabelle. If you make that thing any soggier, it will fall apart. Now it's time for Sussie" —she tapped the pacifier clutched in her niece's chubby little hand— "to go night-night, all right? Can you put him to bed all by yourself?"

Annabelle regarded her pacifier, and then to Grace's relief, she nodded agreement. Dealing with the Sussie issue had been hit-and-miss since their arrival at the cottage, with misses resulting in meltdowns that had likely sent wildlife into hiding for miles around. It wasn't Grace's preferred way of starting the day.

Annabelle gave a forlorn sigh. "Sussie night-night. Annbell down?"

Grace set her down for a second time, and she thundered down the hallway. Grace winced. Perhaps she should have added a caution about noise...not that it would have had much effect on the ebullient toddler. Oh, well. The others would have woken up eventually, right? Scraping back her hair and stifling a yawn, she looked down to find Sean watching her, hands locked behind his head. The opening of his shirt gaped wider, affording her a better view of what had warmed her cheeks earlier. Damn, but the man was in good shape.

Suddenly and acutely aware of her own state of undress, particularly with regard to certain body parts that felt more unfettered than usual, she crossed her arms over her chest and cleared her throat. "Sorry about the early morning company. That's the first time she's managed to escape on her own."

"No worries. She's a cute kid. Very helpful, too." He indicated the pile of books beside him. "I think she emptied half the bookcase."

"I can see that. And I suspect my mornings just got a whole lot more interesting now that she's figured out the Houdini act." Grace sighed, then switched subjects. "How's your leg this morning? Did you sleep at all?"

"I dozed." He shrugged, and hard, smooth muscles shifted beneath fabric. "And it hurts like blazes, but no worse than yesterday."

She tore her gaze from his chest for a third time. "That's good news. And somewhat surprising, after the way you abused the poor thing yesterday. When did you break it, by the way? The cast looks new."

Or at least, most of it did. The foot portion was a little on the disheveled side after their trek through the woods.

"Three weeks ago," Sean replied. "But the cast is only two days old."

"Let me guess." Her voice turned dry. "You ruined the first four or five doing back flips and somersaults."

Green eyes crinkled at the corners. "Not quite. I needed surgery, and then we had to wait for the incision to heal."

"Ouch. That must have been one nasty break. How did you—" Grace broke off, remembering of the rules she'd set the night before, even as a shutter descended over his expression, stirring deeper curiosity. No questions, no answers, and no contact after today. She forced a smile and another topic change. "Sorry. Forget I asked. Coffee?"

"If it's not too much trouble. And my crutches, if you wouldn't mind. Annabelle moved them for me."

Grace followed the jut of his chin to where his crutches lay on the floor by the kitchen table. She carried them back to Sean.

"So, I take it the three older ones belong to your sister, and Annabelle is yours?" He positioned the crutches on either side of himself and scooted forward on the cushions until he sat on the couch's edge.

"Her calling me mama, you mean?" Grace swallowed against the sudden ache in her throat. "I haven't been able to convince her otherwise, unfortunately."

"Ah. Well, I'm sure that will change once her mother's back in action."

The careless words ripped through her with their unexpectedness. She struggled for air, reminding herself he didn't know—couldn't know. It made no difference to the pain. No difference to the stark images that reared up in her mind. Her sister in a hospital bed, unresponsive, unaware, surrounded by machines and wires and tubes.

"Grace?" Sean's voice reached out to her, warm with concern.

Respond, a voice deep in her brain urged. *Say something.*

Her throat worked, but no sound emerged.

Sean struggled to rise from the couch, his gaze becoming alarmed. "Grace—"

She turned and fled.

CHAPTER 8

What the hell?

Sean stared after Grace for a full thirty seconds before he thought to lever himself up from the couch, tucking a crutch under each arm. Then he stood, staring some more. Did he go after her as instinct urged? Stay out of it as she had suggested last night?

She'd made it clear, more than once, that she didn't want to talk. Wouldn't talk.

But her behavior just now made it equally clear she had a great deal to talk about. Hell, he'd never seen anyone turn that white that fast and still manage to remain on her feet. No, something was definitely going on with her. The question was, did he push, or leave her alone?

With a sigh, Sean gritted his teeth against the pain of being upright—damn, he wished he had his painkillers with him—and swung into action. He made his way down the hallway. The first door on the right stood partly ajar, and he tapped gently before nudging it open with the tip of his crutch. Grace stood with her back to him, Annabelle stretched out on a dresser top before her. The toddler grinned at him, waving a stuffed giraffe.

"Man owie!"

Grace's shoulders went stiff. She didn't turn. "Did you need something?"

Her voice wobbled, and Annabelle patted her arm. "Mama cry."

He'd figured as much. Sean cleared his throat. "I just wanted to check on you. You seemed—"

"I'm fine," she interrupted. "I'm just changing Annabelle, and then I'll be out to make coffee. We'll get you back to your cottage as soon as it's light enough."

"I didn't mean to upset you." Hell, he didn't quite know how he *had* upset her, though at a guess, he'd say it had something to do with her sister.

"I'm fine."

"Grace —"

"I'm *fine*, Mr. McKittrick." A sniffle undermined her declaration, but she fired a fierce, tear-bright glower over her shoulder that warned him in no uncertain terms to back off. "I'll be out in a minute."

Tight-lipped, Sean withdrew from the room, closing the door awkwardly behind him. He turned to find Josh standing in the gap of another half-open door.

"Is Aunt Grace all right?" the boy asked.

"She's fine," Sean said, knowing Grace would have his head if he suggested otherwise. "She's just changing Annabelle."

Josh hesitated, then nodded an acceptance not reflected in his solemn gaze. Sean started to scowl, but swiftly wiped his brow clear when the boy took a step back. Damn it to hell, but the kid was jumpy. Josh's gaze slid past him to Grace's bedroom door.

Jumpy and smart. He knew full well something was up with his aunt. And Sean knew full well the boy would be in that room like a shot as soon as the way was clear. He needed to stall him, to give Grace room to recover.

"I owe you an apology," he said gruffly.

Josh's gaze flew back to his.

"I shouldn't have reacted the way I did when I found you on my deck yesterday."

"I was trespassing."

Sean's mouth quirked. "Technically, yes. But you weren't hurting anything, and I didn't need to be that harsh. I'm sorry."

"I'm sorry, too, sir. For making you fall."

Sir? Who the hell taught their kids to say that anymore? Sean coughed to cover his surprise. "You didn't make me fall. I made me fall." He waved one of the crutches aloft. "Truth is, I'm a total klutz on these things. Ask your aunt. If she hadn't caught me at least twice along that path last night, I would have been sleeping in the shrubbery."

A tiny smile pulled at Josh's mouth.

Sean returned the gesture, then balancing carefully, he held out a hand. "Friends?"

Josh's smile disappeared. He withdrew into the bedroom behind him. "I should get dressed," he said. "Aunt Grace needs my help."

Just like that, Sean found himself staring again, this time at the painted panel of a closed door. What was it with this family? He scowled. Grace's reticence, Josh's jumpiness and the distinct alarm in his eyes just now...everything about them was off. Not a lot off, just a little. Just enough to make him curious.

Grace leaned her forehead against the door, listening to the sound of Sean's crutches retreating down the hallway, wrestling with the urge to drag out the suitcases and begin pitching their belongings into them. *Breathe, Grace,* she told herself. *Think this through.*

That they'd aroused Sean's curiosity, she had no doubt, especially after that exchange with Josh and her own flight from the living room. It still didn't mean she needed to go off the deep end reaction-wise. Sean was just a neighbor. A guy who happened to live in the cottage next door. That didn't mean he had any connection to Barry, and it sure as hell didn't mean she had to uproot the kids again.

Besides, where would they even go? She didn't have unlimited funds, and the more they moved around, the more they exposed themselves. Their weekly trips into Perth for groceries were nerve-wracking enough, even though she followed the careful instructions given to her by Paul Kingsley, Luc's private investigator: never go on the same day of the week, never go at the same time of day, never go to the same stores, and never get drawn into conversation. Err on the side of caution.

She made herself inhale. Exhale. Swallow. *Caution, Grace, not paranoia.*

It was a fine line between them these days.

Annabelle tugged at her pajama leg. "Raff," she said, holding up the stuffed giraffe.

Grace dredged up a smile. "It's a beautiful giraffe," she agreed.

No, she wouldn't panic.

"Raff owie."

She'd stay calm...

"Raff owie."

...get Sean back to his own cottage...

"Raff owie, mama. Raff owie!"

...and then they'd all go back to life as usual, because...

"Raff owie, raff owie, raff owie!" Annabelle wailed, wrenching

Grace's thoughts back to the immediate.

She crouched beside the little girl to calm her, but too late. The toddler evaded her and flopped onto the floor with a screech that all but shattered Grace's skull. She regarded her niece wearily. Great. This was just what she needed.

A tap sounded at the door, and she reached up to twist the handle. Josh stood outside, dressed and looking remarkably awake, given the hour.

"Want some help?" he asked.

Grace debated the offer. Normally she'd just plop Annabelle into the crib and wait out the tantrum, but even that seemed too much work this morning. She waved her nephew in.

Josh sat down on the floor beside his little sister and stroked her hair. "Hey, Annabelly," he said over her commotion. "What's the matter?"

Ah, the magic touch of an adored big brother. Grace watched in bemusement as Annabelle stopped mid-shriek and sat up, fat tears rolling down her cheeks.

She held her toy out to Josh, telling him, in between hiccups, "Raff—owie—'eg."

"Giraffe has an owie on his leg?"

Breathing in great sobs, Annabelle nodded. "Raff owie 'eg."

Josh looked over at Grace. "I think she wants it to have a cast on its leg. Like Mr. McKittrick. Can I use a Band-aid from the first-aid kit?"

If it would bring peace back to the house? Grace nodded. "Please," she said. "Be my guest."

Josh popped back to his feet with the nimbleness of youth and held a hand out to his sister. "Come on, Annabelly. Let's go fix Mr. Giraffe."

"I'll be out in a minute," Grace called after them. "As soon as I'm dressed."

The door closed behind the pair. Despite her words, she remained where she was, still crouched, for a long minute. They'd all been keeping it together so well, learning to function as a family, ignoring the specters hovering over them: the very real possibilities that Julianne would die and that Barry would find them. Grace grimaced.

Sean's presence, however, clearly illustrated they hadn't been keeping it together well at all. Josh's reaction to him. Her own knee-jerk paranoia. And worse, the growing, hardening lump in the center of her chest every time Sean asked a question and she held back, too afraid to answer because she knew—with absolute certainty—that she would begin to unravel if she did.

With a groan, Grace pushed to her feet. *Just a little while longer,* she told herself. As soon as it was light enough, they'd get Sean back into his own cottage and out of their lives, and then she'd call Luc. Find out how Julianne was doing, tell him about his neighbor's appearance, and dispel her last, lingering doubts about said neighbor.

But first...

She reached for the jeans she'd discarded on the floor by the bed the night before, then took a clean, long-sleeved t-shirt from the dresser. She pulled it over her head and lifted her hair free. Then she tightened her jaw, swallowed hard, and wiped away another stealthy tear.

First, she needed to get Sean to stop asking those damned, well-meaning questions. And the only way she could do that was to give him just enough in the way of answers.

CHAPTER 9

Sean looked up from pouring coffee into two mugs as Grace entered the kitchen. She wore jeans again today, and a blue long-sleeved t-shirt that hugged a little more closely than the yellow one of the day before. He held up the coffee pot.

"I hope you don't mind."

Her step faltered, and she jammed her fingers into the front pockets of her jeans. Then she shook her head. "Of course not. But do you think you should be doing so much?"

Balancing on his crutches, he twisted to set the pot back on its pad. "I'm supposed to be fending for myself altogether, remember?"

"And you really think you can do that?" she asked as he teetered.

"It's all a matter of practice." He righted himself with a grin. "Now, how do you take your coffee?"

"Just black, thanks."

He slid a cup across the counter and watched her perch on a stool, head bent and face hidden from him. He sighed. "Look, Grace, I'm not trying to be nosy, but—"

"She's in a coma," she said softly.

Sean stared at the dark, bowed head, not sure he'd heard right. "I beg your pardon?"

"My sister. The kids' mother." Grace looked up to meet his gaze, her deep chocolate eyes raw with grief. "She's in a coma."

"Jesus," he breathed. He set his crutches against the counter and leaned forward to rest his elbows on the chipped laminate surface. A glance toward the hallway assured him none of the kids were there. He pitched his voice low anyway. "Grace, I had no idea. I'm sorry. How long?"

"A little over a month."

"Will she—do they—" He didn't know how to continue. How the hell did one phrase a question like that?

"They don't know. There's minimal brain activity, but they say as long there's any at all, there's hope."

"Do the kids know?"

She pressed her lips together. Nodded.

"So that's why you're hiding out here."

She flinched, her eyes widening. "H-hiding?"

"For the kids' sake. I don't imagine they're up to facing school and friends right now."

A quick recalibration took place behind her expression—so subtle, he almost missed it. So fast, he didn't have time to react before she shook her head.

"No. No, you're right. They're not. We don't talk about it. I think we're afraid if we do..." She trailed off and looked away, blinking back a sheen of tears.

Sean reached out to cover her forearm with his hand, pressing gently. "Hey," he said. "Positive thoughts."

Grace sniffled. He nudged her coffee mug closer to her.

"Drink," he said. "You'll feel better. Or at least more awake."

She picked up the mug and rewarded him with a watery smile. A little thrill of triumph ran through him. He smiled back, resisting with every fiber of his being the sudden urge to sweep back that dark curtain of hair. *Whoa there, McKittrick. Down, boy.* He cleared his throat.

"So, tell me—what can I do to help?"

Grace's smile vanished. "What?"

To be honest, the question had surprised him as much as it had her, but he pushed away his misgivings. It was the human thing to do, after all. Nothing more, nothing less. He shrugged.

"I mean it. What can I do to help? I know I'm a little laid up at the moment, but there must be something. Color pictures with Sage, entertain Annabelle, read stories." He gave her his most disarming grin. "I happen to have it on good authority that I do a superior *baaa*."

Grace turned bright red and choked on the coffee. Sean tried to pat her on the back and nearly fell over in the effort, and Grace ended up lunging forward to grab a fistful of his shirt to steady him.

"*Please* don't fall again," she said. "I don't think either my nerves or your cast can take it."

"Not to mention the damned leg in the cast."

Balance restored, Sean clenched his jaw against the wave of pain following the unexpected movement. He closed his eyes and let his head hang between the outstretched arms clinging to the counter. "Freaking hell, that hurts."

"Are you all right?"

He let out a hiss of air. "I will be. Just give me a sec."

He hadn't taken any of Grace's codeine tablets this morning, anticipating a return to his own heavier-duty and much-needed medication. Now he questioned the wisdom of that decision, especially in the face of the trek he still had to make back to his own cottage. He shuddered at the thought. Oh, yeah. Codeine was definitely in order before he did that. At least it would take off some of the edge. Not much, but some.

He finally unglued his eyelids to find Grace regarding him ruefully.

"I think that answers your question about helping, don't you?" she asked.

"I'm fine."

Grace glanced over her shoulder, then back at him. "Bull," she said. "I appreciate the offer, Sean, but you're in no shape to be helping anyone right now. You need to be off that leg and looking after yourself."

She'd called him Sean.

He was still absorbing that—and trying to wipe a second silly grin off his face—when Josh and Annabelle came down the hallway. Annabelle spotted Sean and broke into a trot, making a beeline for him.

"Raff owie," she announced, holding a stuffed toy aloft.

Sean looked to Grace for translation.

"Her giraffe is hurt," Grace said. "She wants you to look at it."

Sean accepted the animal and chuckled. One entire foreleg was covered in adhesive bandages sporting Spiderman in varying poses. He glanced at Josh. "Your handiwork?"

Josh ignored him, looking sideways at Grace. "She kept saying *big owie*," he said. "It took six bandages before she was happy."

"A small price to pay for peace," Grace assured her nephew, tugging him in to drop a kiss on his head. "Especially this early in the morning. Thanks for looking after her for me."

"Raff owie," Annabelle said again.

Sean handed the bandaged critter back to her. "Giraffe has a very nice owie," he agreed. "Josh did a good job."

"Man owie." Annabelle patted his cast, then pushed aside the pant leg flapping along its length. Blue eyes gazed up sadly. "Man owie. No spyman."

"She's sad because you don't have—"

"Spiderman," Sean finished. "Yes, I got that."

"Josh can draw one on your cast for you," a new voice offered. "He's really good at it."

Lillian, the pig-tailed girl from the night before, climbed up on the stool beside Grace. Her other sister—Sage, he remembered—hid behind her, peering at him with those great, dark-fringed eyes. They both wore expectant expressions. Josh, on the other hand, retreated to a position behind his aunt, who stepped in smoothly to cover his obvious discomfort at the suggestion—and to rescue Sean from having to find a polite way of declining the offer.

"Maybe another time, Lilly," she said. "Right now, Mr. McKittrick needs to sit down and put his leg up while Josh and I try to get his cottage unlocked for him."

Saved by a break-in operation. Sean reached for his crutches.

"I'll come with you."

Grace snorted. "And what, watch? In your bare feet?"

Damn. He'd forgotten about the barefoot thing.

"Besides, I need Josh's help and I can't leave the girls alone," she pointed out, "So you'll be far more help if you stay here to watch them for me."

She downed the rest of her coffee in one long swallow, set down the cup, and added dryly, "That way I know you're *all* safe."

"Funny," Sean muttered.

"Truth." She slid off the stool and nudged Josh. "How about

it, kiddo? Feel like crawling through a window for me?"

Sean followed them to the mudroom, hampered by the unforgiving throb in his leg—and by Annabelle's insistence on clinging to one of his fingers as he gripped the crutches. Grace shot him a sympathetic look as she slipped into her jacket.

"We'll be as quick as we can," she said. "I'll bring back your pain meds for you, and then we'll get you home where it's quiet."

He nodded. He had no more argument left in him. "That would be nice."

She tugged open the door, and she and Josh stepped outside into the early morning light.

"Side window," Sean called after them. "The small one. It opens onto the bathroom."

Grace responded with a wave of one hand. Then Lilliane closed the door and the gazes of all three girls turned to him.

Annabelle produced a second small stuffed creature from the pouch on the front of her pajamas. She held it up hopefully. "Bunny owie?" she asked.

CHAPTER 10

"Aunt Grace?" Josh's voice came from behind her as they trudged along the path to Sean's cottage. "Do we have to move again?"

Grace stopped walking. She took a deep breath and turned to her nephew. Meeting his worried gaze, she wrestled with the desire to protect him from more worry—and the knowledge that she couldn't. With all Josh had been through, all he'd known, he'd see through false reassurances in a heartbeat. She couldn't afford to have him question her honesty. But she could—and did—weigh her words with care.

"I don't know," she said. "I hope not, and I'll do everything I can to make sure that doesn't happen, but I can't promise anything, Josh. You know that."

His wire-framed gaze slid away from hers, dropping to the path between them. Grace reached out to squeeze his shoulder.

"As soon as we get Mr. McKittrick back into his cottage, I'll call Luc. He'll know what we should do."

"Will you tell me what he says?"

"Of course. No more secrets, remember?"

It had been their special pact, hers and Josh's, when Juli brought the kids to live with her. She'd seen how damaged Josh was, then, and how much he needed to talk. As much as she'd needed to hear what had been kept hidden from her. No secrets. Not if she'd wanted to help her sister.

And even that hadn't been enough.

Her nephew nodded. He lurched forward and slid his arms around her in a fierce embrace, his face buried against her shoulder. Grace hugged back, equally fierce, and swallowed against the lump lodged in her throat—a tangle of grief, worry, responsibility, and overwhelming love. Josh stepped back.

"I'm good now," he said, blinking too fast.

Without comment, Grace dropped a kiss on his forehead and then turned back to the path.

Getting Josh into Sean's cottage turned out to be remarkably easy. The bathroom window consisted of double-paned vinyl sliders, loose enough in their tracks to be pushed up with the flats of Grace's hands and then wiggled free. Josh was light enough for her to boost, and in short order, he had his head and shoulders through the opening. The toughest moment came when the rest of him disappeared with an ominous, hollow thud.

"Josh? Josh, are you all right?"

No answer.

Grace stretched up on tiptoe, clinging to the windowsill and straining to peer inside. "Josh!"

"I'm okay," came a muffled response. "I just fell into the tub."

"Are you hurt?"

"I don't think so. No. I'm fine."

Relief made her arms shaky. She released the ledge and settled back on her heels again. "All right. Good. Now go open the door for me, and then we'll get Mr. McKittrick."

She replaced the windows in their tracks, and then went around to meet Josh at the door. He sported a large, purpling goose egg on his forehead. Grace swept his hair back to examine it, wincing.

"Ouch. That has to hurt."

Her nephew shrugged. "Not too much."

"Still. Put some ice on it when we get home, all right?" Grace stepped into the cottage and found what she was looking for just inside the door. She scooped up the single, untied running shoe, then hesitated. Should she get a sock, too? He'd be more comfortable...

She shook her head at the idea of going into his room and through his personal things. Not a chance. He'd endured an entirely shoeless journey last night; he'd survive a sockless one today. His pain meds, however, were another story.

"I'll be back in a second," she told Josh, who waited on the deck, rubbing his forehead.

As she'd suspected she would, she found a pill bottle sitting in the open on the kitchen counter. With no kids in the house, Sean had no reason to hide it. She returned to the door, checked to be sure it remained unlocked, and as a last thought, took the key from the hook above the light switch. She needed Sean McKittrick out of their cottage and into his own, and she was taking no chances on any more delays.

"Success!" Grace called out as she and Josh stepped back into their cottage. She slipped off her shoes and headed for the giggles she could hear in the living room. "You can finally go home and get that rest you came for, Mr. McKitt—"

She stopped short, surveying the room in dismay mixed with a tinge of horror, taking in the collection of stuffed animals scattered across the floor and piled around Sean on the couch. Lilliane and Sage followed her gaze and exchanged looks.

Their smiles faded. The mound of toys beside Sean shifted as Annabelle wriggled out from under them. There were so many, Grace hadn't even seen her niece in their midst.

So many, in fact, that it looked as if every stuffie the girls collectively possessed was there. And that was a lot of stuffies.

Seventy-two of them, to be exact. Of every size and type imaginable. Grace knew, because she'd counted them when she'd packed the entire lot for transport to the cottage, not having had the heart to deprive her nieces of that small comfort in the midst of the chaos they'd faced.

"Bunny owie."

Annabelle joined her, holding up a yellow rabbit in one hand. Grace took it from her. A neat cast of masking tape covered one of the hind legs.

"Fwog owie."

The toddler pressed a smiling green frog into Grace's other hand. It, too, wore a cast.

Grace's gaze went back to the living room disaster area. Little bits of masking tape decorated the coffee and end tables. She looked at the animals piled around Sean. Then at him.

"*All* of them?" she asked. Behind her, she heard Josh smother a laugh into a snort.

"Ahh…" Sean cleared his throat, guilt sliding across his expression. "Things kind of got away on me."

"You think?"

"And I may owe you a roll or two of masking tape."

"Three rolls," Lilliane corrected. "Because Annabelle wanted all her animals to have casts like Mr. McKittrick, and then she wanted to do ours, too."

"All of them," Grace said again. A statement this time.

"I take full responsibility," Sean said. Then, with a grimace, he added, "I had no idea two-year-olds could be so loud when they don't get their own way."

Staring down at the frog and bunny in her hands, Grace tried to wrap her head around the idea of seventy-two casted animal legs. Or rather, how she was ever going to get that much masking tape *off* seventy-two animal legs. Fuzzy ones. Her lips twitched. She pulled them straight, digging deep for the modicum of severity the occasion seemed to require.

"Right," she said, directing a pointed gaze at the three main culprits, each in turn. "Here's what's going to happen. I'm going to take Mr. McKittrick back to his cottage before he causes any more trouble—"

Lilliane and Sage giggled, and Grace's heart melted a little. Sage? Giggling? In the presence of a virtual stranger, and a male one at that? That alone was worth seventy-two masking tape casts. She blinked back a sudden sheen of tears and made herself frown—but not too deeply.

"And you two," she continued, "will put all the animals back where they belong and then pick up every little bit of tape. Before breakfast. Understood?"

Both girls nodded, and Lilliane sighed. "Yes, Aunt Grace."

She turned to Josh, who looked like he might burst if he held in the laughter much longer. "You're in charge. Oatmeal for breakfast."

Valiantly maintaining a semi-straight face, Josh nodded. "Yes, Aunt Grace."

Grace handed the frog and bunny back to Annabelle, then took the shoe from Josh that he'd carried back from the other cottage. As the two older girls scrambled to gather up armloads of stuffies, she dug the pill bottle out of her pocket and dropped it on Sean's lap before she cleared a spot on the coffee table for herself.

"I really didn't mean for it to get so out of hand," he said.

"Uh huh." She sat down.

"Hold on." He narrowed his eyes. "You're not nearly as put out as you're letting on, are you?"

She nodded at the bottle in his hand. "You might want to take one of those before we head out. Assuming you didn't take more of the codeine?"

"You're very good, you know. You had me fooled. And no, I didn't take anything."

"More importantly, I have *them* fooled." Grace tipped her head toward the cleanup operation. "Can you imagine the mayhem if they knew how funny I thought they were?"

Sean chuckled, a warm sound that wrapped the two of them in an intimate cloak of shared conspiracy. Grace sat a little straighter and gave the pill bottle another pointed look.

He twisted off the cap and dumped two tablets into a palm. She raised an eyebrow. He recapped the bottle and held it out for her inspection.

"Up to two," he said, pointing to the directions. "Given that I'm about to make a second hike through the woods, the two idea seems wise."

He downed the tablets before she could speak. She sighed.

"And given that you've just taken two heavy-duty painkillers on an empty stomach," she observed in a dry voice, "we should make that hike sooner rather than later. Before you have to crawl home."

"Damn." Sean made a face. "Didn't think that one through,

did I?"

Grace handed his shoe to him as she studied the fatigue lining his face. "I don't imagine you're thinking about much at all besides sleeping in your own bed right now."

He gave her a wan smile. "The thought may have crossed my mind once or twice."

He crossed his good foot over the cast to put the shoe on. A muscle quivered at the corner of his jaw. Grace put a hand over his and took back the shoe. Without speaking, she lifted his foot and guided it to her lap, then slipped on the shoe and laced it up.

"Thank you," Sean said.

She set his foot on the floor and reached to retrieve his crutches. "Give me a few minutes to look after the kids, and then we'll leave."

CHAPTER 11

"You still sure it was wise to take two of those things?"

Sean swayed on his crutches, trying to bring one Grace into focus out of the three before him. They weren't very cooperative.

"The instructions said one or two," he reminded her. Them. He blinked twice. The three Graces stayed.

They sighed. "Yes, but it might have been better to wait until you were home before taking the second," they suggested.

Sean considered the idea. Then he grinned. "Too late."

"You are so hammered, it's not even funny."

He giggled, disproving the latter part of her statement.

The Graces rolled their eyes. "Come on. Let's get you into the cottage before you keel over. I don't have a hope in hell of getting you off the ground in this condition."

"Then maybe you could just join me." He waggled his eyebrows suggestively. Then he frowned. Wait. He *was* waggling his eyebrows, wasn't he? Damn. He couldn't feel them. He balanced on one crutch and put a hand to his forehead. Shit. His eyebrows were gone!

Fingertips encountered fuzz and he gave a gusty sigh of relief.

"They're still there," he told the Graces.

They stooped to pick up the crutch that had fallen away from him. "I'm not even going to ask," they muttered, tucking it under his arm again. "Now come on, Wonder Boy. Home and bed."

He turned his head and nuzzled an ear. "Is that a promise?"

The Graces jerked away. "Oh, for the love of—" They sighed and regarded him narrowly. "If I say yes, will you get your butt in gear?"

"Oh, honey. You have no idea." Sean swung his crutches forward and followed them eagerly across the clearing, bypassing the Graces and heading for the cottage. "Race you!"

"Slow down, Romeo. We'll never make it to the bed if you fall, remember?"

He scaled back his speed, but only a little. "I thought I was Wonder Boy," he said over his shoulder.

"Tell you what." The Graces reached out to steer him straight as he yawed to the left. "You can be Wonder Boy and Romeo if you can get into the cottage in one piece."

It took three attempts to negotiate the stairs. By the time he made it onto the deck, Sean's teeth ached from gritting them, and his shirt was soaked with sweat. He paused at the top to catch his breath, waiting for the pain meds to compensate for the meat grinder he was sure his leg had just gone through. A gentle hand covered one of his on a crutch.

"You okay?"

He opened his eyes onto the three Graces. This time, the middle one seemed more in focus, so he concentrated on her. "That," he announced, "is why I took two pills before coming over here."

"Bad?"

"Very."

"Can you make it into the cottage?"

He studied the distance to the sliding glass doors. Four crutch-strides, maybe five, assuming the meds hadn't skewed his depth perception as well as his inhibitions. He nodded. "I can make it."

"All right. I'll go around and open the door. You aim for the bedroom."

"And you'll follow?"

"Absolutely," the middle Grace told him. "I wouldn't miss it for the world."

In her absence, he made his way across the deck and leaned against the cottage wall, forehead resting on rough cedar siding. He may have dozed off for a second, because when the door beside him slid open and Grace's sharp voice called out, "Sean?" he nearly fell off his crutches.

"Here," he said. "I'm here."

The Graces stepped out onto the deck. There were four of them now.

"Thank God. You scared the life out of me when I couldn't see you."

Four Graces were much better than three.

He grinned. "You care."

"Of course I care. I'd care about anyone in your current condition."

"And you called me Sean."

"What?"

"Twice," he said smugly. "Sean. Because that's my name."

Four sets of hands rested on eight hips, and the Graces pursed their lips as they surveyed him. "Wow. You are getting more blitzed by the moment, my friend. You don't usually do a lot of painkillers, do you?"

"Nope. Clean as a whistle." He pursed his lips to follow up with a demonstration, but only a sad, wet hiss resulted. He frowned. "Hm. That's harder to do than I remember."

The Graces gave a snort of laughter. "All right, enough is enough. We need to get you into bed to sleep this off."

"Bed, yes. Sleep? I don't think so, darlin's." He stretched out an arm to snag the Grace nearest him, but they sidestepped in unison and caught the crutches he dropped. Sean scowled. Now there were four crutches, too? That didn't seem right.

"Darlin's? Plural?" The Graces leaned in to peer at him, frowning. "Just how many of me do you see?"

Oh, wait. He was still holding a crutch, so that was a total of five. Much better.

"Sean?"

He leaned against the cottage again. "Mm?"

"How many of me do you see, Sean?"

"Four," he whispered. "Four beautiful, glorious Graces." He lifted a hand, watched it morph into four, and stroked all the soft, deliciously smooth cheeks before him. "Whoa."

"Whoa is right." She caught his hand in hers and slipped the crutch back into it. "Come on, sunshine, let's move while you still can."

He wasn't sure how he made it through the cottage and into the bedroom. One minute he was standing inside the living room while the glass door slid shut behind him, and a heartbeat later, he was flat on his back on the bed. He stared at the ceiling.

"This is weird," he muttered.

"Which part of it in particular?" Grace inquired, lifting his foot to remove his only shoe.

"How did I get here? To the bed, I mean?"

"Well, it certainly wasn't piggyback." With a grunt, she hefted both his feet and tugged them around until his body had no choice but to follow, putting him more or less straight on the mattress...he thought.

He listened to her come around to the side of the bed. Four of her faces swam into view above him. "And the answer," they said, "is that you walked."

"I don't remember."

Together, the Graces reached down to lift his head and shoulders, and slide a pillow under him.

"I'd be surprised if you remember any of this tomorrow." They smiled and brushed the hair back from his forehead. "Now close your eyes and sleep. You've had a long couple of days."

He caught one of their hands in his and held it to his cheek. "Stay?" he murmured.

He didn't stay awake long enough to hear her response.

CHAPTER 12

Grace stopped in at the cottage long enough to collect her cell phone from the top of the fridge and make sure the kids were safe and settled, and then she headed down to the lake shore. Two Adirondack chairs sat on the grass at the edge of the beach. She turned one so she could look out over the water but still see the cottage. Sean McKittrick's arrival in their lives had resulted in her eyes being off the kids way too many times over the last twenty-four hours. Between that and Sean's presence itself, her paranoia had reached all-new levels.

With luck, Luc could put her mind at rest about at least one of those factors. She flipped open the cell phone and auto-dialed her friend and lawyer.

"Lucien Tremaine," a deep tenor voice boomed in her ear.

"Luc, it's Grace."

"What's wrong?" Luc's voice turned sharp with concern. "The kids—?"

"The kids are fine. I'm fine. It's nothing serious—at least, I'm hoping it's not."

They'd agreed on as little phone contact as possible, she and Luc. The private detective he retained for his law practice had given her a temporary cell phone to use in case of emergency but cautioned her not to call any of her contacts with it. Not her colleagues at the job she'd taken a leave of absence from, not her friends, not even Luc unless absolutely necessary. She was to disappear, completely and utterly, and to stay that way until

Barry was found.

"*There's no such thing as too careful,*" Paul Kingsley had told her. "*Barry's smart. He's been a cop for twenty years, and he knows how to find people. You can't just lie low; you have to be invisible.*"

"Hold on," Luc said now.

Across the connection, Grace heard footsteps, then a door closing. She leaned back in the chair and gazed out over the lake. Fall's brilliant colors were beginning to fade along the shoreline, and many of the trees now stood bare of leaves. High overhead, a flock of geese winged past in their v-formation, their calls to one another made faint by distance. Grace shivered. As warm as the autumn had been so far, it wouldn't last forever. The nights had already turned cold enough that she'd taken to stoking the wood stove again most mornings, and snow was likely less than a month off. Then what? If Barry hadn't been caught—

Lucien Tremaine came back on the line. "All right. Talk."

"Your neighbor turned up." She didn't have to specify which neighbor, because Luc and Sean's cottages were the only ones at this end of the lake. The seclusion had been one of the greatest advantages to holing up here in the first place.

"McKittrick? I didn't think he went up there at this time of year."

"He's recuperating from a broken leg."

"And he came to see you?"

"More like I had to go see him." Grace filled her friend in on the events of the last couple of days, ending with, "I just wanted to know what you and your P.I. thought. Should I sit tight here with the kids, or do I need to worry?"

"Given that McKittrick is one of our finest, I suspect you'll be fine with him there."

Grace blinked. Now there was a tidbit she hadn't expected. "Sean is a *cop*?"

"Fourteen years with Ottawa Police Service, I think he said. So you can breathe again, sweetheart. You and the kids are safe where you are."

Grace closed her eyes, holding back tears of sheer relief. Until Luc had spoken those words, she hadn't realized how worried she'd been. The idea of packing them all up and moving them again, of having to find somewhere else that would be safe from Barry...

But still. A cop? Given the kids' history with their own "finest," she'd have to keep that information away from them.

"Thank God," she said quietly. "I'm not sure what I would have done if you'd said otherwise."

"Rough week?" Luc's voice was gentle. Concerned.

That didn't help ease the whole self-pity thing she had going at the moment. Grace swiped at the tears that spilled over. She tried not to sniffle.

"Challenging," she admitted. "Annabelle is teething, and the girls seem to be taking turns having nightmares. I'm up just about every night with one or the other."

"Hell, Grace," her friend muttered. "You can't keep this up. Not on your own."

"It's not like I have much choice. Even if I could afford a nanny, it's not like I can hire one all the way out here."

"I know. I just wish there was something I could do to help."

She laughed a short, bittersweet laugh. "Besides letting us live rent-free in your cottage, you mean? Or having Paul give me a safety rundown? Or looking after Julianne for me?"

"All things that take next to no effort on my part."

"It's more than you think, Luc, believe me. I don't know what I would have done without you." She took a steadying breath. "Speaking of Julianne…"

"Unchanged."

A single word, filled with so much.

Unchanged. Still in hospital. Still breathing on her own but attached to tubes and wires and machines monitoring the shadow of life that remained.

Still not Julianne.

She glanced toward the cottage where her sister's four children sat at the picnic table on the deck with their drawing materials. It took several attempts to force the next question through a too-tight throat.

"And Barry?"

"Every cop in the city is watching for him. The blue line ends with what he did to Julianne, Grace. They want him caught at least as much as you do."

She curled her free hand into a fist so tight, her fingernails dug into her palm. "I know. But he's smart, and he knows how they work, and—"

"They'll get him. Give them a chance."

"It's been four weeks, Luc. Every single day he's out there puts him closer to tracking us down."

"You're still following all of Paul's instructions? Lying low?"

"Of course. We go to Perth no more than once every two weeks, and I never shop in the same place twice in a row." She extracted her fingernails from her palm and rested an elbow on the arm of the chair. Wearily, she cradled her forehead. "Hell, I don't even gas up at the same station two times in a row."

"Then you're good. The van is rented in my name, Barry

doesn't know about my connection to your sister, you're using a burner phone, you're not in touch with anyone you know… there's no way he can find you, Grace. I promise."

She nodded, needing to believe him.

"Now, about Sean McKittrick," he said.

Grace's heart kicked against her ribs. "What about him?"

"I think you should tell him about your situation. He might be able to help."

"How? By throwing a crutch at Barry if he turns up?"

"I don't know. With the kids, maybe."

"The man is in a full leg cast and on heavy-duty painkillers, Luc. The last thing he needs to be doing is chasing after a two-year-old."

"Right." Luc sighed. "Maybe not. Well, at least he makes for adult company."

"Yes, because he totally came out to his cottage in the woods so he could hang out with a woman who has four young children in tow." The sun had disappeared behind clouds, and Grace stood up, hugging herself against the chill creeping back into the air. "Seriously, Luc, I'm fine. And the less we see of him, the better. You know how the kids feel about cops right now. Especially Josh."

"But if you explain your situation to him—"

"No." The word came out harsh. Strangled. Grace scooped away the hair from her face, holding it back with a shaking hand. "I'm sorry. I know you mean well, but I'm not about to burden a man I don't even know with my sob story. I just needed to be sure we were still safe here, that's all."

Long seconds dragged by, filled with the silence of the lake and the beat of Grace's heart in her own ears.

Then, his voice quiet with more understanding than Grace wanted, Luc said, "You can't keep not talking about it, Grace. Sooner or later—"

Without so much as a goodbye, Grace thumbed the disconnect button. She stared at the cell phone for a moment, then pocketed it and started across the lawn toward the cottage. Talking about what had happened was the one thing she and Luc disagreed on. He insisted it was detrimental to keep things bottled up inside her; she was equally certain she would shatter if she gave voice to what she'd seen. What she'd found when she came home to her condo that day to find the front door off its hinges and Julianne lying bloodied and beaten on the kitchen—

Grace sucked in a shuddering breath.

Oh, no. There would be no talking. Not until Barry was caught, and the kids were safe, and she could afford to fall apart. Except even then, if Juli didn't recover...

Annabelle spotted her approach and squealed a greeting from behind the deck railing. Grace lifted a hand in response and pasted on a smile. With a monumental effort, she pushed away her conversation with Luc. As well intentioned as her friend might be, he had no idea how close to the edge she teetered right now, or how little it would take to push her over.

Tell Sean McKittrick her story and turn into a puddle of hysteria at his feet?

Not in a million years.

CHAPTER 13

Grace held out until seven o'clock that evening before she caved to the urge to check on Sean. With flashlight in hand for her return trip, she left Josh to oversee the screening of a Disney movie and slipped out the side door, headed toward the path through the woods.

All day, a part of her had been preoccupied with their neighbor. She'd assured herself repeatedly it was neighborly concern and nothing more. After all, he'd been pretty doped up when she'd left him—what if he'd tried getting up in that condition, and he'd fallen again? Or worse? Daylight was far enough gone that she should have been able to see a light on in his cottage by now, but there wasn't so much as a glimmer through the trees.

Checking in on him one last time just made sense.

Besides, she reminded the inner voice that snorted at her, she needed to return the key she'd forgotten in her pocket—and the shotgun and shells he'd insisted she carry home last night. All perfectly valid reasons for a trek through the woods at dusk.

Right, the voice responded. *Because wanting to see him again couldn't possibly have anything to do with the idea of having another adult in your life right now, even if it's just as a neighbor. And certainly nothing to do with Luc's suggestion that you talk to him. Tell him...*

She tripped over a root and stopped in the middle of the path, shotgun clutched in one hand, flashlight in the other, staring through the trees at Sean's darkened cottage. Enough, she told herself. She'd been over this a hundred times since her conversation today, and her reasons remained for not wanting to tell Sean her tale of woe. *Valid* reasons.

The inevitable pity would be the worst part. It had been hard enough having Sean feel sorry for her this morning, when she'd told him about Julianne being in a coma. Any more sympathy than that, and she had no doubt she would come completely undone. The very possibility made her gut tighten, and not in a pleasant way.

She'd never been the damsel-in-distress type. She'd made it a point to ensure she could look after herself better than most, and she wasn't about to give that up now. No matter how tempting it might be to fold herself up into a pair of strong arms and let someone else deal with the whole mess.

Blinking back a prickle of tears, she scowled, then straightened her spine and pushed along the remainder of the path to the clearing that marked Sean's property. No pity, no talking, nothing beyond a final check on a neighbor and then back to her own life.

And as for the dream?

Her mouth twisted, half in a grimace, half in a rueful smile. As pleasant as that might have been, she really did have more important things to worry about right now. Not least of which was what she'd do if she found her neighbor expired on his floor. She skirted the cottage—including the poison ivy patch—and picked her way quietly up the steps to the porch. Then she stopped in her tracks.

The door she'd closed earlier stood half ajar.

What the...?

Her gaze lifted from the handle to the dark beyond it. She looked over her shoulder at the SUV sitting empty in the driveway. Goosebumps prickled across her skin. Had Sean gone out somewhere? Come back? Neglected to close the door behind him? Another, more sobering possibility struck.

Oh, hell...had he wandered off into the woods and gotten lost?

For a second, panic glued her feet to the porch. She'd have to call 911. There would be a search party. Television cameras. Publicity. Barry would see. He'd come for them, and he'd find them, and—

And maybe, her inner voice pointed out with exaggerated reasonableness, *he never left the cottage at all. Maybe he's just fine, and you should stop being so ridiculous and just go check.*

She took a deep breath, relaxed her grip on shotgun and flashlight enough that her fingers stopped screaming at her, and nudged the door fully open with the toe of one boot.

"Sean?" she called softly. "It's Grace."

Silence met her.

She stepped inside.

"Sean," she called again, a little louder. "Are you awake?"

Alive? her voice added.

She shushed it so she could listen. No response. The frisson of unease trickled down her spine again. Damn.

She wiped her boots on the mat and then tiptoed through into the kitchen. She laid the shotgun on the counter, wincing at the clatter of the strap's buckle against ceramic tile. Still nothing. Her chest tightened.

She peered into the gloom. Shape by shape, she identified the items in the living area beyond the kitchen. The dining table with its benches, the couch and oversized coffee table, a wood stove, a recliner, a rocker. And there, just off the living room, the door to Sean's bedroom, firmly closed as it had been when she left him.

Her gaze traveled the kitchen, which bore no sign of use in her absence. No way should he have slept this long. Unless he'd woken, taken more pain meds, and gone back to bed again, because heaven knew he had to be worn right out after yesterday. She nodded to herself. That must be it. He was sleeping, and she should just leave him be.

But still she hesitated.

Because what if he wasn't? What if something had gone wrong, and he was...

Dead, her inner voice whispered most unhelpfully.

Grace sighed. She wouldn't rest tonight if she didn't check on him. Just a quick peek in to make sure he still breathed. If she was quiet, he wouldn't even wake up.

Leaving the gun and flashlight on the counter, she tiptoed across the living room, took a deep breath, and slowly, carefully, turned the knob.

Sean jolted awake, his body bathed in sweat, covers pushed aside, the air cold on his skin. Something had woken him, but what? He lay still, staring at the heavily shadowed ceiling, but heard nothing. He turned his head to the window and the trees beyond. He was back in his own cottage, but how—? He frowned. He seemed to recall making his way back from Grace's, but that had been in the morning, and it was almost dark now. Or was it almost light? Had he slept a day, or a day and night combined? He had no idea.

He put a hand up to his bare chest. He might not know how long he'd slept, but he could say with a fair degree of certainty that he hadn't been capable of stripping down. And if he hadn't taken off his shirt...

A corner of his mouth tipped upward. Well. So strawberry-scented Grace had undressed him, had she? An interesting idea, that. Or it might have been, if not for the encumbrance of four—

A soft thud cut off the thought. Sean went still, frowning. That had come from inside the cottage, not out. But no light peeked through at the loose-fitting doorframe, and no voice announced a presence.

Swiftly, Sean ran through the possibilities. Gareth? No, he wouldn't just drive out unannounced—and even if he had, he would have made his presence known on arrival. Grace? Sean snorted at himself. Sheer wishful thinking, that was. That left an animal as the most likely intruder—and if Grace hadn't shut the door firmly enough when she'd departed earlier, it was all too likely.

The sound of a clatter came through the door from the kitchen—something striking ceramic tile. Whatever the intruder was, it was big enough to reach the counter. A thought occurred to him and his blood went cold. Hell. The bear.

He swallowed a curse, remembering the shotgun he'd left at Grace's cottage. He debated the wisdom of trying to scare it off. If he just left it out there, he didn't hold out much hope for his kitchen, but if he tried and failed, and it came after him...

Hell, hell, hell.

Sean pressed a button on the side of his wristwatch and peered at the glowing dial. Seven-fifteen. Had it been nice enough today for Grace to have the kitchen window open? Would it still be? If he opened his own and called loudly enough, would she hear—

The soft, unmistakable scuff of a shoe against carpet filtered through the bedroom's thin wall. Sean rolled to the side of the bed and sat up, his every cop instinct roaring to life. Shit. That was no four-legged animal, it was a two-legged one.

And it was trying hard not to be heard.

He set his foot carefully on the floor and reached for the crutches. He levered himself upright. Empty cottages made a prime target for B&E artists in the off season, and the ones along this stretch of the lake—including his—had been hit twice before. While it wasn't likely someone would break in with a vehicle parked outside, it wasn't impossible, either, especially if there were no signs of light or life this early in the evening.

The footsteps in the living room drew nearer. Sean swung across the floor to tuck himself into the space behind the door. He shifted his crutches to one hand, balanced his weight, and readied for a fight. The door swung open.

Sean reached out and snaked an arm around the intruder's throat.

"You picked the wrong cottage, scum bag," he growled.

Chapter 14

Grace reacted without thinking to the arm around her throat. Years of martial arts practice and some seriously ramped-up paranoia did that to someone. She grabbed her attacker's arm with both hands and pulled, tucking her chin down to protect her throat. In the space of the same heartbeat, she swept her left leg back and locked it behind his, swiveled halfway around, and rolled him over her hip onto the floor.

He landed with a hollow, far too solid thud...and a roar of pain. Her brain stuttered in recognition. *Sean?*

Sean. Cast. Oh, shit.

Open mouthed, she stared at the shadowy form at her feet. A string of profanities followed his bellow, and she dropped the arm she still held, fumbling for the light switch beside the door. The glare of a bare overhead bulb flooded the room. Grace blinked, shielding her eyes for an instant. Then she dropped to her knees beside the man lying on the floor. His jaw was tight, and he'd gone quiet but for his harsh breathing. She covered one of his fisted hands with her own, flinching at its rigidity.

"Sean? It's Grace."

He continued breathing through flared nostrils. She squeezed his fingers. Remorse clutched at her. The man had already endured one tumble. Lord only knew how much damage a second would inflict. Especially one with the force of a black-belt jujitsu throw behind it. She laid her other hand on a forearm slick with sweat and knotted with a pain she couldn't even begin to imagine.

"Sean, can you hear me? You have to talk to me. I need to know how badly you're hurt. Do you need an ambulance?"

Dear Lord, please don't make me call 911. The questions she'd have to answer, the calls she'd have to make...the notice she would bring down upon them...

Sean's entire frame shuddered with an exhale. Forearm muscles flexed beneath her fingers, then began to relax. Fists uncurled. Bottle-green eyes slitted open to glare at her.

"Holy hell, woman," he muttered. "Where in hell did you learn a move like that?"

The normality of his response sent a rush of relief through her that culminated in a prickle behind her eyes. She blinked, her fingers tightening on his arm, his hand. Clinging to his warmth.

"You're okay? I didn't re-break anything?" Her gaze flicked to his cast and then back to his face again.

"I may have jarred half my hardware loose, but other than that, I'm fine." Clenching his jaw, Sean pushed up to a sitting position. His abdominal muscles flexed with the effort, reminding Grace of his state of half undress.

"And you haven't answered my question," he growled, wrenching her attention back up to his face.

He'd asked a question? She flushed, and to cover her embarrassment, asked one of her own instead. "What hardware?"

He grimaced. "Pins. Rods. Enough metal to put airport security on high alert wherever I go." He scooted across the floor on his butt until his back connected with the bed, then sent her a fresh glower. "Did it ever occur to you to knock or call out before you came barging into my house? What if I'd had the shotgun handy?"

Grace tugged her gaze from sweat-slicked muscles for a second time. She sat back on her heels. "You didn't have the shotgun, I did," she pointed out. "And I did call out. Twice."

His scowl deepened. "Well, you should have called louder."

"I thought you were sleeping." She climbed to her feet and scowled back. "Or dead. Excuse me for wanting to check up on you."

"So I'm supposed to thank you for this?" As soon as the words left him, Sean waved them away. "Scratch that. I didn't mean it. Can we blame it on the pain? And maybe the ignominy of having been dumped on my ass?"

"By a woman?" she inquired tartly.

"By anyone. It just so happens I'm a cop, which means I'm supposed to do the dumping."

"I know."

"You know I'm a cop?" His eyes narrowed. "I don't remember telling you."

"I called Luc." As soon as the words slipped out, she knew they'd been a mistake. Fresh heat crawled into her cheeks.

"You called Luc...about me?" Sean asked. "Why?"

Grace shrugged and buried her hands in her jacket pockets, opting for the simplest explanation. "Curiosity, I suppose."

His lips twitched. "Well, I'm flattered, of course, but—"

She cut him off. "Not that kind of curiosity."

Sean linked his hands behind his head, his chest muscles flexing under a dusting of sandy-colored hair. Flat-out amusement danced in the green eyes now. "I see. So I should be insulted instead."

"Of course not. I just meant I'm not—I don't—" Floundering,

Grace snapped her mouth shut and closed her eyes against the view. Had any man's bare chest ever been this distracting? She drew a deep breath and cast about for a change in topic. "Your hardware. Tell me about it."

A heartbeat's worth of utter silence followed her question before Sean roared with laughter. Grace's cheeks reached scorching. Oh, for the love of—

Crossing her arms, she leveled a baleful glare at Sean and waited for him to recover.

"You know perfectly well what I meant," she informed him when he had.

He chuckled some more. "Yes, but you have to admit, your phrasing just then was awfully well timed."

She refrained—just—from telling him where to go. He made another effort to straighten his face.

"Sorry," he said. She didn't believe him for a nanosecond. "And to answer your question, I have two plates and I forget how many screws holding part of my thighbone together, plus several feet of wire."

Grace regarded him for a moment, wrestling with her curiosity. She'd come to check on him, not learn his life history. Or share hers. And now that she'd accomplished what she'd set out to do...

She retrieved Sean's crutches from near the door and handed them to him. "I need to get back to the kids. Do you want a hand getting up?"

"Thanks, but if I'm going to be on my own out here, I should probably figure out how to get myself back on my feet."

She stood back to watch, grimacing at his struggle. More than once, her hand twitched with the impulse to go to his aid, but she held back, knowing he was right about learning to do it alone. At last he stood upright, flushed with exertion and victory.

"Ha!" he said with deep satisfaction.

Grace couldn't help but smile. "Congratulations. Do I dare ask how much pain you're in after that?"

He sank onto the edge of the bed, his chest heaving and sweat gleaming along his shoulders and arms. "More than I would like to be."

She passed him the bottle of painkillers from the nightstand. He took it from her, but didn't open it right away, instead eying her with curiosity.

"You still haven't told me where you learned to drop a man to the ground like that."

"I hold black belts in jujitsu and tae kwon do. I travel a lot for work, sometimes to countries that aren't overly friendly to women. I like to be able to look after myself."

She jutted her chin at the bottle in his hand. "Do you need water?"

"I'm good, thanks." He dumped two tablets into his palm.

She cleared her throat. He looked up.

"Might I suggest just one this time around?" she asked. "Apparently I quadruple in presence when you take more than that."

Sean's brows drew together. "Hell. That was real?"

She fought back a smile. "It certainly seemed so for you."

"Then the rest of it..." Trailing off, he replaced one of the tablets, then re-capped the bottle and handed it back to her.

"How much do you remember?"

"Apart from Wonder Boy and Romeo, you mean? Too

much," he muttered. "Enough to know I owe you an apology. Hell, Grace, I am *so* sorry if I made you uncomfortable."

"You didn't. I knew it was the drugs talking, and believe me, I've had to deal with far worse."

"And you're very capable of looking after yourself. As we've just seen."

Setting the pills back on the nightstand, she glanced out the window. It was full-on dark now. The kids would be wondering where she was. "Do you need anything else before I go? Food? Water?"

"I think I can manage." He patted his cast. "It's easing up already."

"Probably because you're not bashing into things with it."

"Probably."

Grace hesitated. Well then. This was it. Time to say goodbye, with no further need for communication between them, even though they lived just a few hundred feet apart. The small silence between them threatened to grow into something uncomfortable.

Definitely time to leave.

She turned toward the door. She paused in the opening.

"Before I forget, I brought your shotgun back. It's on the kitchen counter. The shells are with it."

"Keep it. I wasn't kidding about finding bear scat beside my driveway. Now that this place is occupied again, chances are good a bruin will give both our cottages a wide berth, but with all those kids you have over there, you should play it safe."

"I'd rather not have a gun in the house."

"And I'd rather you did. It's not like I can run over and do the shooting for you if the occasion arises." He pulled himself up and tucked a crutch under each arm. "You know how to use it, right?"

She hesitated. As long as she kept it well out of the kids' reach, maybe it wasn't such a bad idea. She had to admit there was a certain appeal to having a weapon handy just in case Barry—

"Well?" Sean prodded.

"My uncle taught me when I was twelve," she said. "But I'm not licensed."

"You don't need a license, and even if you did, I'm not about to rat you out for illegal possession of a firearm. You don't have to carry it around with you, just keep it handy. For the kids' sakes."

For the kids' sakes.

He had no idea.

"What about you?" she asked. "As you pointed out, you can't even run."

"Which is why I'm not likely to be wandering more than a couple of feet from a door anytime soon. Take the gun, Grace."

He made a valid point. Several, actually, and so she capitulated with a single nod.

Sean swung past her on his crutches and led the way through the living room, pausing along the way to turn on two table lamps and then the overhead light in the kitchen. Grace picked up the shotgun and shells she'd left on the counter, and then Sean followed her to the door.

"You have a flashlight?"

She patted her jacket pocket in reply.

"Well, then," he said, holding out a hand. "It's been an adventure."

Snorting at the droll summary of the past two days, Grace accepted the handshake.

"That's one way to describe it," she said. "Though I'm sure you'll be glad to get down to the peace and quiet you had in mind when you came out here. Not to mention giving your poor leg a chance to heal."

Sean glanced down at the offending—and offended—limb. "Healing would be nice," he agreed, raising his gaze to hers again. "But I'm glad to have met you. And your brood."

Grace realized he still held her hand, his fingers strong and warm around hers. And that he remained shirtless. She pulled from his grasp.

"It's been nice meeting you, too." She cleared a foreign huskiness from her throat. "And if you do need anything, I usually keep the kitchen window open during the day. If you yell loudly enough, I should be able to hear you from our place. Unless it's raining, of course. Or if it gets any colder and starts to snow. Though I could still..."

She let her babble trail off. *Leave, Grace. Just leave.*

"I'll remember that." Sean reached past her to flick on the porch light. Heat radiated from his bare arm, doing nothing to relieve the frisson of awareness running along her veins. His gaze lingered on hers one last time. "Safe walk home."

Grace made it across the deck to the top of the stairs before Sean's voice stopped her.

"Um, Grace?"

She turned to find the amusement dancing in his eyes again. He nodded at the weapon she carried.

"Those things tend to work better if they're loaded."

He closed the door, leaving her to fumble three of the shells from her pocket into the shotgun's loading port, certain she could still feel his gaze on her.

CHAPTER 15

Sean fought his way out from under a tangle of covers and grabbed for the shrieking cell phone on the bedside table. He squinted at the too-bright display. Scowled. Jabbed the icon to answer the call.

"This had better be damned good, Connor. It's still bloody dark outside."

Momentary silence. Then his cousin's voice, with its signature dryness, said, "It's ten o'clock at night. Just what color did you expect the sky to be?"

Sean did a double take. "It can't be ten. I went to bed at…" he trailed off. "Shit. I slept twenty-three hours?"

"As I'm not there to either confirm or deny, you'll have to go with your gut on that one. Everything okay?"

Sean pushed upright to lean against the headboard. He scrubbed his free hand over his face, pausing to scratch at the three days of growth along his jawline. Man, he needed a shave. It was a wonder he hadn't sent Grace and her brood screaming yesterday morning, the way he must have looked. Especially after a night of not sleeping on that damned couch.

"I said, is everything okay?" Gareth's voice pulled him back to the present.

"Yeah. Yeah, it's all good. I had a couple of rough days, but I'm settled in now." He sensed the gathering concern at the other end of the connection and went for a diversion tactic. "So, how's married life treating you?"

"About the same as ten months of living together did. And before you ask, Gwyn is fine, the kids are fine, and I'm not letting you change the subject that easily. How rough?"

"The drive took a little more out of me than I'd anticipated." It wasn't an outright lie, Sean told himself. Just more of an omission, because if he filled Gareth in on the rest of his adventures here, there'd be no stopping the man from sending a small army of nurses to look after him. "I needed a couple of days to recuperate."

"By sleeping twenty-three hours straight?"

"That just shows how much more relaxed I am out here than I was at the apartment." Okay, that might have been an actual lie. Sean sighed. "Seriously, Gareth, you're like a freaking mother hen. Stop worrying so much. I'm fine."

"Right. Because getting shot in the leg and requiring two separate surgeries has barely affected you."

Sean tried to shift his casted leg into a more comfortable position, but none existed. "Exactly."

"And you're as sharp as ever."

Sean paused. "Is that a note of sarcasm I hear?"

Gareth met his question with another. "Tell me something. How much battery do you have left on your phone?"

"I don't know...fifty percent, maybe? I haven't check—" Sean broke off. "Hell. I forgot my charger, didn't I?"

"I'm standing in your living room with it in hand as we speak," Gareth said. "Pam left some things here, so I stopped by to let her in. I found the charger on the kitchen counter."

"Crap." Sean took the cell phone away from his ear and glanced at the red low battery icon that had popped up on its face. *Crap, crap, crap.* He returned the phone to speaking position. "Yeah, so I may not be calling you much after all. Turns out I'm at ten percent."

Gareth snorted. "This cottage idea of yours just keeps getting better and better, doesn't it? All right. Keep the battery for emergencies. I'll settle for a text from you on Thursday just to let me know you're still alive, and I'll take a run up to bring you the charger on the weekend. Probably Sunday."

"You know I'd like nothing better than to tell you not to bother."

Especially since he knew damned well Gareth would hold this over him for years.

"I'll settle for a *you were right, Gareth, and thanks so much.*" Amusement threaded his cousin's voice.

"How about a *piss off* instead?" Sean grumbled.

Gareth chuckled outright. "See you Sunday," he said. "I'll bring lunch."

The connection went dead. Sean switched off the cell phone and dropped it onto the bed beside him, plunging the room back into complete dark. He tipped back his head to rest against the headboard. Great. Gareth would undoubtedly take one look at his limited mobility on Sunday, and the argument for Sean returning to Ottawa would be on. Now there was something to look forward to.

That, and now that he'd been woken from a twenty-three hour sleep, the probability he'd be up all night, too.

His stomach grumbled. Sighing, he reached to switch on the bedside lamp. Gareth would be looking for signs of self-sufficiency when he arrived. Now was as good a time as any to start practicing.

He made his way out to the kitchen, switching on lights as he traveled so he wouldn't kill himself tripping over furniture. Once there, he opened the refrigerator door and surveyed the contents. He'd kept the groceries simple: eggs, enough fresh vegetables and fruit to get him through to the weekend when he'd planned a shopping trip to Perth, a roast that would feed him for several meals if he ever managed to get it into the oven, and a couple of packages of boneless, fast-cooking chicken thighs. He reached for those now, along with some sweet potatoes and a head of broccoli. Within minutes, even operating one handed as he balanced on crutches, he had the oven preheating and liberally seasoned chicken thighs in a roasting pan. The sweet potatoes went into another pan, scrubbed, unpeeled, and unadorned.

The oven signaled its readiness, and the chicken and potatoes went in. He turned his attention to washing the broccoli and cutting it into uniform florets, then drizzled it with olive oil, tossed it with salt and pepper, and slid the pan onto the oven's top rack. He set the timer for ten minutes, and then smiled with satisfaction.

It felt good to be back on his feet in a halfway independent fashion again. He hadn't cooked since before the shooting— before Gwyn and Gareth's wedding—when he'd shuttled Gwyn out of her own kitchen and made dinner for everyone while she and Gareth caught their breath. He shook his head. Damn, that had been an interesting run-up to marriage they'd had. One more reason he had no interest in that kind of commitment. It looked like way too much work.

He turned to retrieve the dishcloth from the sink, and a jolt of pain shot through his thigh. His breath left him in a whoosh. Halfway independent he might be, but he wasn't quite there yet. He shuffled into the bedroom for his painkillers. A smile pulled at his mouth as he dumped a pill—just one—into his hand, remembering Grace's suggestion the night before. She'd been such a good sport about the whole four-Graces thing. Hell, she'd been a good sport about everything that had happened since he'd first scared the bejeezus out of her nephew.

And she smelled like strawberries.

And she'd kicked his butt.

Strong, beautiful, sarcastic, warm, capable...if he ever did change his mind about settling down, he'd want to do so with someone like—

The thought hit like a shock of cold water. Holy hell, where had that come from? No. No settling down. Not now, not ever.

And in the remotest possible possibility that he did? Strawberries and chocolate aside, someone like Grace was even more strictly off limits. He could admire her all he wanted for stepping in to take on those kids the way she had, but the key word here remained kids. As in not going there.

Between the job and his own growing-up years, he'd seen enough messed-up families to turn him off fatherhood for several lifetimes.

Sean scowled. Why was he even having this argument with himself? It shouldn't be an issue. It *wasn't* an issue. Kids. No. End of discussion. Besides, all of this was moot now, anyway. Grace was gone, back to her own cottage, and he was here. She had no reason to return, and—barring disaster—he had no reason to ask her to. It was done. Whatever it might have been.

He set the bottle of painkillers back on the bedside table and turned to go back to the kitchen. A glint of metal on the floor by the pine baseboard caught his eye. With his cast extended behind him in a careful balancing act, he leaned down to scoop up an unfamiliar key ring with a vehicle fob and three keys attached.

Grace.

She must have dropped it last night when she'd pulled that move on him. Which meant she'd be back to visit.

Warmth tugged at his belly, and the smile returned. Damn. Had his internal lecture meant so litt—

A scream filtered in through the window he kept cracked open for sleep. Thin, high-pitched, and laced with terror. Sean's heart crashed to a stop in mid-beat, then surged against his ribcage. A single thought gripped his mind.

Grace—kids—bear.

He tossed the keys onto the bed, turned, and thudded out of the bedroom. The maze of furniture in the living room ratcheted up from annoying to deadly, nearly sending him sprawling twice before he reached the sliding doors. He pulled aside the glass so hard, the door bounced out of its track and came to rest at a tilt. He didn't pause. Didn't slow down.

He tracked across the deck. The bear. It must have returned. Broken into her cottage. That scream. Had it gotten one of the kids?

The gun, he urged her silently. *Get to the gun.*

He crutched awkwardly down the stairs and across the ink-black ground to the edge of the woods, staggering on the unevenness, searching for the entrance to the path connecting him to the other cottage. Shoving aside tree branches. Cursing under his breath.

Slowly, the night's silence filtered through to him. He paused. Clamped down on the instinct driving him forward. Remembered he was a cop, trained to assess a situation, not to run hell-bent-for-leather into the unknown. He held his breath, peering through the trees, listening through the hammer of blood in his ears.

The other cottage sat dark and quiet.

No screams, no crashing of furniture, no animal growls.

A light came on in the kitchen window. Grace's figure appeared. A cupboard door swung open, briefly blocking her from view before closing again. She stood, framed in the light for a few seconds more, then moved away. The light went out. Sean expelled the air from his lungs in a long, slow hiss. His heart rate slowed.

Behind him, from his own kitchen, came the faint sound of the oven buzzer.

Grace was fine.

The kids were fine.

And the scream?

He filtered through the facts. Kids. Night time. Sleep. Single, high-pitched scream that could have come—no, almost certainly *had* come—from a child. His shoulders descended from around his ears.

A nightmare.

He uncurled his hands from their death-grip on the crutches and winced as he flexed them. Someone had had a freaking nightmare, and he'd been ready to risk life and limb by crashing through the bush, in the dark and on crutches, casting aside everything he knew as a cop, just to get there.

"Goddamn, McKittrick," he muttered into the breeze that stirred against his skin. "You're starting to scare me."

Scowling anew, he turned to answer the oven buzzer's summons.

And to repair the damned sliding door he'd pulled off its track.

Chapter 16

"Aunt Grace, can I have the keys to the van?" Josh raised his voice over Annabelle's shrieks as Grace tried to wrestle her into a t-shirt. "I left my grey hoodie in there the last time we went shopping."

Seated on the floor, Grace stuffed her niece's writhing arm into its armhole for the fourth time. She pinned the limb under her own as she reached for its partner.

"They should be in my jacket pocket," she bellowed at Josh.

Annabelle flung back her head, connecting hard with Grace's chin. Stars burst behind Grace's eyeballs, and she blinked back tears of pain and frustration. The toddler's arm pulled free yet again.

How in the world could a two-year-old be this *slippery*?

"I looked," Josh said. "They're not there."

Hell. Could anything else go wrong this morning? Annabelle had two new molars coming in, and between being up with her half the night and dealing with nightmares for both Lilliane and Sage, Grace figured she'd managed a scant three hours of sleep at best. She brushed a lock of hair back from her sweaty forehead and looked down in despair at her screeching captive.

"Jammy jammy jammy jammy!" yelled Annabelle.

Grace had planned to get outdoors and run the legs off the toddler so she'd nap out of sheer exhaustion, freeing Grace to focus on the other three and their school work for a couple of hours. At this rate, however, aunt would be more in need of sleep than niece.

And all this over pajamas versus real clothes?

"Fine," she growled, trying not to care that she'd just lost to a two-year-old. She set her niece upright and handed over the fleece pajama top decorated with penguins. "You can wear the darned pajamas."

As if someone had turned off a tap, Annabelle's tears stopped flowing and she clasped her arms around the treasured garment. "Jammy!"

"At least they're warm," Josh offered. "And it's not like anyone's going to see her out here."

True on both counts. But Grace's pride still stung, and her confidence in her parenting ability had taken a blow. If she couldn't get a toddler into a t-shirt, how in hell was she going to manage all the other challenges she faced? The teen years, school bullies, homework fights...if Julianne didn't recover, she would face all those and more. On her own. With four kids.

She so hadn't thought this through when Julianne had asked her to be the legal guardian. Had never anticipated that something might actually happen. And now that it had...

Tears of self-pity welled in her eyes. Josh's hand patted her shoulder.

"You're doing a good job, Aunt Grace," he assured her. He nodded at his little sister, who was now tracing the outlines of the penguins on her belly, happily chatting to them. "Mom always said she had to pick her battles with this one. Why don't you let me take her outside for a while? It will give you a break."

Great. Now she was making such a mess of things that a ten-year-old wanted to rescue her. Grace sniffled inelegantly and shored up her backbone. How dared she feel sorry for herself when her nephew had been through so much? Josh had dealt with more than his fair share of responsibility and guilt. He needed a strong, capable adult in his life, not one who folded in the face of a toddler's tantrum, and certainly not one who gave in to self-pity in front of him. She dredged up a smile from beneath the fatigue and worry.

"Thanks, Josh, but Annabelle and I can both use some fresh air." She hauled herself to her feet and gazed down at the curly-headed imp. No wonder Sean had given in to the demands to bandage all the stuffies. The poor man hadn't stood a—

She broke off the thought. Damn. That was at least the sixth time today he'd crept into her mind. She brushed off the seat of her jeans. "Right," she said. "Pity party's over. Annabelle, you and I are going for a walk."

Annabelle fixed her with a suspicious scowl. "Annbell d'ess?"

"No, you don't have to get dressed." Grace sighed. "You can wear your pajamas."

"Find shoes!" the toddler responded enthusiastically. She raced out of the room and down the hallway as fast as her chubby little legs would carry her, announcing to her sisters, "Annbell walk!"

"The keys?" Josh prompted.

"Right. Sorry." Grace cast a look around the room. Dresser top and end tables all sported nothing more than the usual toddler paraphernalia: wipes, a spare pacifier, three stuffed animals complete with "casts," and a collection of picture books. But definitely no keys.

She frowned. "You're sure they're not in my pocket? I know I had them when I went over to—shit."

She scraped a hand through her hair and closed her eyes,

reliving the scene in Sean's bedroom from two nights before. The surprise attack, the jujitsu throw, Sean's hard landing on the floor. Hell, the keys had to have dropped out there. Or else somewhere along the path.

She wasn't sure which she'd prefer, because while crawling around the woods on her hands and knees held little appeal, another visit with Sean had *not* been part of the plan. She opened her eyes to a grinning Josh.

"You know that sounded really bad, right?" he asked.

Grace thought back over her words and rolled her eyes. Only a ten-year-old would have picked up on that. She reached out to ruffle his hair. "Funny. And I think I may have dropped my keys at Mr. McKittrick's. Annabelle and I will walk over there and check, all right?"

Sheer, naked relief flashed behind Josh's wire-framed glasses. She didn't have to ask to know it was because she hadn't asked him to go instead. Hadn't asked him to face a big-voiced man who reminded him entirely too much of his father.

She gave her nephew's thin shoulders a quick hug, then nudged him toward the door.

"Come on. Let's go see how many shoes Annabelle has managed to try on by now, shall we?"

"Man owie," Annabelle said, stepping over the threshold when Sean opened the sliding glass door. She planted an enthusiastic kiss on the plaster cast just above his knee, patted it, and grinned up at him. "Kiss better."

Before he could stop her, she trotted across the living room and climbed up on the couch, leaving a muddy trail in her wake. Sean gazed after the blond curls in bemusement. He'd swear that kid was even cuter today than she'd been two days ago—tantrum aside. He turned back to the door at the sound of a groan.

"Oh, hell," Grace said, her expression dismayed. She stopped just outside and viewed the damage. "I'm so sorry. I was looking for my keys along the trail, and she got away on me. I figured I'd catch up with her on the deck."

She swept back a handful of windblown hair from cheeks made rosy by the autumn morning chill, and Sean's breath hitched in his chest. Damned if the aunt wasn't cuter than she'd been yesterday, too. He swallowed the thought.

Thoughts, plural, because he wasn't supposed to be finding either aunt or kids in the least bit appealing.

He realized Grace was waiting for some kind of response, and he stepped aside to let her in. The faint scent of summer-fresh strawberries followed her. He took an extra step back.

"No problem," he said. "Really. Some of the dirt is mine, anyway. I was out for a walk last night."

Grace looked down at the print of a large, distinctly unshod foot. She lifted her gaze to his. "A walk," she echoed. "On crutches and in the dark. Barefoot. This is a habit of yours, is it?"

Deciding the question was best left ignored, he cleared his throat. "I have your keys here. They must have dropped out of your pocket the other night." He shot a look at Annabelle and dropped his voice to add, "When you tried to kill me."

Already rosy cheeks deepened in color.

"I didn't hurt you too much?" she asked. "I really am sorry."

Sean shook his head. He curled fingers around his crutches, his hand itching to brush back her hair and trace the curve of a cheek. "I'm teasing. And no, no lasting injuries. The keys are on my nightstand. I'll get them for you while you grab Annabelle."

"Annbell s'ay," the toddler announced from the couch.

Grace angled her head to look past him at her niece, heaving a sigh. Sean frowned at the shadows smudged beneath her eyes. The fatigue in the droop of her shoulders.

"Rough night?" he asked. "I heard screams. Twice. Nightmares?"

"The sound carries that far?" Grace winced. "Sorry about that."

"Don't be. Is everyone all right this morning?"

Grace hesitated. Then she nodded, her lips pulling into a brief, tight smile. "They're fine, thanks. Just worried about their mom."

Of course. As she must be, as well. But she'd made it clear she didn't want his help, and he was supposed to be working on letting go of the whole situation, remember? Sean stepped back so she could enter the cottage. On the couch, the toddler paged happily through an old issue of a wildlife magazine.

"Bear!" Annabelle exclaimed. "Rawr!"

"This is so not going to be pretty," Grace muttered.

Sean's lips curved upward. "Would it be easier if you stayed for coffee?"

"Not likely. She's cutting two new molars, so she was up half the night. Tantrums are pretty much a given today."

Sean managed to hold out for all of one-point-five seconds before Grace's glum face and resigned air were more than he could endure.

"Are you sure I can't help out somehow? Maybe you can leave her with me for a little while and go catch a nap or something."

Longing flitted across her expression, but she shook her head. "Thanks, but I'll be fine. I'm hoping the walk will tire her out so she sleeps this afternoon."

"And you'll nap with her?"

"I'll see."

"You need the sleep, Grace."

Her lips thinned into the stubborn line he was beginning to recognize. "I'm fine."

"No, you're not. You're exhausted." He frowned. "Why do you have to be so pigheaded about letting someone else take some of the load for a while?"

"And just whom would you suggest?" Grace scowled back. "The guy who's laid up on crutches, recuperating from a major injury? Or should I call out the forest gnomes?"

Sean regarded her with raised eyebrows. "Forest gnomes?"

She grimaced. "Sorry, that was unnecessary."

"Maybe," he allowed. "But it was still pretty funny."

Unexpected gratitude flashed through her eyes, and she muffled a snort. "It was more snarky than anything, but thank you for being so nice about it. I guess I am a little tired."

"Then let me—"

A shake of her head cut him off. "As much as I appreciate the offer, I really will be fine."

"Pigheaded," he muttered a second time. Then he heaved an exaggerated sigh, taking the sting from his words. "I'll get those keys for you."

Grace put a hand out to his bare forearm. "Let me."

Sean stared down at her fingers, and she snatched them back. Damned good thing, too, because it turned out that skin on skin—hers on his, anyway—had a rather odd effect on his balance. He lifted his head.

"Table beside the bed," he said, and then he tried not to watch the sway of her hips as she crossed the living room.

As predicted, removing Annabelle from the premises wasn't an easy job. The instant Grace scooped her up from the couch, the toddler's bottom lip gave an ominous quiver, and Sean braced himself for the ear-piercing screech he knew was coming.

The little girl didn't disappoint.

Grace grimaced as she rejoined him by the sliding glass door, shrieking toddler in arms and keys clutched in hand.

"Sorry for the commotion," she yelled above the noise buffeting between them. She started to pry the nature magazine from Annabelle's clutches. The toddler's volume doubled.

Sean shook his head. "Keep it," he yelled back. "It's an old issue."

"Are you sure?"

"Annbell s'ay *here!*"

He grimaced. "Quite."

Grace tried and failed to hide a smile. She blocked a small hand headed her way. "We'll leave you in peace, then," she shouted, "and I'll try to keep us out of your way from now on so you can get that rest you came out here for."

"Annbell s'ay man!" The toddler threw the magazine on the floor and out both hands to Sean, her blue eyes overflowing with tears and genuine, heart-wrenching sadness. "S'ay man!"

Grace adjusted her hold, tucking the little girl into her side even as Sean wrestled with the urge to reach for the child. To add his insistence to hers—albeit more quietly, perhaps—that they stay and let him help ease the lines of strain etched around her aunt's eyes.

"Not today, sweetie," Grace told Annabelle. "The man needs to rest."

The toddler's howls resumed. Grace sent Sean a rueful look and raised her voice again. "Still think we'll have a bear problem around here with all this noise?"

He made himself smile. Kept his hands locked on the crutches. "More likely she'll keep every bear in a hundred-kilometer radius at bay."

"That's what I figured, too." Grace stepped out of the cottage and onto the deck. "Well. Thanks again, Sean. Look after yourself."

"You, too," Sean said. He leaned against the doorframe to watch their departure. The slender aunt who had taken on so much, the toddler still wailing to stay with the man. When Grace looked over her shoulder from edge of the woods, he raised his hand in a last farewell, then slid the door closed and turned back to his cottage.

His empty, deafeningly silent cottage.

Damn.

CHAPTER 17

Grace leaned her head back against the sofa cushions and closed her eyes. Thank God Annabelle had finally fallen asleep this afternoon. Last night had been the third in a row of dealing with teething, and Grace didn't know how much longer her body would hold out. It felt as if her brain had detached from the rest of her, watching from a distance as she went through the motions of caring for Julianne's family. How in the world had her sister managed all those years? How would she manage if—

The usual mental door slammed closed on the thought. She couldn't go there. Not yet. *Deal with Barry first, the rest of your life after that.* It was the only way she might stay sane.

Might.

Lifting her head with more effort than should have been necessary, she peered suspiciously at the huddle of children at the kitchen table. The three of them were supposed to be working on a writing exercise, but they'd been whispering between themselves for the last five minutes, casting furtive glances in her direction whenever they thought she wasn't looking. Something was up. The question was, did she have the energy to figure out what?

Before she could decide, Lilliane broke away from the group and came to stand before her, hands folded in the prim manner she had when she was about to ask for something.

"Aunt Grace, may I please bake cookies?"

Normally, Grace wouldn't have hesitated to give permission.

Lilly might only be eight, but she was already an accomplished baker—far better than Grace herself—and required only minimal supervision around the stove. But still...all that huddling for the sake of cookies? She raised an eyebrow.

"Is there some special occasion I should know about?"

Lilly's soft gaze slid away. "Noo...we just want cookies. Raisin ones."

"I see. Do we have all the ingredients?"

Pigtails flopped enthusiastically in response. "I made sure they were on your list the last time we went to town."

"And you're equally sure there's nothing else I need to know about these cookies?"

Hesitation, and then a negative shake of Lilly's head.

"We'll help her make them," Josh offered, urging Sage forward. "And we'll clean up, too. You can even take a nap, if you'd like. I know you were up again last night. You can use my bed, and I'll look after Annabelle if she wakes up."

Understanding dawned, curving Grace's mouth into a smile that pushed away some of the weariness. They were trying to put together a surprise for her. How like them—and how awful of her to suspect anything. She should know better. She did know better, because not a single one of the three had so much as stepped near their boundaries in the entire month they'd been with her.

Apart from the stuffed animal incident, that was, and they'd had help with that one. She smiled at the memory of Sean—

She halted that line of thought, too, and focused instead on the bone-deep craving for the feel of a pillow beneath her head, and blissful, uninterrupted sleep...

"You know what, Josh? I'm going to take you up on that."

Grace levered herself up from the couch. "But wake me in an hour, all right? I don't want to nap too long or I won't be able to sleep tonight."

That should give them enough time to put a batch of cookies into the oven and tidy up after themselves.

Josh and Lilly exchanged a glance, and then he nodded. "Sure, Aunt Grace. One hour."

When Grace woke on her own to long shadows across the ceiling, she knew, instantly and without a doubt, that she'd slept longer than the specified timeframe. Far longer. She groaned at the thought of how much difficulty she'd have getting to sleep that night, then snorted. Really? Given the probability she'd be up another dozen times during the night, she was worrying about the getting-to-sleep part?

She sighed and swung her feet to the floor, then straightened out the covers to her nephew's high standard of neatness. She could just picture them out in the kitchen, shushing one another now that they'd heard her stir, waiting for her to come out and see their surprise. She smiled.

But when she opened the door, absolute silence reigned. No voices, no toddler's feet thudding across the floor. Grace's smile faded. She peered down the hallway to where all the other doors stood ajar. Annabelle was definitely up, and it was definitely too quiet in the cottage for that.

She padded down the hallway to the living room. Empty.

The kitchen beyond was equally deserted. It also looked as if a minor tornado had blown through, opening cupboard doors and scattering bowls and various baking ingredients across the counters in its wake. She crossed to the sliding glass doors. No one on the deck. No one on the lawn that stretched down to the lake. Concern prickled along the back of her neck. What the—

Barry.

Her knees buckled under the weight of the thought, and her brain shattered into a million fragments of fear and fury. Christ. Barry had found them. Come in while she was asleep and taken them. Taken the kids.

Leaden limbs wanted to fold beneath her. She forced them to carry her into the kitchen. Swept the cell phone off the top of the fridge. Headed for the mudroom and her rubber boots, the quickest footwear she could don.

Maybe she could still catch him. Maybe if she drove fast enough and he didn't have too much of a head start—

Luc. A touch of her thumb on the cell phone's touch screen brought up the contact list. Luc would know what to do. She reached for the door and then jumped back as it swung open for Josh, narrowly missing her nose.

She stared. Her nephew's eyes widened behind his wire-framed glasses. In his arms, Annabelle grinned a wide, toothy grin and held out her hands to Grace.

"Mama!" she shouted.

"A-Aunt Grace," Josh stuttered. "You're up."

Grace didn't answer. She couldn't. She was too busy wrestling with equal desires to sweep both children into a hug, collapse in sheer relief, and tear a broad strip off Josh for taking at least a decade off her life.

She took a breath. Then another. Then a third. Only then, her entire body quivering, did she reach to take Annabelle.

Chubby arms rewarded her with a choke-hold on her neck

that Grace had to fight not to return. She shifted her niece to one hip and planted a kiss on a cool cheek that suggested the little girl had been outside for a substantial time. Then she turned her gaze on her nephew.

"You scared the life out of me."

She tried to keep her tone neutral, but her nephew's already thin frame shrank into itself a little more.

"I didn't mean to. I thought you were still sleeping."

"When I woke up and couldn't hear any of you, I thought—I thought—" Grace's words choked off, her throat tightening against the mere idea. She blinked back tears.

Josh's eyes widened and filled with his own tears. He put a hand on her arm. "No. No, Aunt Grace, we're fine. We're all fine."

She nodded. Annabelle squirmed in her too-tight grip, and she forced herself to relax. "I'm glad. But you know the rules. No one goes outside without telling me, if only so I don't have heart failure, all right?"

Josh's gaze slid away. Grace frowned.

"Josh? What's going on?"

"Nothing!" Seeming to realize his denial was too vehement, Josh lowered his voice and gave a shrug. "I was just coming in to clean up the kitchen, that's all."

"Me down," Annabelle demanded. "Me down, Mama!"

Grace set the wriggling bundle on the floor. Was it her imagination, or was Josh deliberately keeping himself between her and the open door? She stepped to the right. He shuffled sideways. Nope. He was blocking her, all right.

She put her hands on his shoulders. He resisted, then, ducking his head, allowed her to move him to the side. She stepped into the opening and looked out. Sage sat on the top step, wrapped in a blanket from the living room, her eyes wide with guilt as they met Grace's. Lilliane was nowhere to be seen.

"Where's Lilly?" she asked.

Neither Josh nor Sage answered.

Grace swiveled on one heel and fixed Josh with a glare. "Now, Joshua Alexander Walsh. Where is your sister?"

Josh swallowed, looking miserable. "At Mr. McKittrick's," he whispered. "She took him cookies."

"She what?"

"She took him cookies. To ask him a favor. But it's okay, because I checked for bears first, and then I watched her go all the way along the path. Enough leaves are gone to see his cottage now. Look! And Sage is waiting for her to come back. She's going to call me when she sees her again."

Grace reached inside and snatched her coat from its hook. She tugged it on. Poised to head out the door, she gave her nephew the fiercest look she had ever directed at him, hardening her heart when the poor boy nearly collapsed in on himself.

"I want that kitchen cleaned by the time I get back," she said. "And keep Annabelle out of trouble. Sage, inside."

Her middle niece jumped up and scurried past her, pressing against the far doorframe to avoid contact. Grace set her jaw, resisting the urge to draw both kids in for a quick, reassuring hug. She closed the door with a distinct bang behind her and went in search of Lilly.

CHAPTER 18

Balanced on his crutches and wiping away the last of his shaving cream with the towel he'd looped around his neck, Sean looked through the sliding door. The beaming, pigtailed girl on the other side of the glass waved at him with one hand. In her other hand, she clutched a foil-covered plate. Sean lifted his gaze to search beyond the deck, but no one else stood within sight. He pulled the heavy door aside.

"Hello, Mr. McKittrick," Lilliane said cheerfully. "Is your leg feeling better?"

Sean raised one eyebrow and furrowed the other. He rubbed a hand over his freshly shaved jawline. "Umm...a little bit, I suppose."

"That's good. I brought you cookies." Lilliane held aloft the plate. "They're still warm. May I come in?"

Sean backed out of the way without comment, and she stepped inside. She shoved the plate at him.

"Could you hold this for a moment, please?"

Sean did as requested, and she stooped to remove her shoes. She straightened again.

"Thank you," she said, taking back the plate. "Do you want me to put them in the kitchen for you?"

"That would be fine," he heard himself say as he peered outside again. Still no one. He frowned. Surely Grace hadn't let her come on her own after his bear warnings.

The little girl carried the cookies through the dining area

and set them on the counter, the plate connecting loudly with ceramic tile.

"Oops. Sorry." She flashed him a grin. "Would you like one now? I can make you tea to go with it."

"Lilliane, does your aunt know you're here?"

"Umm..."

Both his eyebrows drew together. "Yes or no?"

Lilliane straightened her shoulders and lifted her chin. "Aunt Grace is sleeping, but Josh knows I'm here. He watched me walk through the woods so no bears could get me."

Sean absorbed her words. Narrowed his eyes. Watched her look down and scuff a sock-covered big toe against the plank floor.

"Josh knows, but your aunt doesn't," he said. "This isn't about cookies, is it?"

Lilliane didn't look up. Sean crutched over to her and pointed at one of the benches beside the table. She sat. He stood in front of her.

"All right," he said. "Spill."

She looked confused. "Spill what?"

"It's an expression. It means start talking."

Eyes round in her head, she nodded. Then, in a voice small enough that he had to strain to hear it, she said, "We wanted to ask you a favor."

"We who?"

"Me and Sage and Josh. But it's a favor just for Josh."

"I see. And what kind of favor are we talking about?"

Seeming to decide that Sean's bark was worse than his bite, Lilliane scooted forward on the bench until she was at its edge. Feet dangling, she looked up at him earnestly.

"Josh likes to read," she said. "A lot. But Annabelle won't let him. She loves him too much, and she wants him to play with her all the time, and she won't leave him alone. She cries if he goes outside on the deck without her or into his room for privacy. Stuff like that."

Sean suspected he might know where this was going, but he held back his smile and nodded. "It can be tough being a big brother," he agreed, "but I'm sure Annabelle has a nap time. Can't Josh read then?"

Lilliane heaved a sigh. She shook her head sadly. "That's when Aunt Grace makes us do our school work. So we wondered…"

"Go on."

"If Josh is really, really quiet and he only comes over when you're not outside, can he please, please, *please* keep using your hammock? He won't make any mess, I promise."

"I see. So what you're telling me is that the cookies are a bribe." Damn, but it was getting harder by the minute not to laugh.

"No, they're raisin ones. Want to see?"

Sean tried to turn his snort into a cough, but he failed miserably and wound up making an odd honking sound instead. Alarmed uncertainty flared in Lillian's expression.

"Are you choking, Mr. McKittrick?"

Sean gave up. He laughed so hard, he nearly fell off his crutches, and Lilliane jumped up to put a small hand on his arm to steady him. Her face grew hopeful, and when his amusement diminished to a chuckle, she smiled brightly.

"When Aunt Grace laughs, it means yes," she said. "Is that what it means when you laugh, too?"

"Nice try, munchkin." Sean ruffled her hair. "How about we

say I'll think about it? *And* I talk to your aunt about it."

"Do we have to?" Lillian's face fell. "She says we're not supposed to talk to you."

Sean cocked his head to the side at the phrasing. His gaze narrowed again. He would have expected *we're not supposed to bother you,* but *not supposed to talk to you?* Was that a child's interpretation, or an aunt's actual words?

"I think she might notice if Josh disappears, though, don't you?"

Lilliane frowned. "Oh. I didn't think of that."

"Besides, I don't think your aunt meant that you shouldn't talk to me at all," he said lightly. Watchfully. "Just that you shouldn't bother me because of my leg."

Pigtails moved side to side in a negative shake.

Sean considered her response for a long, silent moment. Then he swung himself around and eased down to the bench beside her, careful not to crowd. He rested both hands on the crutches before him.

"I see," he said. "Well, I suppose Aunt Grace has her reasons for that."

A hesitant nod. Big brown eyes met his.

"And you want to do as she says."

A more emphatic bob of the head.

"Do you know what my job is, Lilliane?"

Pigtails shook.

"I'm a police officer. And you know you can trust police officers, right?"

Lilliane's gaze widened, then dropped to the floor. She gave another shake of her head. Sean bit back an oath. Really? Where in hell had a child her age picked up an anti-cop message?

Nothing got his goat faster than parents—or aunts, for that matter—passing on their personal issues to their offspring. Forcing his jaw to unclench, he leaned in to lightly bump Lillian's shoulder with his.

"Hey," he said. "It's true. You know how you can talk to your teacher or your principal if something is bugging you? Well, it's the same for police officers. You can talk to us about those things, too."

Lilliane's feet swung a little faster.

Sean's frown returned. Something niggled at the edges of a brain made lazy by three weeks of inactivity and prescription meds. A few somethings, now that he thought about it. Beginning with Grace and the kids hanging out at a cottage in the woods at this time of year—even if she was homeschooling them, why was she doing it so far away from everything and everyone? And where the heck was Dad in all of this?

And then there was Josh's nervousness around him.

And the global reluctance to answer even the most casual of questions.

And Grace's sister's accident.

Sean blew out a slow breath. Son of a bitch...was this situation what he thought it was? Keeping his voice calmer than he felt, he probed a little further.

"Lilliane, why didn't Josh come over here to ask me himself?"

Lilliane's feet stilled. She shrugged.

"Is he afraid of me?" Sean probed. "Because I yelled at him?"

No response.

His cop instincts revved up to full. "Lilliane, has someone else yelled at Josh? Another man? Was it your dad?"

Face tight with panic, the little girl slid off the bench. "I have to go," she said. "Aunt Grace will be worried. You can keep the cookies. And the plate."

She rushed to the sliding glass door, then skidded to a halt with a dismayed squeak. Sean heaved himself to his feet and joined her, ruffling the top of her head.

"Don't worry, kiddo. I'll run interference for you." He pulled the door aside. "I figured you'd be along soon," he told Grace. "Please, come in."

Tight-lipped, Grace shook her head, her gaze on her niece. "Thanks, but you're supposed to be resting, and I think Lilliane has disturbed you enough."

"She brought me cookies. Cookies are never a bother, right, Lilliane?"

The little girl didn't respond, instead turning her face up to her aunt, her eyes beseeching.

"I'm sorry I left without telling you, Aunt Grace," she whispered. "I was just trying to help Josh."

Sean's heart melted a little more, and he gave himself a mental shake. At this rate, he'd be a puddle on the floor before she left. His decision not to have a family looked sounder all the time, because he was discovering he had remarkably little resistance to a child's big brown eyes. Or blue ones for that matter, he thought, as he remembered the Annabelle-stuffie incident.

He watched Grace's brows pull together.

"What does Josh have to do with this?" she asked Lilliane.

He cleared his throat, drawing her attention to him. "It seems your nephew is feeling a little overwhelmed by the attention of the youngest member of your family."

"Annabelle?"

"She won't leave him alone, Aunt Grace," Lilliane explained.

"Whenever she's awake, she wants to be with him, and you know how much he likes to read."

"I—I—" Grace looked stricken, and her voice dropped to a whisper. "I had no idea."

"I'm sure it's no big deal," Sean assured her. "He's probably just at that age where he needs a bit of space."

"He should have said something."

"He probably didn't want to bother you."

"Then I should have noticed."

Sean resisted the urge to pull her into a hug. Damn. He wasn't doing well with grown-up brown eyes, either. He settled for putting his hand out to her shoulder and giving it a gentle squeeze.

"Hey," he said. "Don't you think you have enough on your plate to worry about? You've taken on an entire family, Grace. I think you can be forgiven for overlooking the occasional small issue."

"But it's not small." Grace sighed. "I rely on him so much— too much—and he never complains. He's such a good kid. They're *all* good kids."

Lilliane threw herself at Grace, nearly knocking Sean off his crutches. He released Grace's shoulder and grabbed for the doorframe instead.

"I'm sorry I broke the rules, Aunt Grace! Really, really sorry!"

Grace dropped to one knee, reaching up to stroke back a strand of hair that had escaped Lilliane's pigtails. "I know, sweetie, and as long as it doesn't happen again, we can forget about it, all right?"

A vigorous nod. Then, "So is it okay, then? Can Josh come over here to read?"

"What?"

"That was the favor," Sean told her. "He'd like to use the hammock on my deck for—"

"No." Grace blushed as he raised an eyebrow at her abruptness. "I mean, thank you, but I don't want him bothering you. I'll make sure he gets time alone at the cottage." She stood again. "We should get going, Lilliane. It's late, and you need to help the others clean up the kitchen."

Lilliane nodded, turning resigned eyes up to Sean. "I'm sorry I bothered you, Mr. McKittrick. I hope you like the cookies."

"You were no bother at all," Sean told her. "And I'm sure I'll love the cookies."

The little girl slipped out the door past her aunt, heading for the stairs. Sean caught hold of Grace's wrist before she could follow.

"Grace, wait. Let Josh use the hammock. I'd be nuts to try doing so myself" —he nodded ruefully at his cast— "so it will just be sitting empty anyway."

Refusal gathered in her eyes. "Thanks, but I'd rather—"

"He wouldn't be bothering me."

"But I—"

"And I'm sure it would be easier on you than trying to keep Annabelle away from him. I've seen her tantrums, remember?" Sean let his hand slide down her wrist to her fingers. It lingered there, as if it had a mind of its own. "Seriously. I'd like to help, and while I can't do much, at least I can let the kid camp out on my deck with a book."

Hesitation replaced the refusal. Sean gave the fingers he held a gentle squeeze.

"Please," he said.

Grace heaved a sigh, but a tiny smile belied her exasperation. "And you call me stubborn? Fine. He can use the hammock. Once in a while." She held up the hand he still held. "Can I go now?"

"Yes. No." He tightened his grip. "Grace, is everything okay? With the kids, I mean?"

"Of course. Why do you ask?"

"Lilliane said you told her she wasn't to talk to me. I wondered why."

She lifted one shoulder in a shrug. "I just didn't want the kids bothering you, that's all."

Bullshit. He didn't think he'd ever seen a smile more forced. But just as he knew she lied, he also knew she wouldn't be pushed. Corner her now and the tiny thread of trust he'd established would snap. Getting Grace to let down her guard was going to take time and patience.

"Right. I figured that must be it." He released his hold on her and watched her cross the deck. Lilliane was already at the edge of the trees, waiting by the path's entrance.

"Grace."

Poised to descend the stairs, she looked back over her shoulder. A woman and four kids camped out in the woods in mid-September. A sister in a coma. Kids walking on eggshells. Josh petrified half to death whenever Sean so much as looked in his direction. A glaringly absent father.

Sean shook his head. He couldn't afford to spook her. Not until he'd figured out whether his suspicions were right.

And what the hell he was going to do if they were.

"Nothing," he said. "Just...take care, all right?"

He stared after her long after she was out of sight, then pulled the cell phone from his pocket. Even though he hadn't used it since Gareth had called, the battery level had still dropped to eight percent. It wouldn't hold out long enough for the calls he needed to make to get to the bottom of this.

He tapped the phone against his cast, then pocketed it again. He'd have to wait until Gareth brought the charger out on Sunday. He closed the sliding door and turned back to his cottage.

"Hell, Grace," he muttered. "What have you done?"

Chapter 19

"I don't have to go." Josh turned at the foot of the stairs to look up at Grace.

She'd taken up position in the doorway to watch her nephew traverse the woods to the other cottage, ostensibly to keep an eye out for bears. For the moment, however, she was wholly focused on Josh, scuffing the toe of his shoe into the dirt path.

"If you're not happy about it, I mean," he mumbled.

Grace sighed. Apparently she hadn't been as adept at hiding her misgivings about this arrangement as she'd thought. She closed the door and walked over to sit on the top step, patting the wood beside her in invitation. Josh came up to sit beside her. She put her arm around him and snugged him close.

"Before Mr. McKittrick came to his cottage, you were used to having a break from me and the girls, and I would love for you to have that again." She pulled back to look down at him. "I'm just concerned, that's all. You're sure you're okay with the idea that he's..."

"A cop like my dad?" Josh finished. Lilliane had already shared the news with him by the time Grace got back to the cottage the day before, and they hadn't really had much of a chance to discuss it since then. Josh nodded. "Yeah. I'm sure. He reminded me of Dad when he yelled at me that first day, but he's different. He's not as angry."

Grace swallowed hard. That was the first mention Josh had made of his father since they'd left the townhouse to come out here. Progress? Lord, she hoped so. She made herself smile.

"You're right. He's not."

"And besides, it's not like I'll be visiting him. I'll just be reading on his deck."

Grace brushed back the hair from the goose-egg her nephew still sported on his forehead from his tumble into their neighbor's tub.

"Then go," she said. "And enjoy your time off."

Josh looped his arms around her waist and gave her a squeeze. "Thanks, Aunt Grace."

Sean had no idea how long Josh had been in the hammock before he noticed him there. He watched the boy from the kitchen window. Josh had extended one skinny leg to push against the deck floor, rocking the hammock gently. Immersed in his book, he pushed the glasses up on his nose and turned a page.

Everything about the kid hinted at the kind of geeky awkwardness that would make him a target for bullies. That alone was cause for concern, but what bothered Sean more were the other possibilities. The signs and symptoms of something bigger. Darker. Far more dangerous.

For the umpteenth time, Sean turned over in his mind the conversation he'd had with Lilliane the day before. If Grace hadn't interrupted when she had, how much more would the little girl have divulged? Would he have gotten any answers?

Could he now?

Sean considered the idea. Josh was awfully skittish around him. He'd likely spook at the very first question. Sean would have to build some trust between them first.

He swung around the dining room table on his crutches and slid open the glass door, leaving the screen in place.

"Good book?" he asked.

The kid's head jerked up, and saucer-shaped eyes stared at Sean for a few seconds before he nodded over the cover of the hefty tome on the birth of the universe.

"Homework?" Sean prompted.

Josh ducked his head and shook it. "I just like science," he mumbled.

Oh, yeah. A definite target for bullies.

A thought occurred to him. "Nature science, too?"

"I guess."

"Ever seen bear scat?"

Josh frowned.

"Poop," Sean clarified.

Interest gleamed behind the wire-framed glasses.

"Leave your book there," Sean said, "and meet me around front, by the driveway."

Without giving the boy a chance to respond, he closed the door again and headed for the opposite side of the cottage. He made it as far as the edge of the back deck when Josh appeared around the corner. Sean hid a satisfied smile. First rule of interview technique: establish rapport.

He swung his way up the path to the driveway and waited for Josh to join him. Hands in fists at his sides, the boy stopped well out of arm's reach. Sean filed away the observation with the others he'd collected, then he pointed with the tip of a crutch to the benign-looking pile at the edge of the gravel.

"It looks like a pile of dirt," said Josh.

"Look closer. See the acorns and seeds mixed in?"

Josh rested his hands on his knees and leaned over to peer at the pile. He nodded. "Is that what they eat?"

"That's what makes up a good part of their diet at this time of year, yes. Apples, too, if they can find them, though it's a bit late for those now. In summer, you'll see more berry seeds—especially raspberries in this part of the country. In spring, there's a lot of green vegetation because that's what they can find."

"What about animals? Don't bears kill animals?"

"Bears aren't particularly keen hunters. Ninety percent of their diet is plant-based. Sometimes you'll get small animal remains—bits of fur and bone from mice or voles—or maybe wasp exoskeletons, if one happens to find a nest of yellow jackets."

Josh looked up at that. "Don't the bears get stung?"

"I guess it doesn't bother them."

"So if they eat mostly plant stuff, why are they so dangerous to people?"

"Mostly because they're protecting their territory. Or in the case of a sow, her cubs. They're also notoriously bad-tempered if they're disturbed." Sean shifted himself closer to the scat and poked it with his crutch.

"Eww," said Josh. "You just put your crutch in a pile of bear crap."

Sean chuckled. "I'll wipe it off in the grass before I go back inside," he promised. "And um...let's not tell your aunt about that, okay?"

The suggestion won him an actual snicker.

"I wanted to show you how dry and crumbly it is," Sean continued. "That tells me it's been here awhile, probably a week or two. A fresh scat looks moist. Kind of shiny. When you're going between your cottage and mine, or just hanging out around your place, that's what I want you to keep an eye out for."

Josh nodded. "I will. And I'll tell Aunt Grace if I see any."

"Good idea." Sean considered inviting the boy in for a snack, but curbed the impulse. Best to let this new level of comfort settle in before he pushed further. He swung around on his crutches and headed back to the path, giving Josh a comfortably wide berth. "And now I'll let you get back to your book."

"Mr. McKittrick?" Josh called out to him as he reached the deck. "Thanks for showing this to me."

Sean glanced back over his shoulder. "My pleasure, kiddo. Enjoy your peace and quiet."

CHAPTER 20

Lilliane frowned at the casserole dish Grace held out to her, then looked up, lifting an eyebrow. "Are you sure you want me to take this to him?"

"Just take your time," Grace said, "and set it down on the ground if you need a rest. I'm sure you'll manage."

Her niece's skeptical expression remained. "It's not me I'm worried about."

"What, then?"

"Is it your macaroni casserole?"

"Is that a problem?"

"It depends." Lilliane wrinkled her nose. "Is it all mushy like the last time?"

"Of course not!" Grace looked down at the foil-wrapped casserole. "Well...not as bad, anyway. I'm sure it's fine. And I'm sure Mr. McKittrick will appreciate it, unlike you rascals. He can't do much for himself right now, remember? Besides, I want to give him something to thank him for letting Josh hang out in his hammock."

"If you say so." Lilliane heaved a long, aggrieved sigh. She zipped up her jacket, lifted her braids free, and took the dish with a shake of her head. "But I'm telling you, he's not going to like it."

"Listen, you ungrateful little imp" —Grace mussed her niece's head— "my cooking is not that bad. You're all still alive, aren't you? Now go. I'll watch you from the porch until you get there. Tell Josh to whistle when you're heading back with him, so I know to watch again."

"Yes, Aunt Grace."

Sean watched Josh and Lilliane conferring on his desk, heads together. Josh shook his head. Lilliane shrugged. Both glanced in his direction. Curiosity getting the better of him, Sean reached for his crutches and hoisted himself out of the recliner.

The kids stepped apart and faced him as he slid the door open.

"Is there a problem?" he inquired.

They looked at one another.

He nodded at the foil-wrapped dish Lilliane held. "Is that for me?"

"Um..." said Lilliane.

He raised an eyebrow. "It either is or it isn't."

Josh sighed. "Aunt Grace sent it for you. As a thank you."

"That was nice of her."

"It's macaroni casserole," Lilliane told him. "But we don't think you should eat it."

"I see. May I ask why not?"

The two children exchanged another look.

"Aunt Grace isn't a very good cook," Josh said at last. Then he hastened to add, "She tries hard, but she hasn't had much practice."

"I appreciate your concern." Sean held back a shudder at the memory of fried sausages and over-salted potatoes. "But it would be rude of me to send it back, don't you think?"

"We could dump it in the woods," Lilliane offered. "And tell her you said thank you. That way her feelings won't be hurt."

"True, but that's also a good way to attract animals we don't necessarily want hanging around, too."

Her eyes rounded and she cast a glance at the woods. "Like bears, you mean?"

"Exactly like bears."

"Oh. But if you put it into the garbage, won't they just find it in there anyway?"

"Not if your garbage is—" Sean broke off. He transferred his gaze to Josh. "You're not just leaving your garbage in bags outside the cottage, are you?"

"We found some cans in the shed. We're using those."

"But you left them in the shed?"

Josh shook his head. "Aunt Grace told me to put them beside where we park the car, so it's easier to put the bags in the trunk and take them to the Dumpster when we drive to town. Is that wrong?"

Sean sighed. How had he not noticed that when he was there? Again, time to get off the damned drugs and clear his head. For now, however, he needed to brief Grace on how to avoid having to use the shotgun he'd given her.

"Lilly, why don't you put that in the fridge for me? I think I'll walk you guys back to your cottage so I can talk to your aunt. Hang on while I get my shoes" —he looked down at his one sock foot— "er...shoe."

Lilliane giggled, and he smiled. Good. He hadn't pushed too hard with his questions yesterday after all. Maybe her relaxation around him would rub off on her brother, and Sean could begin building some real trust. Better yet, maybe it would rub off on their aunt, so he could get some of those answers he wanted.

Grace looked around at the sound of the door opening, ready to reprimand Josh for not having alerted her that he was returning, but the words died on the tip of her tongue when she saw Sean hobble in behind her niece and nephew. He smiled a greeting, and instant warmth curled through her belly, followed swiftly by the panic that dogged every unexpected turn of events in her life these days. She took her hands from the sink of dishwater and wiped them on a tea towel.

"Is everything okay? What happened?" Her gaze traveled over Josh and Lilly, but found no sign of trauma. She raised it to Sean.

"Nothing happened," he assured her. "I just wanted a word with you."

From the living room came a squeal of excitement.

"Man owie!" Unshod feet thudded across the floor toward the kitchen as Grace tried to collect her scattered thoughts.

"It's nothing serious, it's just about your garbage," Sean added.

Grace grabbed for the little girl darting past, but she missed, and Annabelle flung her arms around Sean's cast. He staggered under the onslaught.

"Man owie!"

Grace pried the pudgy hands loose and swung her niece into her arms against the protests. She blinked at Sean. "My garbage?"

"Josh mentioned you've been leaving your cans out by the vehicle instead of in the shed."

"And that's a problem because...?"

"It's one of the things that might make our not-so-friendly neighborhood bruin overlook the noise factor. I assumed you had outdoor experience when I saw you handle the shotgun, but now I think I jumped to conclusions, especially if you don't have bear basics." He raised an eyebrow.

"My uncle taught me to shoot on his farm, but I don't think they had bears there. We didn't stay long with him and my aunt."

Sean gestured at his foot. "Mind if I take my shoe off and come in?"

She realized he was still standing in the mudroom, Josh and Lilliane flanking him. "Of course. Please."

Sean motioned toward the dining area.

"I'll have to sit," he said. "Sorry."

Grace blushed. She knew that. What the heck was with her brain suddenly going offline? She nodded and, with a wriggling Annabelle still in her arms, backed out of the way. Before Sean could advance, Josh intervened.

"Here," he said, dropping to his knees and reaching for Sean's shoelace. "I'll help you get it off."

Grace nearly dropped Annabelle in shock. She stared at her nephew's bent head. Josh? Voluntarily offering to help a man he knew wore a uniform like his father's?

Sean lifted his foot free of the shoe that Josh had loosened. Josh set it aside, then stood and dusted off his knees.

"Thank you," Sean said.

Josh ducked his head shyly and turned away. He came to stand before Grace, poking his finger at his baby sister. "Hey there, Annabelly."

Annabelle pushed against Grace's chest. "Annbell down,

Mama! Annbell down!"

Grace gave herself a mental shake and snapped out of her stupor. She set the toddler on the floor. "Will you read her a story for me?" she asked Josh. "Before she knocks poor Mr. McKittrick right off his feet?"

Trailed by Lilliane, Josh took Annabelle by the hand and led her—willingly, thank heaven—into the living room. Sage, who had sidled closer to Grace at some unnoticed point, tugged at her sleeve. Grace looked down to find her niece's wide eyes fixed on the man they couldn't seem to get rid of.

"Aunt Grace?" she asked in a small voice. "Is a bear going to come and eat us?"

"No, sweetie," Grace reassured her. "No bears are going to come and eat us. They just want our yummy garbage, so Mr. McKittrick is going to tell me how to hide it from them."

Sage screwed up her nose. "Garbage isn't yummy. It's icky."

"Not if you're a bear, sunshine. They like the smelly stuff. Now, off you go and let me talk to Mr. McKittrick, all right?"

"They're nice kids," Sean said as Sage scampered off. "Very polite. Their parents did a good job."

Grace pressed her lips together. She changed the subject.

"Please, sit down." She motioned him toward the paper-strewn table where Lilly and Sage had been working on crafts after their math lesson. And, because it would have been rude not to, she offered, "Tea?"

"That would be nice," Sean said. "If it's not too much trouble."

CHAPTER 21

Grace went through to the table ahead of Sean, stacking homework assignments into one pile and construction paper, scissors, and glue into another. She shifted everything to one end to clear a space as Sean eased himself into a chair. He leaned the crutches beside him and waved a hand at the stacks of paper.

"It must be tough, teaching three different grade levels all at once."

Grace moved into the kitchen. She took the copper kettle from the stove and ran water into its spout. "Easier than you might think, actually. The kids help out with each other quite a bit. Lilliane is teaching Sage to read, and Josh helps them both with math, and there's a ton of stuff online. All I really do is answer questions."

"You have Internet here?"

"Luc has satellite, thank heaven. I don't know what we'd do without it." She set the kettle onto an element and switched on the stove. "Do you take sugar or milk?"

"Both, please."

She spooned loose tea into a teapot, then carried mugs, spoons, sugar bowl, and milk jug to the table.

"You've no idea how nice it will be to have tea while I'm sitting down," Sean said, giving a wistful sigh. "I've misplaced my travel mug, and if there's a way to get an open cup of hot beverage across a room on crutches, I have yet to discover it."

"You have to stand up to drink your tea?"

"And my coffee." His mouth twisted. "No one should have to stand up to drink their first cup of coffee in the morning. It's just not civilized."

Grace returned to the kitchen to take down her travel mug from the cupboard. She set it before him.

Sean looked abashed. "I wasn't hinting..."

She waved away his protest. "Consider it a trade for the bear protection tips. And it seals, too, so it won't leak if you tip it."

The kettle began a low warning whistle. Grace went back to lift it from the stove before it leveled up to ear-piercing shriek. She poured the water into the teapot and set the timer for five minutes, then turned to find Sean watching her.

"What?"

"I'm a little surprised at the precision behind a pot of tea," he said. "For someone with your reputation in the kitchen, I mean."

"My..." She shot a look into the living room, where Josh sat between Sage and Annabelle, reading *The Cat in the Hat,* and Lilliane knelt at the coffee table, working on a drawing she'd started earlier. She scowled. Traitors. Her gaze flicked back to Sean. She shrugged. "I dated a British guy for a couple of years. I was never able to go back to tea bags afterward."

"So what happened to your cooking?"

She bristled. "I'm not *that* bad at it."

"I've eaten your fried potatoes and sausage, remember?" Sean's level gaze met hers, equal parts humor and pity dancing in his eyes. "And Lilliane offered to dump the mac and cheese in the woods so I wouldn't have to eat it. That's what led to the whole bear discussion."

Grace sighed. "Fine," she said. "I admit it. I can't follow a recipe to save my own life. Take-out was invented for people like me."

"Do you have any more?"

"Casserole?"

"Ingredients. Macaroni, cheddar cheese?" Sean reached for his crutches and pulled up onto them.

Grace's jaw dropped. "You want to cook? On crutches?"

"I can cook perfectly well on crutches," he informed her. "But no. I'm not cooking, you are. Under supervision."

"But—"

"No buts. If you don't like the idea of a cooking lesson, think of it as a rescue mission on behalf of your kids." Sean swung around the peninsula to join her in the kitchen's suddenly tight space, and Grace sidled out of the way as he opened the refrigerator door. "Good. You have cream cheese, too. We'll do the shortcut version today, and I'll teach you the white sauce way another time."

Another time?

Before she could wrap her head around the words, or their implications, the stove timer sounded for the tea she'd made. Sean reached past her to switch it off, his chest brushing against her arm. His hard, muscled chest, if memory served from seeing it the other night.

Which it totally didn't.

Couldn't.

Wasn't allowed to, damn it.

Sean stepped back and motioned for her to take his place at the open fridge. "You'll need both the cream cheese and the cheddar. Oh, and get the broccoli, too. We'll add some of that."

She wrinkled her nose. "To mac and cheese?"

Sean's hard, heated pecs leaned in again. He waggled his eyebrows. "Trust me."

The warmth in Grace's belly climbed up to scorch her cheeks. She covered her discomfiture by taking out the ingredients he'd requested and setting them on the counter by the stove. Sean retreated a couple of steps to lean against the peninsula, and from there, he started issuing orders.

"First, a pot of water. Bigger than that. You need lots of water for cooking pasta or else it clumps together."

"Do you have some kind of broth? Bouillon cubes are fine. You'll need to dissolve one in boiling water."

"Grate your cheddar while you're waiting for the water to boil."

"Add your macaroni to the water and turn the heat down so it doesn't boil over. Now set your timer so you don't overcook it."

The instructions came at a steady pace, interspersed with gentle reminders to stir this, wash that, add something else. Twenty minutes later, Grace stared down in astonishment at the steaming pot of completed macaroni and cheese before her, chunks of vibrant green broccoli sprinkled throughout.

"That's it?" she asked, shooting Sean a suspicious look. "That's all I have to do?"

"It's the...quick and easy method," he responded diplomatically, but the light dancing in his eyes assured her he'd meant *idiot proof.* Mindful of the young faces that had gathered on the other side of the peninsula to watch the proceedings, she refrained from sticking out her tongue.

"Cooking doesn't need to be complicated to be good," Sean added. He glanced over his shoulder at their onlookers. "Lilly and Sage, why don't you two clear the table for dinner? Josh, can you put Annabelle in her high chair and get out some bowls?"

A bemused Grace watched her nieces and nephew spring into action, unsure what she found most surprising: Sean's ease at issuing requests, her own comfort with letting him do so, or the kids' unquestioning acceptance of his authority, with not a single one of them looking her way for confirmation.

"Are you staying for dinner, Mr. McKittrick?" Josh asked, coming between them on his way to get the bowls.

Sean raised a lazy eyebrow in Grace's direction. "I don't know. Am I invited?"

She hesitated. Damn. Every time she resigned herself to what she felt certain was a final goodbye with this man, they somehow ended up seeing one another again. That in itself was bad enough. But dinner? She glanced at her nephew's expectant face and groaned inwardly. Well, it *would* be rather rude to say no after he'd supervised the making of the meal…

Her gaze moved to Lilly and Sage waiting by the table for her answer. Even Annabelle sat quietly, as if sensing some impending decision. Grace held back a sigh.

"Of course you're invited," she said, hoping her voice didn't reflect her reluctance as much as she suspected it did. She forced a lighter note. "You still have to tell me how to do the bear-proofing, remember?"

A shadow flickered in Sean's green gaze. Disappointment? Of course. After a couple of days of peace and quiet, relatively speaking, he would have had a chance to rethink his impulsive offer of help with her *brood*, as he called them. He hadn't really wanted to stay for dinner, and he'd hoped she'd give him an easy out. Grace wondered what it said about her that she found a perverse satisfaction in his discomfort. Then she reminded herself yet again how it didn't matter whether he wanted to be with the kids or not, because *he* didn't matter.

Despite what her dratted hormones tried to tell her.

Holding out her hand, she signaled for the bowls Josh had taken down. He handed them over, and then, without being asked, counted out forks for everyone and passed them to Sage to put on the table. Water glasses followed, with Lilliane distributing those. Grace's heart warmed as she left them to it and began piling mac and cheese into bowls.

Only a month, and already their thrown-together family had little routines in place. To her, it seemed a mark of security in the kids' lives. Small progress, but good to see nonetheless. Sean's hand relieved her of the bowl she held, interrupting her reverie and giving her a start.

"Everything okay?"

"It's fine, thanks. Just daydreaming. You can give that to Josh for Sage."

Sean quirked a skeptical brow at the heaping bowl. "A five-year-old can eat that much?"

Grace's face flamed with heat for a third time—or was it the fourth?—and she pressed her lips together. "Of course not," she mumbled. "I wasn't paying attention. Josh, you can give that one to Mr. McKittrick, please. He can have my place at the table."

"I don't want—" Sean began.

"I can't offer you the bench for your leg," she said. "But at least the chair has arms, so it will be easier for you to get up."

And so, despite her very best intentions, Sean McKittrick joined her family yet again.

Chapter 22

Sean listened to the murmur of voices floating down the hall from the bedrooms. Lilliane, calling to Sage to bring her a towel. Josh, chanting "Annabelly with the big round belly" to the delighted giggles of his baby sister. Grace's warm, melodic tones urging everyone along toward their bedtime.

He stared down at his hands, buried up to their wrists in hot, sudsy water. It was all so...

Domestic.

Sean waited for the shudder that inevitably accompanied the thought. It didn't come. In fact, about all he felt right now was a warm, comfortable glow in the pit of his belly. Well, that and a buzz of anticipation, knowing that Grace would return to join him. With the kids tucked into bed, it would be just the two of them. They could make tea—or maybe she'd have a bottle of wine kicking around somewhere, and they could sit and...

Sean yarded his libido back to reality. As attractive as his neighbor was, and as much as he might want to see whether his instincts were right where the kids were concerned, maybe staying wasn't such a good idea after all. Or necessary.

Once his cell phone was functioning again, he'd have the answers he needed in ten minutes or less. He didn't need to be involved with Grace on any level. He was out here to rest and recuperate, not to...well.

Certainly not to do whatever his traitorous body kept suggesting he do. Not with someone like Grace, who screamed commitment and domesticity and all the things he'd made it a mission to avoid in his life.

A door closed at the end of the hall. Anticipation kicked in Sean's gut. Mouth tight, he washed the last bowl, rinsed it, and placed it in the rack. He needed to get out of here before he did something stupid. Needed to go home, back to his own cottage, and—

And then he remembered how, in a moment of weakness, he'd promised Lilly he'd give their aunt another cooking lesson tomorrow. Hell. He'd really screwed that up, hadn't he? How would he extricate himself from that brilliant idea?

Really, McKittrick? You're not some horny teenager anymore. You can't trust yourself to keep it light and friendly? Just neighbors?

Another door closed, and Grace's footsteps came down the hallway toward him. This was it. Just her and him. Parts of his anatomy tightened, and Sean scowled in disgust at the involuntary response.

He might not be a horny teenager anymore, but apparently he made one hell of a horny thirty-seven-year-old. He slapped the dishcloth into the sink, spraying water down his shirtfront, and finished washing the macaroni pot as Grace entered the living room. Her gaze met his, and her step faltered. Stopped. Slow seconds dragged by as neither of them spoke. About the same time as Sean decided it was a damned good thing he was on crutches and unable to cross the room to her as quickly as he'd like, she cleared her throat.

"Shouldn't you be sitting down?"

Mundane. Mundane was good.

Sean pulled the plug from the sink and reached for a tea towel. "I'm good, thanks. I wanted to hang around to say goodbye, so I thought I'd make myself useful."

"Oh...you're going already?"

Anatomical things stirred again. His fingers tightened on the towel he held.

Bloody hell, Grace.

She nodded in answer to her own question, turning brisk. "Of course. You must be tired. I'll get my coat and a flashlight and walk you back."

"I brought a headlamp."

"Ah. Smart thinking." She scuffed a toe against the floorboards and crossed her arms over herself. "Well, then...thank you again for rescuing the kids from another disastrous meal. And for the bear advice. I'll take down the bird feeders in the morning and put the garbage cans back in the shed."

Sean draped the tea towel over the edge of the sink to dry. He reached for his crutches and tucked them back under his arms. "What time would you like me back here?"

"Back...?"

"For tomorrow's cooking lesson?"

"Oh." Grace wrinkled her nose. "You really don't have to do that. Despite what the kids might think, we'll manage."

His jaw clenched. Unclenched. Clenched again. She was giving him an out. This could end here. It *needed* to end here. But already his head was shaking, his lips stretching into a smile of betrayal.

"I don't mind," he heard himself say. "A few more lessons, and you'll be well on your way to chef-hood."

A *few* more lessons? Oh, this just got better and better. It was one thing to want to build trust, but quite another to let things become too personal. And working this close to Grace definitely strayed into *personal*. Sean gripped the handholds on the crutches and formulated a polite correction—*actually, just one more lesson will do*—but Grace's smile wiped it from his mind before he could speak it.

"If you're sure it's not too much trouble," she said. "I suspect we'd all appreciate it. And I have to admit I'll appreciate the grown-up company, too."

Sean swallowed. So much for backing out of his offer. At least it would give the cop in him a chance to dig deeper into the family's mystery...assuming his inner teenager could be convinced to stay on track.

"It's no trouble," he assured her. "I'm happy to help."

"Annabelle naps between two and four, if you'd like to come over then. We'll get more done without her underfoot."

He nodded. "Sounds good. But I really should go now."

Before I get myself into any more trouble.

"Of course. I'll get your things."

Grace returned from the entrance with his one shoe and his jacket. She stood with the latter hugged against her as he sat to put on his running shoe and tie it, then handed the garment to him when he straightened in the chair. Acutely aware of her warmth imprinted on the fabric, he slid his arms into it, then stood again to rest on his crutches. The silence between them teetered on the verge of uncomfortable. Sean cleared his throat.

"Thank you again for dinner."

Her cheeks dimpled. "Thank you again for teaching me how to make it."

More silence. Damn, he hadn't been this tongue-tied since grade school. He scowled. Grace's hand came down on his forearm.

"I knew you'd overdone it," she said. "You're in pain, aren't you?"

He stared down at her fingers, slender and pale against the deep khaki of his jacket. Felt their combined strength and fragility, their gentleness. The faint scent of strawberries slipped across his senses and wove through his veins. Sean tightened his grip on the crutches.

"I'm good," he replied. He cleared the hoarseness from his throat. "But I should get going. Leave you to your peace and quiet."

Grace hesitated as if she might say something, but then she nodded and dropped her hand. She led the way to the door and opened it, stepping out onto the porch with him into the pool of light cast by the light over their heads. Sean tugged the headlamp from his jacket pocket. He slipped it on, then looked up to find Grace holding a hand over her mouth. A grin peeked out from behind her fingers. He grimaced.

"That bad?"

Amusement danced in chocolate-brown eyes. "Let's just call it functional rather than fashionable."

"I see. Well. Good thing the bears won't care, right?"

Her gaze flicked to the dark beyond the porch. "Are you sure you're okay walking back on your own?"

As much as he'd rather stay? Sean nodded. "I'm sure. I make enough noise crashing through the trees on these things, I guarantee I'll scare off any wildlife."

Silence fell, then, and in the space of a heartbeat, turned awkward. Expectant. Grace's gaze turned back to him, lifted to his. Softened. Sean sucked in a ragged breath and stepped back. His crutch-tip landed on a fallen leaf and skidded out from under him, and Grace leaped forward to grab hold of his jacket.

"Are you all right?" she asked, propping him up while he regained his balance.

Her warmth wrapped around his chest, squeezing the air from his lungs. Sean closed his eyes. Could the damned universe make this *any* more difficult?

"I'm fine," he muttered. "Just tired. It was a longer day than I'm used to."

Instant contrition flashed across her face. Great. Now he felt like a heel. He put a hand out to hers, intending to apologize. Skin brushed skin, and Grace inhaled as sharply as he had a moment before. Sean pulled back. To hell with apologizing. If he stayed here another minute, he was going to do something they would both almost certainly regret. Without a word, he swung away and headed for the stairs down to the path, pausing long enough to switch on the headlamp before he pointed himself toward the trees and home.

CHAPTER 23

"Mr. McKittrick is here!" Lilliane's voice sang out from the cottage.

Grace poked her head out of the shed and looked across the clearing to where Sean stood on the porch. She gave a wave, held up one finger, then returned to trying to squeeze the garbage can into the already overstuffed space...and to trying to slow the sudden increase in her heartbeat. She'd dreamed about Sean again last night. About hard muscles and smooth skin, hot and silken to the touch. About his hands, strong and capable and—

Her cheeks heated, but not from exertion.

"Damn it to hell, Grace," she muttered under her breath. She gave the garbage can a final shove, wedging it in beside a lawn mower. She'd wrestled with unwanted flutters and tremors all morning, every time she thought about the pending cooking lesson. To her increasing dismay, no amount of severe discussion with herself had any impact on hormones that seemed to have taken on a life of their own.

She slammed the shed door and looped the padlock through the hasp, then snapped it closed. Sneaking a peek over her shoulder, she found Sean still on the porch. He was waiting for her. Wonderful. Now she wouldn't even have the walk of a short distance to pull herself together. She curled her fingers into her palms, took a deep breath, and pasted a smile on her face as she started across the grass toward him.

A headache. Maybe she could plead a—

No, if she did that, he'd just want to stay and do the cooking for her. Same if she said she was too tired. Flu? If she said she was coming down with something, surely he'd keep his distance so he wouldn't catch it, too. She tripped over an exposed root. Damn. She was stressing way too much over this entire thing. Sean's flight from her porch last night had made it abundantly clear he wasn't interested in anything more than friendship, and neither should she be.

She firmed up her spine. And she wasn't, because she had four kids to look after, her sister was in a coma, and she was hiding out from Barry...and in what universe did that leave room for a man in her life? In any capacity?

But still her steps slowed as she drew closer to the cottage. She wiped damp palms against her jean-clad thighs and forced herself to keep going.

"Chicken," Sean announced.

She stumbled, and her smile faltered. Crap. Was she that obvious?

He held up a grocery bag. "I checked out your spices yesterday, and you have curry powder, so I brought over some of the chicken I roasted a couple of days ago. And some rice. Chicken curry sound good?"

Oh. That kind of chicken.

Sean tipped his head, narrowing his eyes. "Everything okay?"

"Of course." She climbed the stairs to his side. "And yes, chicken curry sounds great, but I can't let you provide groceries as well as lessons."

"I was actually hoping you could pay me back. With a favor."

Still not recovered from last night's all-too-vivid dream, Grace's hormones chose a wholly inappropriate interpretation of *favor*. Her heart skewed sideways. "F-favor?"

Sean lifted a lazy eyebrow. "Of the running an errand kind. Picking up some groceries for me the next time you go to Perth, so I don't have to drive in myself."

Her face flamed. His eyebrow rose higher.

"Are you sure everything is okay? You seem...jittery."

"I'm fine. Everything is fine."

"Is it your sister?" he asked.

"What?"

"Your sister. She hasn't taken a turn for the worse, has she?"

"No. No, she's still the same, as far as I know."

Now Sean frowned. "You don't stay in touch with the hospital?"

Holding still, Grace closed her eyes and took a deep breath. She pulled her chaotic thoughts and traitorous hormones together. Pasted a smile on her lips that she hoped would pass for bright and not terrifying. Opened her eyes again.

"Sorry," she said. "It's been a long day already, and I'm a little out of it. Yes, of course I stay in touch about my sister, and no, there's been no change. And I'd be happy to get groceries for you. I was actually going to make a run into town tomorrow. If you're serious about these cooking lessons, I'm going to need something more to cook with than what's currently in my fridge."

Sean regarded her, his green eyes narrowed. Then he nodded. "Good plan. I'll help you make a list."

Sean dipped a spoon into the simmering curry, blew on it for a moment, then tasted. He let the spicy sauce roll over his tongue.

It was milder than he would have made for himself, but most likely perfect for the kids. He swallowed and aimed a sidelong glance at Grace, grinning at her anxiety.

"Perfect," he declared. "We'll make a cook out of you yet."

A delighted smile spread across her face. "It's really okay?"

"It's delicious. It'll knock the kids' socks off." Sean set aside the spoon. "You just need to remember to start the rice about half an hour before you want to eat, and then you'll be set. There should be enough left over for lunch tomorrow, too."

"You're not staying for dinner?"

Was that disappointment underlying her surprise? He shook off the thought and steeled himself to stay strong. After that supremely awkward parting on her porch last night, he'd given the whole Grace-and-her-family thing a great deal of thought—and he'd concluded that he needed some time and space to regroup and get his bearings. Even if he hadn't been determined to stick with the whole idea of not ever settling down or having kids—which he was, he assured himself—there was too much else going on.

Too many questions, and too much growing certainty that his suspicions about her were right. In which case, he didn't dare get involved. Not if it meant compromising himself as a cop.

"Thank you for the invitation," he replied, "but as long as you can handle things from here, I think I'll opt for an early night. I didn't sleep well last night."

Instant remorse and worry shadowed Grace's eyes. "You've been overdoing it, haven't you? I knew it was too much for you, back and forth along the path all those times. I shouldn't have let you—"

"Stop," Sean interrupted. Playing the sympathy card had

seemed a legitimate way to excuse himself, but Grace's guilt slid under his ribs like the blade of a knife. She had more than enough on her plate without him adding to her stress levels, and he didn't need any more reason to feel sorry for her.

His judgment was already clouded enough.

"It has nothing to do with you…" he started to add, but then he let his voice trail off. It actually had everything to do with her, just not in the way she thought. Or in a way he needed to think. Damn.

He flexed his jaw and sought neutral ground.

"It's the cast," he said. "It gets in the way when I'm trying to sleep."

Grace wrinkled her nose. Sean buried an impulse to lean over and kiss it. Tightening his grip on his crutches, he held back a curse.

"I can imagine," she said. "I broke my arm when I was a kid, and the cast nearly drove me nuts. How much longer are you in it?"

"I go back for an MRI next week. They don't normally cast a broken femur, but even with all the metal they stuck in me, mine wasn't healing as well as it should. They're hoping the cast immobilizes it a bit more."

Guilt returned to her expression, underlined by horror. "Good God, Sean, you've been standing in my kitchen for two days straight, you've fallen twice, and you've made multiple trips through the woods over uneven ground—and *now* you tell me you haven't been healing properly?"

She marched around the counter peninsula, pulled a chair out from the table, and pointed. "Sit."

Josh, Sage, and Lilliane—all working on homework

assignments at the table—traded looks, their eyes round. Sean gave them a reassuring smile, then flapped a dismissive hand in Grace's direction.

"It's all good," he said. "I can barely wiggle my toes in this thing, so I can assure you I'm quite immobile. *And* I'm off the painkillers as of this morning, which proves things are healing."

"You fell," she repeated, placing hands on hips. "Twice. I don't think they designed either your cast or your hardware to withstand that."

He had to concede that point.

Josh cleared his throat. "When did you fall the second time, Mr. McKittrick? When you were going back to your cottage?"

Sean raised an eyebrow at Grace. "You didn't tell them?"

Her cheeks flushed pink. "I didn't see the point."

"The point is to let them know self-defense works." Especially Josh, whose intelligence and awkwardness would make him an obvious target for bullies—if it hadn't already.

Sean met the boy's wide, wire-framed gaze. "I thought your aunt was an intruder when she came over to check on me the other night. When I grabbed hold of her, she threw me to the floor."

All three sets of kids' eyes grew rounder.

"But you're bigger than she is," Lilliane said.

"And you're a police officer," Josh added.

"Are you going to arrest her?" Sage asked.

Sean pressed his lips together against a smile. Then he shook his head. "No, Sage, I'm not going to arrest her. And being a police officer doesn't automatically protect me, Josh. Your aunt is well trained in martial arts. Even if I'd expected a fight from her and I didn't have a cast, I suspect she would have still taken me down."

The boy's gaze flicked back to his aunt. "Did she hurt you?"

"Not counting my pride? Only a little. And I'm fine now." Sean directed the last bit at Grace, who still scowled at him. "Seriously. Things feel better than they have since I was—since it happened. Barring any more gymnastics on my part, I'm sure it will stay that way."

"Maybe. But even so, you and I both know you're doing too much. I refuse to be party to that."

He raised a lazy eyebrow. "So you don't want me to come over anymore?"

"That's not what I said."

"So you do want me to come over."

Fire, McKittrick. You're playing with fire.

Grace crossed her arms. "Would you please stop twisting my words? I'm just concerned about your leg, that's all."

Given the bright flags of color that so attractively stained her cheeks, Sean suspected that *wasn't* all, but he abandoned his teasing anyway, reminding himself he was supposed to be keeping his distance.

He waved a hand in apology, his voice gruffer than he intended. "Sorry. My sense of humor gets a little carried away sometimes. So...I'll see you tomorrow?"

"I'm getting groceries, remember?"

"Right. I forgot." A thought struck him. "Why don't I sit with the kids for you? Give you a chance to have some time to yourself?"

Bad idea, bad idea, bad idea! his voice of self-preservation screamed at him. He brushed it off. It was just a neighborly thing to do. Hell, Grace wouldn't even be present, so how could it be interpreted as anything but the most casual of gestures?

Grace directed a pointed look at his leg. "Leave you with four kids to look after? I doubt that's what your doctor had in mind for immobilization."

"I'd have Josh and the girls to help me with Annabelle, and I'm sure—"

Sage slipped out of her chair and buried her face against Grace's waist.

"I don't want to stay with him," she whispered. "I'm scared."

Scared? The questions with which Sean wrestled reared up again. He struggled not to let them show in his face. Patience, he reminded himself. He still didn't have a usable cell phone. If he went all cop on Grace, she and the kids were likely to disappear beyond his reach. Beyond his help.

And she was going to *need* that help.

"You don't have to stay, Sage. Why don't you and Josh and Lilly go with your aunt, and I'll just keep Annabelle company?" Sean met Grace's gaze and shrugged. "I'm sure you'd find it easier to shop without a two-year-old in tow."

Indecision flickered in her expression for a second before she shook her head. "It would be infinitely easier," she agreed, "but I don't dare leave you on your own with her."

"I'll stay," Josh volunteered. "I don't mind. I don't feel like shopping anyway, and if Annabelle wakes up, I can get her out of her crib for Mr. McKittrick."

"Well, then," Sean said, filing away Grace's look of utter astonishment with all the other clues he'd collected, "that's settled. Now, I don't suppose you have a spare raincoat, do you? The day got a little soggy out there."

Grace followed Sean out onto the porch, shivering in the afternoon's damp chill. Holding the umbrella over Sean's head to protect him from the steady drizzle of rain, she did her best not to dwell on the memories of their parting here the night before. *Friends, Grace. You're just friends. That's what's best.*

Sean picked his way across the wooden surface carefully, wet leaves slipping beneath his crutches. She made a mental note to have Josh rake them up for her when he finished his homework. The last thing she wanted was to be the cause of yet another fall for their neighbor.

Sean reached the top of the stairs and turned. "You really don't have to do this."

She shook her head inside the hood of the rain cape she wore. It was the only adult-sized one in the cottage, and Sean had refused to borrow it and leave her without. Hence the umbrella.

"It's the least I can do. I'd never forgive myself if you caught pneumonia on top of all the other trouble we've caused."

"You haven't caused any trouble, Grace. And I won't melt if I get a little wet. I'm tougher than you think."

"You have to be, around us."

He chuckled. "I suppose, yes."

He picked his way down the stairs, and she trailed behind, one hand half outstretched in case he slipped. Together, they started along the path toward the trees, Sean's garbage-bag-encased cast rustling with each step. Grace shifted her grip on the umbrella.

"You never told me how it happened," she said.

Sean paused and looked back over his shoulder. "This?" He indicated his leg and shrugged. "You never asked."

Because she hadn't wanted to know. Hadn't wanted to invite

confidences. And sure as heck hadn't wanted to be close enough to him to care. She held back a sigh.

That ship had sailed.

But still...*just friends.*

"It never seemed the right time," she lied.

Sean looked up at the umbrella she held over him, then around at the dripping trees. Thunder rumbled overhead. But he was polite enough not to comment on the obvious.

"Work," he said. "An accident."

She frowned. "Car?"

Sean turned to continue picking his way along the path. "I was shot."

Grace stumbled and almost knocked him over. "Seriously?"

"Unfortunately." Sean balanced on one leg and a crutch, and pushed the umbrella out of his face. His jaw had flexed, and the bottle-green eyes had gone flat.

"I—wow—I don't know what to say," she murmured. "What happened? Or don't you want to talk about it?"

Sean shrugged. "It was a domestic dispute with suspected weapons involved. And kids. The guy had a high-powered rifle. I got in the way."

A domestic. Grace shuddered. Just like her sister and Barry, only no one had been there to call the cops for Juli. She thrust away the horror that never quite left her anymore.

"How bad?" she asked Sean.

"A direct hit on the femur. A lot of bone fragments and some soft tissue damage, but fortunately the artery wasn't touched."

"And the prognosis? Will you be able to go back to work?"

Would he want to after an incident like that?

"If I stop falling on it?" Sean quirked a half-grin at her.

"More than likely. I'll be off for a few months, and I have a lot of therapy ahead, but all in all, I was lucky."

Lucky. Grace bit the inside of her bottom lip. She supposed that was one way to look at it, but—

Sean raised an eyebrow. "What?" he asked.

"I've just never really thought about how dangerous a cop's job is. I mean, I read the stories, of course, but I don't think about it."

"Few people do—including cops. We function better when we *don't* think about it."

A gust of wind threatened to turn the umbrella inside out, and Sean tipped his head toward his cottage. "Come on. We'd better get me inside so you can get home again and out of this."

Grace walked with him to the sliding door he'd left unlocked. She held the umbrella over him until he'd stepped inside, then watched him strip off the dripping plastic Josh had helped him taped over the cast.

"Did it survive?" she asked.

"Seems intact. Josh did a good job. Tell him thanks for me?"

"Of course." She half turned to go, then looked back at him. "About tomorrow—"

"Just after one," he said. "I'll be there."

That wasn't at all what she'd been going to say, but the unfurling warmth in her chest somehow rendered argument impossible. He was lucky to be alive—and she and the kids were lucky to know him at all. She nodded.

"See you then."

"Aunt Grace?"

Grace looked up from diapering Annabelle to find her nephew hovering in the bedroom doorway. "Yes, Josh?"

"Why did you learn jujitsu?"

Grace did up the Velcro tabs on the diaper wrap, then secured them with diaper pins. They'd had no more messy surprises since she'd bought the pins, and she intended to see it stayed that way. She reached for her niece's pajamas and glanced again at Josh.

"You know I do a lot of traveling, right?"

"I kept all the postcards you sent me, but Mom said we didn't have room to bring everything with us when we moved in with you. I like the ones from China best. And India."

Grace smiled. She'd known the kids would love those countries. Somehow, when all this was over, she'd get that collection back for Josh.

"Well, traveling alone can be dangerous sometimes, especially for a woman. I wanted to be sure I could protect myself if I got into trouble."

"Trouble like my mom, you mean?"

The knife that resided permanently in her heart these days gave a vicious little twist. God, how she hated that conversations like this were needed. Wished she knew better how to handle them.

She nodded. "Kind of like that, yes."

Her nephew digested her words while she slid Annabelle's legs into the footed pajama onesie and then stood the toddler up on the dresser top. Annabelle bounced enthusiastically.

"Why didn't Mom learn, too?"

With one of Annabelle's arms in a pajama sleeve and the other eluding capture, Grace blew out a long breath, puffing out her cheeks. Annabelle giggled and tried to imitate her. Grace seized on the moment of distraction and slid the second sleeve into place. She zipped up the onesie and set her niece on the floor. Then, the knife wound in her heart aching, she leaned against the dresser, hands gripping the top on either side.

"Not everyone is interested in learning. Most people don't think they need to. Your mom and I never really talked about it, but I suppose she felt safe with your dad when they first met, and then when she had babies to look after, she was just busy."

And in denial, apparently. So much denial.

Josh's thin shoulders hunched, and his throat moved convulsively. "I'll bet she wishes now that she'd learned."

Grace crossed to his side and wrapped him in a wordless hug, not knowing what to say. Not sure there was anything she could say. But she could hold him. She could hold him—all of them—and keep them safe.

Josh sniffled and lifted a hand to wipe the tears from under his glasses. "She's not going to wake up, is she?"

Grace squeezed her eyes closed. God, what she wouldn't give to be able to tell him Juli would wake up and be herself and be his mom again. But she wouldn't lie. She couldn't lie, because if Juli died, or lived but wasn't ever Juli again, Grace would be all Josh and the others had. And if he couldn't trust her...

She dashed away her own tears. "I don't know, Josh. I wish I did, but I don't."

A shudder traveled through his slight frame, and his arms went around her waist in a fierce hug. Annabelle wedged herself against their legs.

"Jossa sad?" she asked.

Josh stepped back, wiped his eyes again, and then heaved his baby sister into his arms. "Joshua is fine," he told her. "We're all fine."

His face took on a determined look, and he met Grace's gaze. "We're fine because you're here with us, Aunt Grace, and whatever happens, you're doing your best."

"Oh, Josh." Grace ruffled his hair. "You're an awesome kid, you know that?"

He ducked his head and shrugged awkwardly around his armload. "Do you want me to read Annabelle a bedtime story?"

"That would be lovely. Thank you."

He headed out the door, then turned. "Aunt Grace?"

"What, sweetheart?"

"Is it okay if I learn jujitsu, too?"

"It's more than okay, Josh. I think it's a great idea."

CHAPTER 24

Grace unloaded the shopping cart onto the conveyor belt, separating Sean's groceries from her own with a bright red stick emblazoned with *Thank you for shopping with us!* Sage and Lilliane assisted, carefully lining up boxes of pasta and bags of produce. It was nice, being out with just the two of them, but weird, too. She felt lost without Josh and Annabelle. She hadn't been away from any of the kids in more than a month. Never been more than arms' reach away or not known exactly where they were and what they were doing.

Well, except for their cookie escapade.

Grace's mouth tipped upward. She had to admit she was rather glad the kids had taken matters into their own hands, keeping Sean in their lives. She wouldn't have done so herself. She still meant what she'd told Luc about not spilling her guts to the man, but Luc had been right about having another grownup around.

And a grownup willing to take a two-year-old off her hands for the afternoon? Pure gold.

The girls set the last of the groceries on the belt, and Grace turned her attention to her lists—one for her family, one for Sean. She scanned them one last time to be sure she had everything. The conveyor lurched forward as the cashier began processing the order. Sage and Lilly moved ahead to watch her scan the items. Grace followed.

"It's two separate orders," she told the cashier, "but if things get mixed up in the bags, it's not a big problem."

"Sure thing, hon." The middle-aged woman didn't slow down, whisking items through at a steady pace.

Cheerful and efficient, the woman—Dana, according to her name tag—was by far one of the best cashiers Grace had ever run across. She'd found herself in the woman's lineup once before and was only too happy to have her again today. No unnecessary chatter, no fumbling to find codes, just a quick, friendly delivery of service and—

"You're short a couple today."

"Pardon?"

Dana nodded at Sage and Lilliane. "You only have two along. You're short a couple."

Cold pooled in Grace's belly. "Excuse me?"

"Last time I saw you, you had four in tow." Dana chuckled, running three more items over the scanner in quick succession. "Lord, I love that little one. Such a cutie, with all those blond curls. And so good-natured. Did she and your young man stay home with dad today?"

As if sensing the panic swelling in Grace's chest, Lilliane's hand slipped into hers, and Sage's arms stole around her waist. Grace fought down the urge to scoop up both girls and bolt from the store.

"Don't do anything to attract attention," Paul Kingsley's voice rang in her ears. *"You don't want anyone to notice you or remember you."*

Anyone such as a too-observant cashier in a store they'd only visited twice before. She forced herself to smile at Dana. To squeeze Lilly's fingers in reassurance. To gently rub Sage's shoulder.

"She is a sweetheart, isn't she?" she replied to the cashier's question. "And yes, they stayed home today."

Dana reached the stick dividing Sean's groceries from her own.

"You know what?" Grace said, blood thundering in her ears. "I'm in a bit of a rush, so let's just put both orders together."

"Are you sure? It's no trouble for me, and it will only take a few extra minutes."

With what she considered astonishing restraint, Grace managed not to scream at Dana. Or to reach across the counter to grab her by the shoulders and shake her until her teeth rattled. She smiled again.

"I'm sure," she said. "But thanks."

Back at the minivan a few minutes later, Grace did up Sage's seatbelt with trembling fingers.

"Aunt Grace, is the lady going to tell Daddy where to find us now?"

Grace swallowed against the bile rising into her throat at the worry in her niece's voice. At knowing what lay behind that worry. Composing her features, she pulled back to look down at the five-year-old with a confidence she didn't feel. "No, sweetie. The lady doesn't even know your daddy."

That much was almost certainly true. The chances of a direct connection between a cashier in Perth and a cop on the run in Ottawa were infinitesimal at best. It was the possibility of indirect connections that made Grace's blood run cold. For all that Perth might be nearly an hour from Ottawa, and Ottawa might be a sizeable metropolis, the entire valley was surprisingly well connected.

Frighteningly so.

People knew each other. They were related to one another. They would talk. And the friend of a friend of someone's third cousin twice removed would mention something in a coffee shop, and another friend would overhear, and then Barry would know, and—

Grace expelled a shaky breath. *Stop it,* she scolded herself. *Barry will be found long before word of a woman with four children in Perth ever reaches his ears. You're being ridiculous.*

But even so...

She tapped Sage's nose with the tip of her finger and looked over at Lilliane in the other seat. "What say we skip the ice cream cones today, and we make hot cocoa at home instead? Just in case Mr. McKittrick needs rescuing from Annabelle."

Both girls nodded agreement. Then Lilliane giggled. "At least there's no more tape to make casts for her animals."

Grace laughed. "True, that. And a good thing, too."

Still grinning, she withdrew from the minivan and slid the side door closed. Then she climbed into the driver's seat, started the vehicle, and put it in gear.

Ridiculous, her voice reminded her.

But she cast a last glance around the parking lot anyway.

Just in case.

Sean studied the Spiderman figure on his cast.

"Your sister is right," he told Josh as the boy put the finishing touches to it. "You're very good."

Josh mumbled a thank you, the tips of his ears turning as red as Spiderman's mask. Hiding a smile, Sean glanced at his watch. Grace and the girls should be back any minute from their grocery expedition into Perth, and Annabelle would likely be up soon, too. Grace had told him the toddler would sleep for two hours max, but they'd passed that time allotment a good half hour before. He'd considered waking her, but Josh assured him Grace would want her to sleep. It was weird, having a ten-year-old giving him instructions on how to handle a toddler, but Josh was far more competent than his age suggested. All the kids were.

In the three days Sean had been coming over to deliver the promised cooking lessons to Grace, he'd had ample opportunity to observe them in their daily activities. He'd seen the level of self-reliance each of them possessed, watched the way they came together to function as a unit. Grace hadn't been kidding when she said they pretty much managed their own lessons. Lilliane appeared to be as proficient a reading teacher for Sage as she was a reader, and Josh had infinite patience when it came to their math lessons. And significant aptitude in that subject, too, from what Sean could see.

"Advanced algebra?" he'd asked Grace, holding up a text from the table on the first day. "Isn't that high school stuff?"

"Grade eleven," Grace had agreed, looking up from the eggs she whisked for a frittata. "Now you know why I let him teach the math around here. Science, too."

"He must have a hard time of it in school."

"Surprisingly not. Yet, anyway." Her gaze had flashed to the living room, where the three kids were immersed in watching episodes of *Horrible Histories* on a laptop set up on the coffee table.

Mouth tightening, Sean had filed away the information with the other tidbits he'd gleaned. A level of maturity in the three older kids that went well beyond their years; their pronounced care not to step out of line; Josh's hyper-developed sense of responsibility for his siblings; his knee-jerk over-apologizing if he thought he'd done something wrong.

Someone had seriously damaged these kids, and if it was who he thought…

Josh returned a black marker to its zippered pouch. Looking satisfied, he sat back in the chair he'd pulled up beside the casted leg Sean had propped up on the coffee table.

"I'm done."

"Thank you. Annabelle will be thrilled when she sees it. Do you do a lot of artwork?"

"Cartoon stuff, mostly." Josh shrugged one shoulder. "Superheroes."

Sean leaned back against the couch cushions and locked his fingers behind his head.

"So if you could have a superpower, what would it be?"

"Strength," Josh said without hesitation. "So I could protect people."

Such as his mother? His sisters?

Sean kept a carefully neutral expression. "Good one. Good reason, too."

Josh eyed him. "Can I ask you something?"

"Sure."

"Do you like beating up on people?"

Sean's eyebrows twitched together in surprise. So much for neutral. "Not particularly, no."

"But you *have* beat up on them."

"Because I'm a cop, you mean?"

Josh nodded.

Holy hell, this kid had a twisted perspective.

"I became a cop to help people, Josh, not to beat up on them. Sometimes force is necessary if I'm trying to stop something bad from happening, but cops don't like when that happens. We try to avoid violence whenever we can."

Josh stared at the hands he'd clenched in his lap. His voice dropped to a whisper that Sean had to strain to catch. "Some cops like it."

Before Sean could respond—hell, before he could recover enough to *think* of a response—the crunch of tires on gravel came from the driveway. Josh bolted from the chair like a startled fawn, all legs and eyes. He stood in the middle of the living room, fists clenched, every line of his body rigid not just with tension, but with terror.

Sean reached for his crutches, biting back the multitude of questions he still had. And the many more that had just been raised.

"Sounds like your aunt is back," he said easily. "Why don't you give her a hand with the groceries?"

"But what if it's not—" Josh broke off. He sidled closer to the uncovered window overlooking the driveway and peered out at its edge. His fists uncurled. "Never mind. You're right. It is her."

He turned and headed through the kitchen to open the side door. From outside came the high-pitched voices of Sage and Lilliane, the lower pitch of their aunt. A vehicle door slammed. Sean stayed where he was, listening, thinking, weighing his choices. The decision he was going to have to make.

Josh's reaction just now had been the last piece of the puzzle Sean knew now he'd been trying to avoid putting together. A completed picture he couldn't ignore—and one he didn't need his cell phone to confirm. Grace had taken her sister's kids from their father. They were hiding from him. And no matter how well intentioned her motives might have been after her sister's accident, her actions put *her* in the wrong. They made her a fugitive.

And they made Lucien Tremaine—who as a lawyer should have known better—an accomplice.

And they put Sean in the most difficult position he'd ever occupied in his life.

Hell.

CHAPTER 25

"Grace, can I ask you a question?"

Grace looked up from stirring the thick, fragrant soup on the stove.

"Um...I suppose," she said. She took the bowl of chopped kale Sean handed to her.

"Stir that in, then turn the heat off and just let it sit until you're ready to eat," he said. "The kale cooks fast."

She did as instructed, then slanted him a glance. "You had a question?"

"Why are you here?"

"Because I'm cooking...wait." Her gaze narrowed suspiciously. "Did you take too many painkillers again?"

A tiny smile tugged at the corner of Sean's mouth. He pulled it straight. "I didn't mean why are you here in the kitchen. I meant why are you here at this cottage? In the middle of nowhere with four kids, three of whom should be in school?"

Grace swallowed the flutter in her throat. "I told you—"

Sean shook his head, cutting her off. "No more half-truths. When you and the girls pulled into the driveway, Josh damn near died on the spot until he realized it was you. Who else was he expecting?"

The ever-present knot in Grace's chest grew three sizes, squeezing out her voice. Shit. She dropped her gaze to the pot of soup again.

"Tell me, Grace." Sean prodded, his voice gentle but insistent.

The flutter of panic spread, coating her palms in sweat. She set the wooden spoon on the counter and wiped her hands against her denim-clad legs. He wasn't going to give up until she told him, was he? But if she did, if she started talking, started telling him about Julianne and Barry, about the door hanging off its hinges when she returned home with the kids, about the battered form she'd found on her kitchen floor...

If the rigid control she maintained began to unravel...

Her gaze went to the sliding glass doors off the dining area, to the kids seated around the picnic table on the deck beyond. Three of them there, another sleeping peacefully in her cot; all depending on her to keep it together, to look after them, to be their anchor in a world that had turned upside down and inside out for them. She drew a shaky breath.

She couldn't. Didn't dare. Because if she couldn't put herself back together again—

"I can help you, but only if you tell me everything. Has a warrant been issued for you?"

Her startled gaze shot back to his. "A what? Of course not! Why would there be—" She stopped short as understanding dawned. "You think I took them. The kids. You think I *kidnapped* them?"

Sean's lips drew even tighter. "I think you meant well," he said. "I've seen how Josh and the girls are, and I know you're trying to protect them. To do the right thing. But Grace, there are laws. Channels. You can't just up and circumvent those—and I can't ignore the fact that you have."

Grace's mouth flapped wordlessly. *That* was the problem?

"Look," Sean said. "Let me help you. I'll walk you through turning yourself in, make sure the kids get the help they need from Children's Aid so they're safe until their mother recovers. I'll even testify on your behalf, but—"

"Stop," she whispered. She scraped her fingers through her hair, squeezing them against her head so her brain wouldn't explode. "Just stop. It's not what you think."

"I think it is. At first I wanted to believe it was just the trauma of their mother's accident, but over the last few days—"He broke off and rubbed the back of his neck. "Damn it, I know what the symptoms of bullying look like, Grace, and those kids have all the signs."

The bile of panic rose in Grace's chest, pooled in her throat. She was going to have to explain. To tell him everything. Talk about finding Julianne, about hiding from Barry, about everything. The edges of her heart frayed and began to unravel. Her toes curled against the floor.

"You were concerned for them," Sean persisted. "I get that, but you still can't just up and take them away from their father like that. Not without the authority to do so."

Breathe, she told herself. *You can do this. You'll be okay, because you have to be.*

"Aunt Grace? Is everything all right?"

Josh stood on the other side of the counter, his face pale, eyes wide behind his glasses, and hands bunched into fists. *How much did he hear?* Grace fought back the roll of her stomach. She made herself smile a reassurance. But it took three tries to unglue her tongue from the roof of her mouth and find enough voice to lie to him.

"Everything is fine, Josh. Mr. McKittrick and I are just talking."

"You look upset."

"I think I'm a little stressed by this whole cooking thing. It's harder than it looks, but I think I'm getting the hang of it. How are you and the girls doing? Are you ready for a snack?"

Josh hesitated, his gaze flicking from her to Sean and back again, clearly undecided as to whether he should accept her explanation, but at last he nodded. A grim-faced Sean moved out of the way, his impatience palpable. He leaned against the counter as Grace took a plate of cut-up vegetables and a container of hummus from the fridge. She set them on a tray along with a handful of napkins, feeling the burn of Sean's gaze between her shoulder blades the entire time. Silence sat thick over the kitchen.

She knew she should speak, if only to reassure Josh that all was well, but she couldn't find the words, never mind the voice. The best she could manage was a smile as she slid the tray across the counter. With a last, lingering glance between her and Sean, Josh carried the tray to the sliding door and tapped with his foot to summoned Lilliane to open it. When the door closed again, Grace took a deep breath, steeling herself to face Sean, to meet the sympathy warring with accusation in the green gaze.

"It's not what you think," she said. "I have papers. Custody papers. I'm their legal guardian."

Sean's jaw dropped. "You—what?"

"You're right about the abuse. It wasn't physical," she added hastily as Sean's hands curled into fists, "at least it hadn't been that I know of. Not at first. And not with the kids."

"Go on."

She shivered. So that was how a voice like ice sounded. She looked away from Sean, unable to meet his gaze. The anger, the horror, the pity she knew she would find there when he heard.

The pity would be the hardest. It would be her undoing, and she couldn't come undone. That was why she hadn't told the story since that awful, awful night when she'd given her statement to the police and then called Luc for help, desperate to protect Julianne's kids. Why she was terrified to retell it now.

But she had no choice, not if Sean thought what he did, and so she dredged up the words she needed—and the memories that came with them.

"Julianne left her husband in July. She and the kids moved in with me, and she started divorce proceedings. He'd been having anger issues at work, and things had been escalating to the point where he'd been suspended. Based on his history, the court awarded her temporary custody. It was enough to tip him over the edge." Grace's voice cracked, and she paused to swallow. Breathe. Wrap her arms once again across her middle.

Sean remained silent, waiting. After a moment, she continued.

"Barry started turning up at the house in the middle of the night and calling at all hours. Julianne finally took out a restraining order against him. The decision was hell on her. She wasn't eating, she wasn't sleeping—and the kids were just as much of a mess. One day, just before school started, I took the day off work to give Julianne a break. She needed some time alone, so she stayed home, and I took the kids to a museum. We were out for the whole day and didn't get home until dinnertime. When we pulled into the driveway, the front door was hanging off its hinges."

"Christ," said Sean softly. "Did the kids see?"

Her fingers dug into her ribs, distracting her from the memories. The all-too vivid images. The blood. The bruises.

So many bruises, black and purple and livid against her sister's unnatural pallor. She looked past Sean's shoulder to the trees beyond the window. She shook her head.

"No. I made them stay in the car while I went in and called 911, and then a neighbor took them for me overnight while I went to the hospital with Juliahne."

"Grace."

She met Sean's gaze again—no, his scowl—and knew that he knew.

He would have heard the story at work. It would have been impossible for him not to hear. A cop who'd beaten his wife into a coma and then fled; a cop who was being hunted by his colleagues.

Of course he knew. But he asked all the same.

"Barry who?" he asked. "What's his last name?"

"Walsh," she replied. "Barry Walsh. And yes, he's a cop."

CHAPTER 26

Rather than leaving after dinner as he had the three previous evenings, Sean stayed late that night. He didn't ask if he could, but Grace didn't say he couldn't. It was simply how things unfolded.

He had planned on offering to help ready the kids for bed, but there'd been no need. Together, the three eldest functioned like a well-oiled machine. A single request from Grace, and they all departed down the hallway without question to don pajamas, brush teeth, and read quietly in their beds for a while, leaving Grace with only Annabelle to look after and Sean frowning in their wake.

"Will you be okay on your own for a few minutes?" Grace asked, tugging his attention back to her and away from his rumination over what the kids had to have been through with their father.

Sean's mouth compressed further as he saw her gaze focused somewhere just beyond him. She hadn't looked directly at him since Annabelle had woken from her nap, just after she'd dropped the bombshell of her brother-in-law's identity on him. Or rather, confirmed it, because the pieces had already begun clicking into place for Sean as she told her story. Her paranoia. Lilly's reaction to finding out he was a cop. Josh's observation that some cops liked to beat up on people. It had all made so much sense when it came together. Heartbreaking, sickening sense.

And it made him want to kick the living shit out of the man responsible.

"Sean?" Grace prompted. Her chocolate-brown gaze touched his, then slid away again. Annabelle waved an enthusiastic goodbye at him from her arms. He roused himself to a smile.

"Of course," he answered her question. "Take your time. I'll make tea."

"You don't have to stay."

"Yes," he said. "I do."

Grace hesitated as if she might argue, then she nodded. "I'll be back in a few minutes."

Sean remained seated on the couch after she left, listening to the murmur of Grace's voice and Annabelle's cheerful chatter on the other side of the wall behind his head. From down the hall came the click of a door closing. A faucet turned on in the bathroom.

All normal sounds. All bizarrely out of place in such a deeply fractured family.

His brain still reeled from Grace's revelations. From putting two and two together as all the pieces fell into place. He'd known immediately who Barry Walsh was, of course. The man's temper was legendary—as was his reputation for skirting dangerously near the use of excessive force in his job. Sean had already been laid up by the shooting when Barry had gone off the deep end and beaten his wife to a pulp, but he'd still heard the stories from his colleagues. Still shared their utter contempt for the man, and their desire to see him hunted down.

And he still felt sick at the thought that Grace and the kids were in Walsh's crosshairs.

Daniels, he thought suddenly. Grace Daniels. Someone had

mentioned an aunt to him, but he'd forgotten that detail until just now. Poor Grace. If his brain hadn't been so fogged up, he would have remembered sooner, and he wouldn't have put her through the trauma of this afternoon. Or at least he would have been gentler about it, because he would have still needed details if he was going to help.

Annabelle had woken just as Grace had finished her story, preempting further discussion and leaving him with so much more he wanted to know. Needed to know, if he was going to help.

And he *was* going to help, whether Grace liked it or not, because no way in hell would he leave her to fend for herself. That's was why he was still here. Why he was going to make tea and sit with her and insist she tell him as much as she could remember. Then, once Gareth brought the cell phone charger out to him tomorrow, he'd make some calls and find out—

Sean let his head drop back against the couch. Find out what? Where Barry was? If his colleagues knew, the son of a bitch would already have been arrested. And even if Sean *could* find him, what would he do—trip him with his crutches? Hell.

He leveled a fierce glare at his encased leg. He'd never felt so helpless in all his life. Not even when he'd been on the floor of that house, lying in a pool of his own blood, waiting for the gunfire around him to cease and someone to notice he'd been hit. Jaw going tight, he pushed back the memories. He'd be damned if he'd leave Grace feeling that vulnerable.

He reached for the crutches and heaved himself to his feet. Tea might be a poor substitute for peace of mind, but at least it was something...and at least she wouldn't have to feel alone.

By the time Grace returned twenty minutes later, he had a

tray laid out in the kitchen with two mugs, a couple of lemon wedges, the honey he knew she preferred as a sweetener, and a pot of black Assam tea. He gave Grace a lopsided smile.

"I got as far as I could with it, but you're stuck with the carrying."

She grasped the tray without comment but paused before lifting it. She sniffed at the amber liquid he'd splashed into one of the mugs.

"Is that whiskey?" She raised an eyebrow.

"I found it in the cupboard over the fridge. I don't think Luc will mind."

"Should you be drinking? You might still need one of those painkillers when you get home."

"I'm not drinking. You are."

She opened her mouth, then snapped it shut again on whatever objection she might have been about to make. Without comment, she carried the tray into the living room and set it on the coffee table. Sean followed.

They settled with the length of the couch between them, their silence heavy with waiting. He didn't have to be psychic to know Grace was a heartbeat from folding under the pressure of the day. Nor did he need a degree to tell him this was a woman in serious need of unloading. By his calculations, she'd been out in this cottage with the kids for more than three weeks now. Waiting to see if her sister would live, hiding from her brother-in-law, jumping at every snap of a twig in the woods.

His jaw tight, Sean poured tea into Grace's whiskey mug. He added a glob of honey and squeeze of lemon, stirred, and handed it to her. She accepted it with a mumble of thanks, then settled back against the arm of the couch to face him, her knees drawn up before her.

Nothing protective about that body language.

Sean squeezed the remaining wedge of lemon into his own tea. He twisted in his seat, too, but only far enough that he could still rest his casted leg on the coffee table beside the tray. He cleared his throat. Grace looked away.

"What's her prognosis?" he asked. "Realistically."

Grace's eyes closed. Her lashes shadowed her cheeks. Weariness etched itself onto her brow. She took a deep, tremulous breath, and her fingers tightened to white on her mug.

"It's not good," she said. "Even if she lives—which is doubtful—she'll never be the same. She'll most likely never even wake up."

Sean let the information sink in. He tamped down the slow burn of fury at his core. How any man could strike a woman at all, never mind beat her that severely, he would never understand. Ever.

He took a swallow of too-hot tea. Coughed against the sear of it in his throat. Returned his attention to Grace.

"So this—you and the kids—it's going to be permanent."

"Yes."

"That's a lot to take on."

Grace's resolute gaze met his at last. "Our parents died when Julianne was nine and I was six. Over the next ten years, we were shuffled from one relative to another—six months here, a year there—because no one wanted to take us both on at the same time. Julianne was the only stability in my life. She fought tooth and nail to make sure we stayed together. I owe her nothing less for her kids."

Admiration warred with sadness in Sean as he studied the

woman on the couch beside him. The circles underscoring her eyes, the fine lines of worry and fatigue etched into the corners. "You know it won't be easy."

She snorted. "I think I had that figured out, yes."

His mouth curved. "I suppose you did. So what will you do? After this, I mean. After Barry is caught and you can go back to Ottawa."

"Damned if I know. I haven't been able to think that far ahead. I still haven't got a handle on the whole idea of providing three meals a day and making sure there's clean clothes for everyone." She ran one hand through her hair and sighed. "I'm hoping that part gets easier with practice."

"What about your job? I assume you have one?"

"I was—am—a business systems analyst. I'm on indefinite leave at the moment."

"But the job is waiting for you. That's good."

"Yes and no…it's waiting, but it requires a lot of travel. I don't see being able to go back to it. I wouldn't want to be away from the kids that much, even if I could afford the child care."

"So you'll have to find a new job?" he asked, only just holding back the *on top of everything else* that wanted to follow.

She gave him a lopsided smile, and a tiny spark of amusement lit her eyes. "You're more concerned about this than I am, for heaven's sake. It's not as bad as it sounds. I'm very good at what I do. Finding another job will be the easiest part of all this."

"It'll still be tough financially. I don't suppose there will be any income assistance…?"

In the blink of an eye, Grace's face turned haggard again. "That depends."

Sean cursed his insensitivity. Of course. Life insurance. If

Julianne died, Grace and the kids would be financially cared for. If she lived and didn't recover, however…

Hell.

He reached out to cover Grace's clenched hand with his own. "Hey," he said softly. "It's going to be okay."

Grace blinked rapidly, her jaw flexing. "I keep telling myself that. I'm just having a hard time believing it."

Without giving himself time to reconsider the impulse, Sean took the mug of tea from her and set it on the coffee table, then tugged her over to join him at his end of the couch. She stiffened in surprise as he slid his arm around her. He rested his chin on top of her head.

"It *will* work out," he said gruffly. "I promise."

Grace remained rigid for another few heartbeats, then, as if the air had been let out of her, relaxed into his side with a shuddering sigh.

"Thank you," she whispered. "I think I needed to hear someone else say that."

He squeezed again. "You're doing an amazing thing for those kids, Grace Daniels. I'll tell you that anytime you need to hear it."

Silence crept between them, this time soft and comfortable, measured by the tick of a wall clock Sean hadn't even noticed until now, the stir of branches against the cottage wall as the wind lifted them, the rhythm of Grace's breathing.

For the life of him, he couldn't have pinpointed when it changed. Became more. But change it did, and suddenly he found himself aware of more than just Grace's warmth against him. He knew without looking exactly what part of her anatomy pressed against his ribcage. Felt the warmth of her breath through his t-shirt. Inhaled the headiness of her strawberry scent.

And knew by her stillness that something had shifted for her, too.

His throat went dry.

Damn.

This was so not supposed to happen. He'd already had this conversation with himself. Multiple times. He didn't get involved with women like Grace. Didn't do commitment. And sure as hell wasn't about to take on fatherhood...in *any* guise.

"Grace..."

Her breathing stopped.

He closed his eyes and gritted his teeth, trying to find the words to explain why he couldn't do this. Hell, trying to remember why. He sucked in a steadying breath and pulled back to look down at her, at the liquid heat of dark-chocolate eyes, the flush of heightened color across her cheeks. A low, heavy ache spread through him. Grace's lips parted. Reason crumbled.

"Aunt Grace? It's after nine. Are you coming to tuck us in?"

Josh's voice from down the hall slammed between them like a shock of ice water. Sean would have been hard pressed to say who moved away from the other faster, him or Grace. Or who was more shaken. Grace looked about as shattered as he felt. But for the same reasons? He sure hoped so, because bloody hell, that had been close. Too close.

"I'm coming, Josh," Grace responded to her nephew. The quiver in her voice made Sean's toenails curl. The way she avoided his gaze made him curse himself as all kinds of idiot.

That was twice he'd almost slipped up. He couldn't afford to do so again. Friendship with this woman might be acceptable now that he knew her whole story and no longer needed to act in his capacity as a cop, but anything beyond was not. Never had been. Never would be. Not when he had this many hang-ups about kids and commitment.

He'd done her a grave disservice in letting her think otherwise.

"Grace," he began.

She stood up from the couch. "I'll be back in a minute," she said. She still didn't look at him. "And then you should leave."

"Thank you again for staying with Annabelle and Josh today." Grace's words were as stiff as her spine, and Sean's fingers stilled for a second in their adjustment of the straps on his headlamp. She willed him not to comment, to just leave and let her recover from what had almost happened between them.

Again.

Twice now he'd come close to kissing her, and twice he'd backed off, the state of panic in his expression both comical and traumatizing. There wouldn't be a third time. Not if she could help it.

"You're welcome," Sean replied. "It really was no trouble. And I'm glad we finally had a chance to talk."

That made one of them. Grace put a hand to her chest and rubbed at the ache in the center.

"I'm glad I was wrong," he added. "And I want to—"

"No."

"You didn't let me finish."

"You were going to offer more help, but no. Thank you. You've done enough."

"Actually, I wanted to suggest we go over safety precautions," he said. "To make sure you stay as hidden as possible."

"Luc had his private detective do that with me before we came. I'm good." She reached past him to twist the doorknob. "It's getting late. You must be tired."

"Grace." Strong fingers closed over hers, warm, gentle, paralyzing, threatening to undo her.

She closed her eyes. Shook her head. "Don't."

"We need to talk," he said gruffly.

"There's nothing to talk about."

"What happened tonight—what *almost* happened…"

She tugged free of his grasp. "Was a mistake. For both of us. It won't happen again."

A muscle flexed in his jaw. "You have kids," he said. "Probably permanently. I'm just not—I've never been—"

"Sean. Let it go." Grace lifted her chin. "The very fact you'd rather talk about what almost happened instead of acting on it tells me everything I need to know. And honestly, I think it's for the best. I don't have room for complications in my life right now, anyway. So can we please just forget about it?"

Sean's hand lifted, as if he might reach for her. She stepped back. The hand settled to his side again. It formed a fist. He sighed.

"Of course," he said. "You're right."

He pulled open the door, and he and his crutches stepped out onto the porch. Arms wrapped around herself, Grace watched him cross to the steps. He looked over his shoulder.

"I won't see you tomorrow. My cousin is coming up to visit, and I need to clean up enough that he thinks I can look after myself, otherwise he'll pack me up and take me back to Ottawa." He grimaced. "He and his wife think I ought to move in with them until I've recovered."

An automatic offer of help leapt to her lips. She bit it back. A day's break from Sean would give her a chance to regain her bearings. Her perspective.

Her sanity.

And if his cousin did drag him back to Ottawa? Well. That might not be such a bad thing, either.

"Of course," she said. "Enjoy your visit."

She closed the door.

CHAPTER 27

On the road. Arriving noon. Bringing lunch and a surprise. Please still be alive.

Chuckle-snorting at the text message, Sean thumbed in a quick reassurance to his cousin, sent it, and switched off his cell phone. He pocketed the instrument, then crutched across to the kitchen, where he tugged the travel mug Grace had loaned him from his other pocket. He filled it with the last of the coffee, screwed on the top, and turned off the coffee machine. Then he glanced at the digital clock on the stove. Five past eleven. That gave him almost an hour to kill...by doing what?

With a sigh, he pocketed the sealed, coffee-filled mug and turned back toward the living room. The last three mornings, he'd been on the path to Grace's cottage by this time, greeted by Annabelle's squeals of delight and the administration of kisses-better to his cast. Yesterday after dinner, Lilliane had told him she didn't mind that he was a police officer, because he was still nice, and quiet little Sage had presented him with a drawing of a man on crutches, wearing an apron and stirring a pot of what she'd told him was mac and cheese—her favorite.

Damned if he hadn't had to swallow a lump over the latter.

He pulled the mug from his pocket and set it on the coffee table, then dropped onto the couch with a sigh. It was good that Gareth was coming today. His leg could probably use the break from rough paths and standing around Grace's kitchen. And God knew he and Grace could do with a bit of distance between them after last night's episode. Damn, but he'd come close to kissing her. Too close. Again.

He shook his head at himself. Those lapses were so out of character for him. He wished he could blame it on her situation—the whole damsel in distress thing—but he couldn't even do that. First of all, he'd never had the slightest inclination to rescue someone before—not outside his job, anyway—and second, as overwhelmed as Grace might be, she was far too strong to want or accept rescuing.

So what in the hell had gotten into him?

He looked again at the clock on the stove, watching its glow change from eleven-oh-seven to oh-eight. He tried—and failed—to remember what he used to do with his mornings when he'd come out here before. Before he'd discovered the potency of strawberry-scented shampoo and dark-chocolate eyes, and the magic of belly laughs and reading stories and coloring pictures.

Would Annabelle miss him today? Would the others?

Would Grace?

Eleven-oh-nine.

Hell.

"Man owie?"

Grace looked down at the toddler tugging on her pant leg. Annabelle's hopeful gaze met hers and then traveled back to the door. It was the fourth time they'd been through this routine since breakfast. There hadn't been any accompanying meltdowns so far, but Grace found herself bracing, just in case. She should find something to distract the child, but the headache that had been sitting behind her eyes all morning didn't leave much room for creative thought. Or coherence, for that matter.

Especially after that repeat dream performance after Sean left last night.

Because it wasn't just a headache that she fought. Her entire body ached with dissatisfaction. Restlessness. Plain old take-me-now need such as she hadn't felt in—well, forever, if she was honest. Not like this. Not like Sean brought out in her.

The same Sean who'd made it abundantly clear he wasn't interested in—

Annabelle tugged on her pant leg again. "Man owie?" she repeated.

Grace sighed and crouched beside her. "Not today, sweetie. Sean is busy. He has visitors."

The toddler digested the words, then changed tack. "Go see man?"

Damn. So far Annabelle had been satisfied with the busy explanation. This new suggestion did not bode well for the day's peace. Or Grace's headache.

"Not today, love. Let's find something else to do, shall we?"

Annabelle's bottom lip began an ominous quiver.

Grace swallowed a groan. She sought frantically for a way to head off the looming tantrum. Preferably something that would allow her to stretch out on the couch for a few minutes, and maybe give the acetaminophen she'd taken time to kick in. Then Annabelle's face cleared.

"Lake?" she suggested. She trotted around the counter to point out the sliding glass doors to where her sisters and brother sat at the picnic table, and beyond them, the glistening water. "Annbell s'im lake."

Grace chuckled. "I wish we could, darling, but it's too cold for swimming. Annabelle would turn into a popsicle."

And there, like magic, was the distraction she'd needed.

"Poppicle!" The little girl danced on the spot, then turned to bang on the glass to get her siblings' attention. "Poppicle poppicle poppicle! Jossa! Sage! Lill'ane! Poppicle!"

Well. The level of excitement didn't do much for a headache, but it beat the alternative. With a grin, Grace waved the three others into the cottage and then turned to the fridge. Five minutes later, leaving Josh in charge of the table proceedings and subsequent cleanup, she retreated down the hall to lie down and deal with her now-throbbing head. Annabelle's voice floated after her.

"Jossa, Annbell s'im," she told her brother. "S'im lake."

Grace sighed and closed the bedroom door. That battle could wait until after the explosions stopped going off inside her skull.

Sean teetered on his crutches as a small missile surged through the door he'd just opened and wrapped arms around his waist. A second one followed in its wake, and Sean grabbed for the doorframe.

"Uncle Sean, Uncle Sean!" two voices cried in unison.

A strong hand clamped down on Sean's shoulder, steadying him.

"Told you I had a surprise for you." Gareth grinned. "They've been asking about you every day. I figured you'd be tired of the peace and quiet and ready for a little noise."

Sean snorted but didn't bother enlightening his cousin as to how wildly off base he was with that assumption. Instead, he leaned a crutch against the wall to free up a hand so he could ruffle the blond heads belonging to Maggie and Nicholas, the youngest of Gareth's step-kids.

"I'm always up for a little noise where these two are concerned," he replied. He reached out to pull their older sister into the hug. "And for a visit from my Katie-girl, of course."

Katie smiled up at him over her siblings' heads. "Hi, Uncle Sean. Are you feeling better?"

Before Sean could answer, Nicholas tugged aside the open pant leg covering his cast. "Oh, cool! You have a Spiderman on your cast! Hey, where's your bullet hole? Does it still bleed?"

"All right, Nicky, that's enough for now," a woman's voice said. "Remember what we talked about. Give Uncle Sean some room, please, and no pushing."

"But, Mommy, he has a *Spiderman*."

Gareth's hand settled on Nicholas's head, tipping it back. "Your mother asked you to do something, Nicholas."

"But—" The little boy broke off and heaved a sigh. "Fine. But can I see the Spiderman later?"

"Of course," Sean agreed. "As soon as I'm sitting down, all right? And maybe you can draw another one for me."

Nicholas's eyes went wide. "Really? *Cool.* Can I see the bullet hole, too?"

Sean swallowed a snort of laughter. "Sorry, no hole. The cast covers it up."

"Oh, man." And with that final complaint, Nicholas divested himself of coat and shoes, dropped the items on the floor, and darted into the cottage.

Maggie tugged at Sean's arm. "Can I draw, too? I can make a T-Rex. A purple one."

"I would love a purple T-Rex."

More shoes and another coat landed on the floor, and Maggie followed in her twin brother's wake.

"Katie—" Gareth began.

"I know." Katie handed her coat to Sean and slipped out of her shoes. "I'll make sure they don't touch anything."

With the three smallest bodies removed from the entry, Sean turned his attention to the adults who had accompanied them. "Well," he said. "Hello. Good to see you."

Gwynneth, mother to the kids and new wife to his cousin, stepped into the cottage and gave him a one-armed hug, her other arm wrapped around a grocery bag.

"One day," she said, "I swear we'll arrive at your place without the whole stampede thing."

Sean grinned. "I'll believe *that* when I see it." He returned her hug and then let her relieve him of Katie's coat. "So how was the honeymoon? Worth the wait?"

"Most definitely." Gareth's voice was a low growl of pure male satisfaction that made Sean laugh and Gwyn blush. "Though I'm sure it would have been just as good without the delay caused by my cousin getting himself shot."

"I'm sure most things would have been just as good if I hadn't got myself shot," Sean said dryly. "Maybe even better."

Unless, of course, he thought about Grace and the kids, and how he never would have met them if he hadn't been sidelined by an injury and come out here to—

He realized Gwyn had disappeared into the kitchen and Gareth was frowning at him. Waiting...as if for a response.

"Sorry, I missed that."

"I asked how the leg is doing. You seem a little loopy still. Not off the painkillers yet?"

Sean took the crutch he'd leaned against the wall. He still felt a little loopy, to be honest, but it wasn't because of pain meds. Nor was it something he cared to discuss with his cousin. "Not entirely, but I'm down to just one at the end of the day. I can make do with over-the-counter stuff the rest of the time, so it's definite progress."

Gareth hung his coat on a hook, then reached down to retrieve Maggie and Nicholas's garments. "And you're managing okay on your own? Getting lots of rest like you're supposed to?"

Something else Sean didn't care to discuss.

"I'm good," he said. "Really."

Gareth's gaze met his. It narrowed. An eyebrow lifted.

Sean rolled his eyes. "You're worse than a mother hen. Look at me. I'm fine. The place is clean, I'm fed, I'm off most of the meds...what more do you want?"

"I want to know what you're trying so hard not to tell me."

Damn. He'd forgotten just how good Gareth had become at seeing through any attempt at hiding something. Fatherhood had definitely changed the man. And not altogether for the better, Sean thought sourly. Not when he himself was on the receiving end, anyway. He opened his mouth to deny Gareth's words, but Nicholas's voice, high-pitched with excitement, interrupted.

"Mommy, come quick! There's a *baby* at the door!"

CHAPTER 28

"Aunt Grace, wake up! Wake up, Aunt Grace!"

Grace struggled upward through sleep, the remaining vestiges of her headache tugging at her skull, threatening to return if she moved too quickly. It had been worse than she'd thought, bordering dangerously on the edge of becoming a full-blown migraine. Even now she hesitated to open her eyes, afraid the daylight would—

"Aunt Grace!" Small hands shook her and pulled at the covers. "Wake up! Annabelle's gone!"

Grace's eyes shot open. She stared at Lilliane's panicked face as the little girl's words sank in, twisted through her, took root in her heart. She bolted upright, then gripped the mattress as the world swam out of focus and tipped before righting itself. Then she transferred her hold to her niece's arms.

"What do you mean, gone? Gone where?"

Tears spilled from Lilly's eyes. "We don't know. We can't find her. And the back door was open!"

Grace was down the hall and in the mudroom before she even registered movement. Joshua met her at the door, panting and fighting back tears.

"I don't know what happened, Aunt Grace! We were watching a movie, and then suddenly I realized she was gone. I've called and called, but she won't answer me. I'm so sorry!"

Grace tugged her coat from its hook. "Do you have any idea how long she's been missing?"

Josh shook his head. "I'm sorry," he whispered again.

Grace swallowed against the heart that had taken up residence in her throat. "Let's not panic, okay? I'm sure she's just wandered off into the woods" —where at least one bear lived— "or down the driveway to the road. Or maybe to Mr. —"

"I found her mittens on the chair beside the lake. She kept asking to go for a swim after you went to lie down. You don't think—"

Grace bolted from the cottage, screaming her niece's name.

"Nicholas was right," Gareth observed from behind Sean. "That is definitely a baby."

Sean looked down at the toddler patting his cast and grinning up at him.

"Man owie," said Annabelle cheerfully. Then she peered past him at the family gathering and pointed a chubby finger. "Who dat?"

"I'm Nicholas," said Gwyn's son. "What's your name?"

"Her name is Annabelle," Sean said. "She belongs to my neighbor."

"What in the world is she doing here all by herself?" Gwyn asked.

A faint call reached through the still-open sliding door. A woman's voice, underscored by panic. Sean grimaced.

"Besides giving her aunt a heart attack, you mean?"

"Aunt? Not mother?"

"Long story." Sean glanced over his shoulder at Katie. "Would you be a sweetheart and grab my coat from the hook by the door? It's the black one."

Gareth's hands closed over his upper arms and shuffled him sideways, away from the door. "I suspect it will be faster for me to get her. Especially with a toddler in tow."

"There's no way Annabelle will go with you. She pitches a fit if her own aunt tries to take her away before she's ready."

His cousin's dark eyebrow ascended. "I see. And she and her aunt visit often enough for you to know that from experience? Why, Sean McKittrick, you dark horse, you."

"Blow it out your—" Sean broke off at the sound of Gwyn's cleared throat reminding him of the presence of tender ears. He shot her an apologetic look, then scowled at Gareth. "Well? Are you going to get her or not?"

"Just waiting for a name and a direction, cuz."

"She's that way," said Sean, pointing out the door, "and her name is Grace."

The initial paralysis gripping Grace's brain gave way to the tumble of a thousand thoughts and possibilities, each more horrific than the last. Annabelle lost in the woods, cold and hungry, curling up and going to sleep, never to wake again. Annabelle at the bottom of the lake, her blond curls tangled in the weeds. Emergency crews dredging the water. Divers bringing up the body. How could she have failed Julianne so horribly?

Grace cupped shaking hands around her mouth and shouted again.

"Annabelle!"

Her niece's name echoed across the water and bounced back to her. She waited for a response, listening with every fiber of her being. Nothing. She slipped her hand into her pocket and clutched Annabelle's tiny mittens, abandoned on the chair as Josh had said. For the hundredth time, her gaze raked the sand between the chair and the waterline. Dozens of footprints marred the surface from the kids playing down here under her supervision, skipping rocks, building sand castles. If there was any way to tell whether some were fresher than others, she didn't know it.

She needed help.

Sean. He would know what to do.

Grace scanned the unbroken stillness of the water a final time, then turned back toward the cottage. She drew up short, the breath leaving her lungs in a hiss when she found an unfamiliar man blocking her way.

"You must be Grace," he said. "I'm Sean's cousin Gareth. I believe you may have misplaced something."

CHAPTER 29

Sean slid the glass door open as Grace ran across the deck, her face pale and taut with worry. He shifted out of her way, and she stepped past him into the cottage, took one look at Annabelle, seated on Sean's living room floor with a pile of wooden blocks and Gwyn and Gareth's brood, and promptly burst into tears. Sean leaned one of his crutches against the wall beside the door and reached for her with his free arm.

"Hey," he soothed. "She's safe. Everything is fine."

"I thought—I thought—" Grace gulped and buried her face against his shoulder.

Over the top of her dark head, Sean saw Gwyn and Gareth exchange looks. Gwyn raised an eyebrow. Gareth shrugged. Sean ignored them both. He bent his head and focused on the woman he held, her body wracked with trembling so fierce, he feared she might fall apart. He tightened his arm around her.

"She's okay, Grace," he whispered, willing her to hear him, feeling her terror, aching for her. "It's all good."

Grace nodded against him and snuffled. "I know," she mumbled. "I know she is. It's just—I was just—Josh found her mittens beside the lake, and..."

Fresh tears flowed, wetting Sean's shirt further. He unlocked his arm long enough to accept the wad of tissue Gwyn plucked from the box on the counter and held out to him. Then he set the other crutch beside its mate, balancing on his good leg.

"No sudden moves," he warned Grace, "or you'll dump me

on my ass again."

"Again?" Gareth drawled. "This sounds interesting."

"Mommy, Uncle Sean said a bad word!" Maggie piped up, her eyes round.

Grace giggled into Sean's wet shoulder, and he felt his heart lighten. He tucked the tissue into her hand and stuck his tongue out at his step-niece.

"Traitor," he told the little girl, adding a wink.

"*And* he stuck out his tongue!" Nicholas added indignantly.

"I'm sure Uncle Sean is sorry," Gwyn said. "Go back to your blocks."

"But—"

"Blocks," she repeated, and argument ceased. She patted Grace's shoulder. "I'll put on some tea, and you can join us for lunch. It will give you a chance to get your bearings again."

Sean felt Grace's concerted effort to pull herself together. She lifted her head, blew her nose, and summoned a watery smile.

"Thank you," she said, "but I can't. I have to get back to the others. They'll be worried."

"There are more?"

"Three," Sean said.

His cousin stared at him. "Three more *children*."

"My other nieces and my nephew," Grace volunteered, still sniffling. She stepped back, leaving a chill along Sean's body in her wake except for where one hand remained on his arm to steady him. "I'm looking after them while my sister is in hospital."

"I see. And Sean is...helping?" Gareth's voice remained neutral, but his expression could only be described as sardonic. Sean scowled at him, knowing full well this was payback. Gareth took every opportunity he could to remind him how wrong he'd been about Gwyn. No doubt he saw this as another chance to rub it in...especially if he imagined something going on between Sean and Grace.

"He's been a tremendous help, yes." Grace wadded up the used tissue. Her gaze flicked to Sean's famous cousin, hovered, turned uncertain. She gave a small shake of her head, as if denying whatever thought had formed.

"He's been giving me cooking lessons," she added. "Without him, I think the kids would have mutinied."

She glanced up at Sean, her chocolate eyes and the increased pressure of her hand on his arm signaling her intent to let go. He recalculated his balance, then accepted the crutches she reached for.

"How very kind of him," Gareth said. This time, there was no mistaking the underlying sarcasm.

Grace shot Sean an uncertain look. Sean shot his cousin a glower. Gwyn poked her husband in the shoulder.

"Behave," she told him. Then, without flinching, she reached out to pluck the soggy tissues from Grace's fingers and replace them with fresh ones. "The kids can come for lunch, too. Can we send Gareth to get them, or will having a strange man turn up on the doorstep freak them out? Maybe Katie could go with him for reassurance."

Grace used the new tissue to blow her nose a second time. "I appreciate the invitation, but I'm fine, and you came to visit with Sean, not to get involved in a drama. I'll get Annabelle out of your hair and—"

"Nonsense," Gwyn said. "We brought enough to feed a small army, and our crew will be delighted to meet new friends. How old are yours?"

"Josh is ten, Lilliane is eight, and Sage is five. And the little escape artist there"—Grace nodded toward Annabelle—"is two. But really—"

"Perfect. And we insist. Right, Gareth?"

"Oh, we do," Gareth agreed, directing his words to Grace but a sideways glance at Sean. "In fact, we would like nothing more than to get to know you and your kids."

Sean swallowed a groan. He knew that look from his cousin. The raised eyebrow, that glint in his eye. Both said Sean was in for some serious harassment later on. He would have to correct Gareth's misinterpretation of Grace's presence in his life...soon.

Gareth, however, had already turned his attention elsewhere. "Katie, would you like to come with me to fetch Ms.—" He stopped. "Hold on. Here we are dragging you and your kids along for lunch, and we haven't even been properly introduced. Sean?"

Sean glanced at Grace. Would she want her name shared, or—? Grace gave the slightest of nods, indicating agreement—and trust. A small core of warmth formed in Sean's chest. Gareth cleared his throat, and Sean wrenched his attention back to the present.

"Of course. Grace, this is my cousin Gareth Connor and his wife Gwyn. Gareth and Gwyn, my neighbor Grace Daniels."

"Delighted to meet you, Grace Daniels." Gareth held out his hand.

Beside him, Grace's breath hitched a little as she accepted the handshake. She glanced at Sean uncertainly. "Gareth...?"

"Yes," Gwyn answered the unfinished question, her voice wry. "He's that Gareth Connor, but we try not to let it go to his head."

"She makes me clean toilets to keep me humble." Gareth wrapped an arm around his wife's waist and tugged her close, dropping a kiss on her forehead.

Sean chuckled. "Still haven't won the housekeeper argument, huh?"

"I've been allowed a once-a-month service," Gareth said. "It's a start."

A small body pushed past Sean to the center of their group.

"I'm Nicholas," Gwyn's son announced, planting himself in front of Grace. He pointed at his siblings. "And that's my big sister Katie, and that's Maggie. She's my twin. But we're not identical twins. A boy and a girl can't be identical, because a boy has a —"

"That will do, thank you, Nicholas," Gareth interrupted. "I'm pretty sure Ms. Daniels is familiar with the male anatomy."

Nicholas frowned. "The what?"

"How little boys are built."

"Oh. Can I come with you and Katie to get Grace's kids?"

"That's Ms. Daniels to you, Nicholas," Gwyn said.

"Grace is fine with me," Grace offered. "That is, if it's okay with you."

"Or I could call her Auntie Grace," Nicholas said. "Because that's what she'll be when she marries Uncle Sean, right?"

"M-marr—" Grace stuttered, turning red.

Sean inserted himself into the conversation. "Grace and I are just friends, Nicholas. We're not getting married."

"Why not? She's pretty. And nice. And you look at her all lovey-dovey like Gareth does with Mommy."

Grace made a strangled noise beside Sean. Her blush turned

neon.

Looking very much like he might explode with pent-up laughter, Gareth set a hand atop Nicholas's blond head, turned him firmly around, and said, "That's quite enough, Nicholas."

"What'd I do?" the boy asked in genuine perplexity. "Katie told me—"

"Enough," Gareth repeated. "Katie told you quite enough, and now she and I are going to go and get Grace's kids. I'd like you to stay and help entertain Annabelle. Can you do that for me?"

"But I—"

"Nicholas."

Nicholas shoved his hands into his jeans pockets and heaved a sigh. "Oh, all right."

Head down, he shuffled away.

"And on that note," Gareth's voice quivered with amusement, "I think I'll go fetch the rest of our lunch party. Katie?"

Already dressed and waiting, the eldest of Gwyn and Gareth's kids slipped past Sean and out the door. Gareth slanted a look of mixed exasperation and amusement at his wife.

"I keep telling you that girl is entirely too observant for her own good," he said. "Never mind anyone else's peace of mind. I'll be back in a few minutes." He turned to Grace. "Josh, Lilliane, and Sage, right?"

Grace nodded. "I'll stand on the deck so they can see me through the trees."

"Let Sean do that," Gwyn said. "I'll put you to work in the kitchen."

Sean quirked a smile at Grace's look of inquiry. "Makes sense to me. My kitchen is smaller than yours. I'd just get in the way with these things."

Grace followed Gwyn toward the kitchen, and Sean trailed Gareth onto the deck. He caught hold of his cousin's sleeve before Gareth stepped out of reach. "Grace and me...it's not what you think."

Gareth glanced toward the two women in the cottage, and then met Sean's scowl with a slow, delighted grin.

"Actually," he said, "I suspect it's not what *you* think."

CHAPTER 30

Organized chaos.

That was the only way Grace could think to describe the lunch scene. Kids seemed to be everywhere—no, kids were everywhere. With seven of them crammed into Sean's small cottage, along with four adults, how could they not be? Gwyn, however, was a marvel. Raising her voice just enough to be heard over the commotion, she divided the kids into teams, putting Nicholas and Sage to work clearing the living room coffee table, having Lilliane and Maggie set places there for the kids, and asking Josh and Katie to put out dishes for the adults at the dining table.

Sean was relegated to Annabelle-care, and once instructions were issued, Gwyn's husband Gareth—the Gareth Connor—stepped in to supervise completion. Grace couldn't help but follow him with her gaze, marveling at the presence of a Hollywood mega-star at a cottage in the middle of—

"He doesn't bite, you know."

Grace jumped at Gwyn's voice. She blushed. "I—uh—I—"

Gwyn chuckled. "Don't worry. I'm used to it. He has that effect on everyone." She handed Grace a casserole dish wrapped in a dishtowel. "Thai chicken and rice. It has a bit of heat to it, but not much. My kids aren't fans of spicy food."

"Mine, either."

"If you want to set that on the table and come back, I have a second one to go out, along with some veggies and a salad."

Grace eyed the sizable dish already in her hands. "You brought an awful lot of food for a lunch."

"I made extra so Sean would have leftovers for a few days. I don't know why I bothered, really. He's a far better cook than I am, and I should have known he'd be coping just fine. He's just been so good to me and the kids since Gareth and I got together...I wanted to do something nice in return."

"Sean told me you and your husband wanted to take him in while he recovered. That seems nice."

"I'm not sure *nice* is how Sean would define it." Gwyn sent an amused look to where Sean sat on the couch, paging through a back-country hiking magazine with Annabelle tucked into the crook of his arm. "As good as he is with kids, he makes no bones about not wanting to be around them too much. Or about not wanting his own."

Grace almost choked at the thinly veiled warning. Gwyn grimaced.

"Too direct?" she asked.

"Um..." Grace had no idea how to answer. Gwyn sighed.

"Sorry. I have a habit of being rather blunt," she said. "I'll butt out now. Besides, it's not like you have to worry, because the kids aren't yours to begin with, right? How long is your sister in hospital for?"

Sudden tears blurred Grace's vision, and the casserole in her hands tipped precariously. Gwyn leapt forward to take it.

"Oh, Lord," she muttered. "I've put my foot in it again, haven't I?"

Grace shook her head, swallowing hard, aware of Sean's concern from across the cottage and Gareth Connor's frown as he tried to steer the kids clear of the conversation. She pulled herself together, mustered a smile. "No. No, it's okay. Really. I'm fine. It's just a delayed reaction to losing Annabelle, I think."

Gwyn regarded her for a moment, and then, with an acceptance that brought a fresh welling of tears, turned Grace toward the bathroom and gave her a little push. "We'll watch the kids and finish up here. You go wash your face and take a few deep breaths. It helps. I promise."

"Is Aunt Grace okay?" Lilliane perched on the couch beside Annabelle and looked up at Sean, worry shadowing her brown eyes.

His heart gave a little squeeze at the trust there as well. "She's fine," he reassured the girl, ruffling her hair. "She just had a bad scare with losing your sister, and she needs a few minutes alone."

"It wasn't her fault that Annabelle got lost. She had a headache, and she needed to lie down. We were supposed to be watching Annabelle, but we forgot. And we didn't know she could open doors."

Sean's mouth tilted up at one corner. "It was no one's fault," he said. "It was just something that happened."

"But what if it happens again?" Lilly frowned.

"Tell you what. Tomorrow, while Annabelle is napping, I'll bring over a new latch for the door, how's that? We'll put it up really high, where she can't reach. Will that help?"

"It will help loads," Nicholas said, joining them. He patted Lilly's shoulder comfortingly. "When I was little, Mommy had to put a latch on our door because I kept getting out of the house, too."

A snort reached them from the kitchen.

"I had to put a latch on *everything* to keep you contained, you little monkey," Gwyn said, making her son giggle. "Now, everyone come and get your plates, before things go stone cold and I need to reheat everything again."

Six kids traipsed obediently into the kitchen, and Sean twisted around to lift Annabelle down from the couch.

"Here," said Gareth. "Let me."

He hoisted the willing toddler into his arms, then stooped and handed Sean his crutches. But he didn't move away. Sean braced himself for the harassment he felt certain was coming.

Instead, Gareth said simply, "Spill."

Sean didn't pretend not to understand. "It's not my story to tell."

"But there is a story. And not a pleasant one, I'm guessing."

You have no idea.

"Yes," he responded to Gareth's statements. "And no."

"Will she be all right?"

She will if I have anything to do with it.

The sheer ferocity of the thought caught Sean off guard. So did the twist of his stomach at the idea of any other possibility. His jaw went tight. "She'll be fine."

Gareth regarded him for a long moment, still holding Annabelle. Then he tipped his head toward the bathroom door behind which Grace had disappeared. "Why don't you check on her? I'll get Annabelle settled."

As Gareth carried the smallest of their company over to the table, the other kids began making their way back to the living room. Sean pulled himself up onto his crutches and moved out of their way, and the six of them settled around the coffee table he'd once thought too big but that only just accommodated them. Funny how that had worked out.

He crossed to the bathroom door and tapped gently.

"Grace? It's Sean. Can I come in?"

Grace wiped her face dry and stared into the mirror at her reflection. Hell, her under-eye circles had circles at this point. She'd never looked—or felt—so tired in all her life. Or so helpless. Or so completely overwhelmed.

More tears spilled over onto her cheeks.

Crap. She'd already spent a good ten minutes hiding out in Sean's bathroom. At this rate, she'd never make it out for lunch. She took another of the deep breaths Gwyn had recommended, although so far they hadn't done much more than make her lightheaded. The thoughts that kept her pinned in the little room kept spinning through her head: How on earth was she going to manage? How could she be a good parent to those four kids? With all they'd been through, all their trauma, how could she hope to be enough for them?

She put a hand to her chest, pressing against the tightness of panic. Ever since she'd told the story to Sean yesterday, she'd been slowly unraveling at the seams, just as she'd feared. As if talking about it had suddenly made it bigger. More real.

Infinitely more terrifying.

She was so not ready for this. So not capable of handling what was already happening, never mind what was still to come.

A tap sounded at the door.

"Grace? It's Sean. Can I come in?"

She tried to suck back the tears, she really did. Tried to breathe. Tried to hold herself together for the kids' sakes. She tried—and then she pulled open the door, buried her face against Sean's shoulder, and burst into yet more tears.

CHAPTER 31

"Better now?" Sean handed another wad of tissues to Grace. She sniffled from her perch on the edge of the bathtub and nodded.

"I'm fine," she whispered. "And I'm so sorry for all of this."

"Don't be." Seated on the closed toilet, he shifted his casted leg to another position, trying to ease the pins and needles in his foot. "You've been under a lot of pressure. I'm surprised you've held up as long as you have."

He kept his voice pitched low, so it wouldn't carry beyond the door to the others. If Grace had a lot to deal with, so did those kids.

"I've had no choice." She blew her nose. Her resolute gaze met his. "I *have* no choice."

"You can let me help."

"You have helped."

"I meant help more." He reached forward to take one of her hands in his. "Grace, I've been thinking. Last night—"

"No." She pulled away and stood up, but she couldn't go anywhere, because his outstretched cast blocked the door.

He didn't move. "We can't just ignore—"

"Yes," she said. "We can."

Frustration reared in him. "Damn it, will you at least let me finish a sentence?"

"I can't." Her voice was ragged. "Look, I won't deny there's chemistry between us, Sean, but I told you last night, I don't have room for this right now. Not with the way things are. Not with the kids."

He caught her fingers and twined them in his, feeling her warmth. Her fragility. Remembering the way her fear for Annabelle had cut through to his own core. He scowled. "What if it's more than just chemistry? What if—"

"What if you're just caught up in my circumstances? What if half of what you feel is some misguided sense of responsibility? Sympathy for them"—she nodded at the bathroom door—"and for me? What if what I feel is utter terror at the thought of raising four kids on my own?"

"We don't know that's what it is."

"And I can't take the chance that it isn't. I don't know how I'm going to handle what's already going on in my life, Sean, but I do know that anything more will break me—and them. So please—just don't."

He thought about how much he'd missed the kids that morning. How quiet his cottage had seemed without them. He thought of the men his own mother had paraded through his life when he was young. His absolute determination never to be one of those men in another child's life.

And then he hesitated.

Closing his eyes, he turned her hand over in his and pressed his lips—gently, briefly—to her palm. Felt her shudder. Heard her indrawn breath. "Don't," her whisper echoed in his heart. He swallowed against the lump it left behind. Releasing her hand, he pulled himself up to stand beside her.

He hated to let it go at this, but now wasn't the time. Not with the others waiting and Grace so defensive. And not when he needed to work through her words, to see whether he could refute her logic—or whether he should.

"We should get back to the others," he said.

Her face pale and drawn, she nodded. "I'll be out in a minute."

Sean turned the doorknob, then hesitated, every fiber of his being screaming for him to reach out to her. To let her know he was there for her.

"Can I at least still help?" he asked. "As a friend?"

A tear sparkled on the edge of her lashes. It fell when she nodded and gave him a wobbly smile.

"I'd like that."

Lunch was delightful. Despite Grace's misgivings about staying on after her meltdown, Gwyn and Gareth managed to make her feel relaxed and welcome—and more normal than she'd felt in what seemed a lifetime. Warmth radiated between the two of them, drawing her in and filling the entire cottage. Annabelle was thrilled with her new audience—particularly Gareth; Lilliane and Katie became fast friends within the space of an hour; and Nicholas and Maggie collectively took quiet little Sage under their wing, accepting her shyness without question or comment.

And Sean...Sean laughed and joked and shared in telling boyhood stories of summers with Gareth's family in Wales. He handed her the salt and pepper, made sure all the dishes were passed to her, and stooped to retrieve her napkin when she dropped it. Later, when Gareth offered her cream and sugar for the coffee Gwyn had poured, he shook his head on her behalf.

"She takes it black," he said, and then he turned to lift

Annabelle into his lap so he could clean her sticky fingers and face.

Grace's cheeks warmed as she caught the look that passed between Gareth and his wife. *It's not what you think,* she wanted to tell them. *We're friends. That's all.*

But Nicholas arrived with a question, Lilliane wanted seconds on the fruit salad dessert, and the opportunity to speak up passed. It was just as well, she decided. She wasn't likely to even see Sean's family again, so there didn't seem to be much point in expending energy on explanations. They'd figure it out for themselves sooner or later, or else Sean would set them straight.

Her gaze lingered on her neighbor as he swiped a damp facecloth across Annabelle's nose, making her giggle. Friends. The word made a part of her heart ache with heaviness. Another time and place, other circumstances, and—

She cringed internally at the traitorous thought. She looked over at Josh and Sage and Lilliane, guilt twisting through her heart. How could she even go there? They deserved so much more from her. So much more from life...

A hand waved in front of her nose, making her jump.

"Earth to Grace," said Sean. "Are you okay?"

"Sorry, I must have zoned out for a minute. Lack of sleep, I guess."

Green eyes held hers for a moment, looking inside her, seeing more than she wanted them to see. More than friendship. She sat up straighter. Forced a smile. Made herself glance away to the others.

"What did I miss?"

Gwyn and Gareth exchanged another of their looks. Grace

gritted her teeth. Did they *have* to keep doing that? She was becoming downright paranoid about what they might be thinking.

"Sean and I were thinking of taking the kids down to the lake to skip rocks off the dock. Josh said he'd run home for Annabelle's coat, if that's all right with you."

She'd missed all that? Grace held back a sigh. No wonder people were exchanging glances over her. She turned to Sean. "Is your leg up to it? Maybe I should go instead."

Sean set Annabelle on the floor. "I'm fine. I haven't been anywhere today, so the exercise will do me good."

A flurry of activity followed as coats and boots and various other articles of clothing were produced and donned. Gareth volunteered to watch Josh traverse the woods to get Annabelle's outdoor wear, Sean helped Sage with the zipper on her coat, and Grace helped Gwyn begin clearing the table. By the time everyone had trooped out the door, the silence they left in their wake seemed positively deafening.

"Well," said Gwyn. "*That* was an adventure."

"And probably not what you'd anticipated when you came out for a visit," Grace replied with a twinge of guilt.

"No, what I'd anticipated was having three kids whining about being bored after the first hour." Gwyn's voice was wry. "So before you go thinking you intruded, please let me say thank you for saving my sanity. And possibly my children's lives. Now, would you rather wash or dry?"

Grace opted for the novelty of drying—something that rarely happened in her life now that she'd taken to letting nature do that chore for her. She and Gwyn worked in companionable silence for a few minutes. Then, without warning, Gwyn tossed the dishcloth into the sink, spraying soap bubbles everywhere. She turned to face Grace, wet hands on hips and lips compressed.

"If my husband asks, I tried to stay out of this," she said. "I really did, but I can't. Grace, what is going on with you and Sean?"

"I—uh—" Grace stood frozen, damp tea towel in one hand and plate in the other.

"Because I meant what I said earlier, about him not wanting kids, and if he hasn't been honest with you—"

"He has," Grace interrupted. "Very honest. And I've been honest with him. We're friends, Gwyn. Nothing more."

Gwyn raised a slender eyebrow. Her hands remained on her hips. "Are you sure about that? Because the two of you together..."

Grace clutched the towel tighter. "The two of us what?"

"You just...work. If I didn't know you'd only just met, I would have thought you'd been together for years."

The past week rushed back at Grace in a whirl of images. Touches. Laughter. Tears. Ease. Sean's trek through the woods to see them each day. Josh kneeling to remove his shoe. Sage sidling up to perch on the edge of the couch while he read to Annabelle. Lilliane serving him tea as she chatted about her school science project. Sean pulling her into his strong, warm arms and assuring her everything would work out. Except not everything would.

She closed her eyes.

Gwyn touched her hand. "I'm right, aren't I?"

"Yes...and no." Grace set the tea towel and plate on the counter. She scooped back her hair with both hands, then crossed her arms and leaned back against the cupboard. "I do like Sean. A lot. And under other circumstances, things might have worked out differently. But I have four kids to think of, and yes, he's made it clear that might be a problem."

Both of Gwyn's brows shot up. "Might be?"

"He skirted around the possibility of seeing where things went, but I can't. I don't have room in my life for that right now. We've agreed I need a friend more than...anything else."

"Sean. Sean McKittrick skirted around the idea of—" Gwyn shook her head. "I can't even make sense out of those words."

Grace could think of no response. She picked up the plate again and dried it.

"And you're sure," Gwyn said. "That you want to be just friends?"

"I have no choice," Grace said quietly. "It's not just me I have to think about."

"They're permanent, then." Gwyn's voice softened. "The kids, I mean."

The admission took everything Grace possessed. "Yes."

"I'm sorry."

Grace nodded, unable to reply past the thickening in her throat. She gazed out the kitchen window overlooking the deck and the lake beyond. Down on the dock, Sean balanced on one crutch while he showed Sage how to skip a rock across the water's surface. Josh had already mastered the skill and appeared to be coaching Nicholas and Maggie. Katie and Lilliane were on their bellies staring down into the water. Gwyn's husband patiently followed Annabelle from shore to dock-end and back to shore. For a heartbeat of a moment, everything felt normal. Ordinary.

Grace almost smiled.

And then her cell phone rang.

Sean watched Gareth swing Annabelle into his arms as he strolled down the dock to join him. All the others were at the far end, on their bellies along the edge, peering into the water while Josh explained to them how the frogs would burrow into the mud to survive the coming winter.

"Pinecone!" Annabelle announced as she and Gareth reached him, holding out her find to him. Not seeming to need a response, she went back to examining her treasure.

Gareth cleared his throat. "Well?" he asked.

"Well what?"

"Well, what are you going to do about Grace?"

"There's nothing to do. We're friends. Nothing more."

"Bollocks," his cousin said bluntly. "You're more than halfway in love with her, and you know it. And anyone with half a brain can see she feels the same about you."

"We may have chemistry, but that's not the same as love. And it's certainly not enough to make either of us throw away our good sense."

"So you've talked about it. With her."

"Not that it's any of your business."

"And you've agreed on this friendship thing."

"Yes."

"Then you're both idiots," Gareth said.

Sean sighed heavily. "The kids are permanent, Gareth."

The words stopped his cousin in his tracks. Gareth stared at him. "Their mother...?"

"In a coma. Beaten by their father. It doesn't look like she'll recover."

"Bloody hell." Gareth looked over at the kids lined up along the dock edge, then at the little girl he held in his arms. "Bloody, bloody hell," he said again. "That poor woman. What will she do?"

"Raise them as best she can, I imagine."

"With the help of *friends*?"

Sean bristled at the distinct sarcasm in the last word. "Just because we're trying to be responsible about this—"

Gareth waved him silent. "I don't know what Grace's issues are, but you're just plain scared. You're more than a product of your upbringing, Sean. Or you could be, if you'd give yourself half a bloody chance."

"This has nothing to do with my upbringing."

"It has everything to do with your upbringing. Your entire life has been lived around that damned upbringing, Sean, and it's time to let it go. I've known you since you were in diapers, and I've never seen you like this around a woman. You know how she takes her coffee, for God's sake. When have you ever known what one of your girlfriends takes in her coffee?"

Sean scowled, but he had no answer.

Gareth sighed. "You and Grace could have something special here, if you'd give it a chance. Anyone can see that just by looking at the two of you. Do you really want to lose that—to lose *her*—because you're afraid of making a mistake?"

Honestly? Sean didn't know what to think anymore, beyond wishing Gareth and his questions and theories would just go away and stop making his brain hurt. He scowled and tried to regroup. To explain what had made such perfect sense to him when Grace had put it forward.

"Grace doesn't want me getting involved with her because I feel sorry for her and the kids," he said, "or to get involved with me out of desperation."

His cousin's eyebrow rose. "And you're okay with that as an excuse?"

"Her life has been turned inside out, Gareth. Sane people don't fall in love and commit under those circumstances."

Gareth snorted and set a wriggling Annabelle down as the others made their way back, causing the dock to buck and shift beneath their feet.

"I have news for you, McKittrick," he said, taking the toddler's hand in his so she didn't topple. "Sane people don't fall in love, period. The insanity's what makes it so much fun."

CHAPTER 32

"Grace," Luc's voice said in her ear.

"When?" she asked. It was her only question, because she didn't need to hear him say it. She already knew. Had known the moment the cell phone rang in her pocket. She stared at the fingers gripping the counter beside her. Fingers that were attached to her, but weren't hers. The world had moved off to a distance, leaving her alone. There, but not there. Living, but not alive. Breathing and talking, but not thinking. Not feeling. Not capable.

"About a half hour ago," said Luc.

While I was talking and laughing and not thinking about her. Grace examined the knowledge, but she didn't know what to do with it, and so she set it aside until later.

"Was anyone with her?"

"A lot of people. She coded and they tried to revive her, but..." Luc's voice trailed off.

"She would have hated that. All the fuss."

"I know."

She closed her eyes. "Are you there now?"

"I'm on my way over to take care of...whatever needs taking care of."

She nodded. Remembered he couldn't see her. Found more words. "Good," she said. "Thank you. And thank the nurses and doctors for me, will you? For looking after her."

"Of course."

"And once everything is arranged, you'll let me know when?"

Luc didn't answer.

Grace checked the cell display. It still showed a connection, and she put the phone back to her ear. "Luc?"

Her friend sighed. "Grace, Barry was seen hanging around the hospital a couple of days ago. They think he's watching for you."

"I'm not missing Julianne's funeral, Luc."

"Sweetie, you could be putting yourself and the kids at—"

"She's my sister," Grace said, and just like that, the feeling returned. It slipped into her core, paused as if surprised to find itself there, and then shattered into a million shards of glass. A million razored edges. A million reflections of all that she had lost. All *they* had lost.

The kids.

Oh, dear God. The kids.

Her knees folded and she sank to the floor, her back against the cupboard and fingers tangled in her hair.

She would have to tell the kids.

She gulped for air.

"Grace? Sweetie, are you okay?" Luc's voice held equal parts sharp concern and compassion. "Look, I'm going to give McKittrick a call and have him come and give you a—"

"No." She rested her head on her drawn-up knees. "I'm fine, Luc. Really. And I'm at Sean's now."

"Oh. Then he knows?"

"He knows."

"Good. I'm glad. Let him help? Please? Or I can come out—"

"I'll let him help," she whispered. "Just stay there. Stay and look after Juli for me?"

"You know I will," he promised gruffly. "But I'll take a drive out tomorrow to see you, all right?"

"All right. I'd like that."

"Good. And about the funeral, Grace..."

Outside the kitchen window, multiple pairs of feet thundered up the stairs onto the wooden deck. Grace picked out the voices that belonged to her. Sage. Lilliane. Josh. Annabelle. All hers now. All without a mother.

All still vulnerable because of their father.

She tightened her grip on her hair. Squeezed her eyes shut. Breathed past the shards. "I'll stay away," she said. "But I still want to know."

Without waiting for a response, she lowered the phone from her ear and disconnected the call. Then, with a mighty effort, she packaged up her grief until later. Until after the kids were in bed, because they came first. They had to come first.

She opened her eyes.

Gwyn silently extended a hand to her, pulled her to her feet, and drew her into a fierce hug.

"I'm so, so sorry, Grace," she whispered.

Grace let herself be cradled, borrowing the other woman's strength to shore up her own. "I don't know how to tell them," she said, her voice breaking. "I don't know what to say."

Gwyn drew back as the glass door in the dining room slid open. Her eyes shining with tears, she gripped Grace's shoulders and squeezed. "You'll find the words," she said. "I promise."

Then she turned to the arriving horde. "All right, listen up. My three—leave your shoes on and head back outside to the van. It's time for home."

Half a dozen voices lifted in protest. A single deep one cut across them all.

"Grace?" said Sean.

She met his gaze, dark with concern, clouded by questions. Clamping down on both lips to stay the tears that threatened, she shook her head in answer. Sean inhaled sharply. One at a time, the babble of children's voices died away as the atmosphere in the cottage shifted. Even Annabelle became quiet, leaning her head on Gareth's shoulder and watching with wide blue eyes.

Gareth cleared his throat. "You heard your mother, kids. It's late. Say goodbye to everyone, and then out to the van, please."

The two families exchanged quiet goodbyes and hugs. Katie, Nicholas, and Maggie included Grace in their rounds, and Nicholas paused to look up at her solemnly.

"It was nice meeting you," he said.

Grace couldn't help but smile. "It was nice meeting you, too, Nicholas."

He glanced over his shoulder at the other adults, then back at her. "Are you *sure* you and Uncle Sean aren't getting—"

"Nicholas!"

The boy jumped at the sharp tone in his mother's voice. Without another word, he disappeared out the door.

Gwyn was next in line for a hug, pressing a piece of paper into Grace's hand as she ended the embrace.

"My phone number," she said. "Call me if you have questions about"—she glanced toward Grace's bunch—"well, anything. Or if you need to talk or you just want to get together with the kids."

"They'd like that," Grace murmured. "Thank you."

Gwyn hesitated, seeming at a loss for more words. Then she hugged her again. "Call me," she said again.

Then she and Gareth and their family were gone, and the cottage fell silent, and Grace faced the kids—*her* kids—and searched for the words to tell them their mother wouldn't be waking up after all.

Not ever.

Sean met Grace in the hallway outside the bedrooms as she pulled shut the door to Josh's room and he did the same to the girls' door.

"How is he?" he whispered.

"Better than I thought he'd be, but that's probably because he's trying so hard." She nodded at Sage and Lilliane's room. "What about the girls?"

"Sleeping. Lilly sang Sage to sleep and then nodded off within seconds." Sean swallowed at the remembered image of older sister comforting younger while he'd looked on, hurting for them but helpless to make things better. He cleared his throat. "And you? How are you holding up?"

Grace leaned against the wall. "I'm okay, thanks. I don't think it's entirely sunk in yet." She shook her head. "A part of me expected it—I knew she couldn't survive what Barry did to her—but I still hoped. Still thought she might be one of those miracles you hear about."

The helplessness returned, tightening around his chest.

"I'm so, so sorry, Grace."

"Me, too." Grace sighed, a tremulous whisper of sound. "Thank you for your help, by the way. I don't know what I would have done without you."

"You would have managed the same way you've managed all

along," he told her gruffly. "Because that's what you do."

She laughed without humor. "I suppose. But you made it easier, so thank you."

"You're welcome." He tipped his head toward the living room. "I made tea. I thought you could use a cup."

"Is there whiskey in it?"

"Will that help?"

Chocolate eyes filled with pain. Then with tears. Grace's lips trembled, and she shook her head. "No. No, I don't suppose it will."

"Ah, Grace..." Sean set aside his crutches and reached out. He pulled her into his arms, resting a shoulder against the wall for balance and his chin against her head. Her slender frame shook with sobs. He closed his eyes against the pain in his own heart. And then, because he could do nothing else, he simply held her until the tears ran out.

She pulled away at last to wipe swollen eyes with her fingertips. "I've made you soggy." She sniffled. "I'm sorry."

"I'm sure I'll dry." He smoothed back the hair from her forehead. "Why don't you go wash your face, and I'll make fresh tea? I suspect it's gone cold by now."

"It's late. You should go home and get some sleep."

"I'm not going anywhere. Not tonight. I've already snitched a pillow and blanket from your bed for the couch."

"But—"

He put a finger across her lips. "I'm staying, Grace."

She smiled the tiniest of smiles behind his finger. It still managed to light up his core.

He dropped his hand again. "I'll see you in the kitchen."

She nodded acceptance and turned toward the bathroom.

Then she looked over her shoulder. "Sean?"

"Yes...?" Just in time, he caught back the all-too-ready *my love* that wanted to follow.

Grace's eyes widened slightly, as if she'd heard the words anyway. She gave an almost imperceptible shake of her head—a warning?—and then another small smile. "Nothing. Just... thank you."

Grace took her time in the washroom, splashing cool water onto hot, swollen eyelids and gazing at her dripping reflection in the mirror over the sink. So that was it. Julianne was gone. It was just her and the kids, now. Her and four broken, wounded children. Though she supposed Annabelle would be too young to be greatly affected. And in all likelihood, the girls would recover fairly fast as well. Sage in particular. Josh, however—

She leaned her hands on the counter, thinking of the guilt she knew her nephew carried over his mother's beating and now her death. He'd never come out and said as much, but he'd hinted at having wished he'd stood up to his father. Intervened somehow. Grace had seen the self-blame again tonight in the hollowness of Josh's eyes when she'd tucked him into bed. Ten years old, and he'd seen so much; suffered so much. How would she ever begin to put him back together?

She turned on the water again, splashed a final handful over her face, and then reached for a hand towel. She'd figure it out. Somehow, because she had no choice, she would figure out what to do. How she would manage. How she would heal this broken family.

But she would start tomorrow, because tonight...she met her

gaze in the mirror and smiled sadly at her reflection. Tonight, she was tired. Tonight, she had lost her sister and her best friend. And tonight—she reached up, switched off the light, and opened the door. Tonight, Sean had made tea for her, and that would be enough.

She looked in on each of the kids as she made her way to the kitchen. Josh had fallen asleep curled tightly into a fetal position; Sage and Lilliane were spooned together, with Lilliane's arm around her sister's waist; and Annabelle slept soundly with both her arms thrown over her head. For the moment, each had found peace, and for that, Grace felt supreme gratitude. She closed the last door softly and then went to join Sean.

He glanced up at her approach, his mouth curved in a smile but his brow creased in concern. He nodded at the hallway from which she'd just come. "All quiet down there?"

"They're out cold," she replied. Sean had already spread a blanket over the couch and placed a pillow there, so she took the tray from the counter and carried it to the table.

Sean joined her, easing himself into a chair. He reached for the teapot and poured for both of them. Grace watched, envying the quiet strength emanating from him, wishing she knew how to absorb it for herself. For all of them. Sean slid her cup toward her.

"Penny for them?" he offered.

She shook her head. "They're not worth it. Not tonight. I'm just..."

"Worn down to nothing?"

"Yes. That."

"I'll make breakfast for the kids in the morning," he said. "You can sleep in. It will do you good."

"Thank you, but I doubt I'll sleep much at all, to be honest. And Luc is coming out to check on us tomorrow. I don't know when he'll get here, but I should be up for him."

"Will he make the arrangements for your sister?"

Grace nodded, then swallowed. "Yes, but I won't be going."

Sean's mouth formed a hard line.

"Barry." It was a statement, not a question.

"He was seen at the hospital a couple of times. They think he's been watching for me. I can't take the chance, not with the kids." She stared out the window into the dark beyond, her jaw flexing. "He kills my sister, and then I can't even go to her funeral because of him. Do you know how wrong that is?"

"They'll get him, Grace. They'll get him, and he'll pay for what he did. I promise."

"Not enough, he won't. Not for the damage he's caused."

"It's never enough," he said. "But you'll find a way to reconcile yourself to that and move on."

"Will I?" Disbelief sat bitter on her tongue.

Sean's hand covered hers. Squeezed. She let his silent compassion wash over her. Through her. For a moment—a heartbeat—the words *hold me* hovered on her lips. Then she returned the gentle pressure of his hand, pulled away from his grasp and set her cup back on the tray.

"I'm tired," she said. "If you don't mind, I think I'll skip the tea and just turn in."

Sean remained at the table long after Grace disappeared down the hallway and closed her door. Staring out into the night, he rested an elbow on the table, thumb hooked under his chin and fingers across his mouth. Every fiber of his being ached to go after her. To hold her and comfort her and tell her it would be all right. Except she was right. It wouldn't be, not even when Barry was caught and put behind bars.

Because even then, Julianne would still be dead, and those poor kids would still be without their mother, and Grace—Grace would still need to be stronger than anyone should ever have to be.

Small comfort that reminder would be to her.

Sean's fingers curled into a fist over his mouth. Fourteen years as a cop, and he'd never before felt this helpless. Never before had he wanted to toss the law he served to the four winds, track down a suspect, and mete out the brand of justice Barry Walsh *really* deserved.

The realization he might be capable of doing just that was a sobering one. So were the reasons behind it. All five of them. Four of whom slept peacefully—for now, at least—and one he suspected would lie as wide awake tonight as he did. Although likely not for the same reasons.

He sighed and twisted around in his chair so he could reach his crutches, then levered himself upright. Turning off lights as he went, he moved through the kitchen and into the living room, ending at the couch. He settled there, plumping up the pillow he'd brought from Grace's room. The faint scent of strawberries lifted from it as it had the first night he'd stayed here. His fingers stilled for a second, then smoothed the fabric where her head would have rested. He pictured her alone in bed, lying awake, trying to make sense of a life that had been ripped apart.

Damn it to hell and back.

Helpless didn't even begin to describe the knot in his chest.

With a sigh, he pulled his t-shirt over his head and dropped it on the coffee table. Then he switched off the lamp beside the couch, stretched out, and pulled the blanket over him.

Standing with her back pressed to the bedroom door, Grace listened to the soft breathing of her niece in the playpen nearby, the sounds of Sean settling on the couch in the living room. She hadn't been able to tell him, but she was glad he'd decided to stay. Just knowing he was near made a difference. It made the world a little less empty...at least for now. Her breath caught in a half sob. She pressed a hand over her mouth. Squeezed her eyes closed against the burn of yet more tears.

Juli was gone.

She'd been there a moment ago.

And now she wasn't.

Now she was just...gone.

Grace slid to the floor. She hugged her knees, her chest aching and lungs on fire with a grief that wanted to wail and scream and gnash its teeth, but couldn't.

Couldn't because she was needed. Relied on. Because someone had to stay strong for Josh and Sage and Lilly and Annabelle, and she was their only remaining someone. All that stood between them and the monster of a father who had killed their mother.

All they had left.

Across the room, Annabelle moved in her sleep, took a deep breath, sighed. A single tear escaped Grace. She looked over at her bed, captured in a moonbeam that filtered through the trees outside. With its mound of pillows and flannel-covered duvet, it should have looked inviting, but instead it looked cold. Stark. As empty as the world felt without the one person in it who had always been there for her.

The endless loop in her brain started again. How would they manage? How would she ever learn to be both mother and father to four damaged children? What if she wasn't enough? What if—

Grace pressed the heels of her hands against her eyes and groaned. Dear God, could she please—just for a little while— stop *thinking?* She sucked in a deep breath. Held it. Released it in a quavering sigh. Maybe she should have had that whiskey after all. Maybe she should have had the entire damned bottle, if only to knock herself out for the night.

But she had been right. It wouldn't have helped, because nothing would have changed. Juli would still be dead, and Barry would still be hunting them, and the kids would still need her, and she would still be alone and scared and—

Hold me, her brain whispered.

She froze. For the first time since the phone call from Luc, her mind stilled. And then, in the midst of the fear and the chaos— and now the grief—that defined her life, a single thought rose above all others. A need.

The soul-deep ache for the touch of another human being.

A desire to feel alive and whole and grounded and...

Sean.

Of their own accord, her legs propelled her upward. Her hand turned the doorknob. Her feet carried her silently from the room. Down the hall. A full moon shone through the uncurtained windows, bathing the room in cold white light. Bright enough to see Sean look over at her approach. To meet the concern in his gaze.

"Grace? What's wrong?"

She wrapped her arms around herself. Shivered. The temperature had dropped tonight. She should have thought to start a fire in the wood stove. It would be cold in the morning without it.

Sean sat up, pushing the cover aside. "Grace?"

She pressed her lips together. Inhaled through flared nostrils. "Don't judge me," she said. "Please don't. Because I know I'm asking a lot, and I know it's wrong, but I need—I need—"

"What, sweetheart?"

Her jaw locked. Her shivers increased.

I need to be held.

Sean grabbed his crutches and raised himself up on them. Real worry creased his brow now. "Grace, what's wrong? What do you need?"

Her teeth chattered. She shook her head mutely.

I need not to think.

Sean crossed the floor to her. Crutches pinned in place under his arms, he lifted his hands to her shoulders. "Damn it, Grace, you're starting to scare me. Talk to me."

I need...

The thought faded, half-formed, eluding her. She closed her eyes. Dug deep for a fragment of the fortitude that had kept her going all day, and whispered, "Hold me?"

Sean exhaled in a gust. "Is that all?" he murmured, pulling her into his arms as he had before and resting his chin against her hair. "Of course I'll hold you. I'll hold you for as long as you need, Grace Daniels."

His chest was bare. Muscled. Solid. Grace inhaled his clean

male warmth.

"Not like that," she said. She felt him draw back a little. The scattering of crisp hairs across his chest prickled her cheek.

"I don't understand."

She found another scrap of strength and lifted her head, leaning back until she could meet his gaze. Even in the bright moonlight, it was shadowed and hard to read. She hoped hers was equally hidden by the night. She shook her head.

"I don't want you to hold me like that."

I need...

Again the thought escaped. She lifted a hand. Smoothed it along the line of his shoulder. Felt him go still.

"Grace—"

"I need to be held," she said. That wasn't quite it, but it would do. She trailed fingertips down the center of his chest and over the lines of his rigid abdomen, traced along the edge of the jeans he had unsnapped. His breath turned ragged.

I need...

"Grace, I—"

"I need to forget. Just for tonight. No strings," she said. And then the wisp of thought that had been hounding her, half formed and fragile, finally completed itself. "I promise. I just need you, Sean. Please."

CHAPTER 33

Grace left him in the middle of the night. Sean felt her stir, felt her warmth draw away from his side, felt the care in her movements as she tried not to wake him. Part of him wanted to whisper her name, to reach out and pull her back into the nest of covers they're created on the floor of the living room, to wrap her in his arms and hold the world and her pain at bay for just a little longer.

A greater part held him silent, knowing she would resist. *No strings,* she'd said. This had been a one-time thing. A need he had been only too willing to fulfill for her. But every touch, every kiss, every whimper of pleasure he'd drawn from her had wrapped another gossamer-fine thread of steel around him and around his heart.

Or perhaps they'd just revealed the bonds already in existence.

Gareth's voice came back to him from the previous afternoon. *"You're more than halfway in love with her."*

He'd known then that Gareth was right. Tonight had proved it.

But he still didn't call Grace back to him as, slender and ethereal in the moonlight, she gathered up her scattered clothing. He still didn't let her know he was awake as she padded down the hallway toward her room, her footsteps nearly soundless. He didn't speak. She didn't look back. Her bedroom door closed with a soft click.

His thoughts followed her on a sigh. *I love you, Grace Daniels.*

He stared up at the shadowed ceiling. *I love you.* So many times tonight, the words had nearly spilled from his lips, but he'd caught them back for a multitude of reasons. A multitude of doubts. Grace came as part of a package deal he'd sworn never to take on. As wonderful as the kids were, they were still a permanent fixture in her life—and not one that he could afford to take lightly. For all their sakes. He'd seen too many families crumble under the weight of poorly thought-out good intentions. He'd been on the receiving end of those intentions himself as a kid—more times than he cared to count.

Love Grace he might, but would that be enough?

Grace slid into bed, shivering at the cold of the duvet cover against her skin. Skin warmed by Sean, still bearing his scent, the imprints of his touch, his kisses. She stared at the outline of the window and the tangle of branches it framed, black against the moonlit sky. A sigh trembled from her lips. Damn. That had so not worked out the way it was supposed to. Oh, it had served the purpose she'd intended. For a little while—a few moments suspended forever in time—she'd achieved exactly what she'd wanted. Forgetfulness. Life. Connection. The very thorough fulfillment of her needs.

What she hadn't expected was the all-new sense of loss that came with it. The realization, as Sean's hand glided over her belly and the curve of her hip, that this was it, this was all she would get. And she wanted so much more. Within a heartbeat, the act of sex she'd sought had become something else. Something more. Something so bittersweet that it had taken away her breath.

Grace closed her eyes.

She loved him. She loved him, but nothing could come of it because she wouldn't risk the kids—couldn't risk them. Not for him, not for anything. So right in the middle of losing Julianne, she would have to give him up, too.

She waited for the tears, but none came. At last she decided that perhaps she'd just done all the thinking and feeling one person could manage in one day. Perhaps some part of her brain—wiser than the rest of her—had shut itself down out of sheer self-preservation, knowing she had reached her limits. Surpassed them. With another sigh, she rolled over to face the wall and let sleep reach up from the depths of exhaustion to claim her.

Tomorrow she would deal with Juli and the kids and the rest of her life.

Tonight, it was enough to allow the memory of strong arms to hold her and grant her the illusion of security.

They met again over pancakes in the morning, a discombobulated bunch held together by the cheerful chatter of their youngest member. Sean flipped pancakes at the stove. Grace carried them to the table as they were done. The three eldest ate in silence.

It was a day like any other, but not. The thread of hope they'd all guarded—silently, carefully—had disintegrated, leaving them in the same life they'd been living for the last month, but one that had irrevocably changed. They all felt it. All but Annabelle. It left Grace floundering, at a loss as to what to do, what to say...

How to fix it.

She returned to the kitchen with the empty platter and

watched while Sean loaded it up with fresh pancakes. His fingers closed over her wrist when she would have turned away.

Reluctantly, she lifted her gaze to his. They'd exchanged only the most mundane words so far: *good morning, would you like coffee, how many pancakes will the kids eat, are you hungry?* Somehow, it made the new awareness between them bearable—even as the thought of losing him became increasingly less so.

Sean pitched his voice low. "They'll be okay, you know. Kids are stronger than we give them credit for."

She nodded. Having survived the loss of both her own parents at a young age, she knew that. Knew—in her head—that as awful as this time was for them, they would survive. Her heart, however, was a whole other matter.

"I just wish I could make it all go away," she murmured, looking over at the table. "They're all so young. Childhood isn't supposed to be like this."

"You're right. It's not. But it will get better."

"Will it?"

Sean cupped her chin and lifted until her gaze met his again. "I have absolute faith that it will," he said, giving her a smile that warmed her a little. "Because you'll make it better. Just give yourself time and—"

"And?"

He hesitated, then shook his head. "Trust yourself," he said. "Give yourself time, and trust yourself. You can do this."

It hadn't been what he'd started to say, she was sure, but she accepted the words with a nod. Partly because she wanted to believe him, and partly because she didn't want to think about what she'd hoped he'd say. *Give yourself time and let me help you. Let me be there for you.* She turned away to carry the platter to the table.

Sean left after breakfast. She saw him to the door, waiting as he shrugged into his jacket, at a loss for words. What could she say to the man who had helped her cope with the magnitude of yesterday in the way that he had? The man who had so readily been there for her children in one moment and then for her in another? *Thank you* seemed inadequate on some levels and just plain wrong on others.

The *please stay* that hovered was even more wrong.

Digging her fingers into her ribcage, Grace shored up her resolve. *No strings,* she'd promised him, and she would keep that promise. No matter how much it made her battered heart bleed.

Sean zipped his jacket and tucked his crutches back under his arms. "I'm going to make some calls today," he said. "To find out where things stand with the investigation."

"You can do that?" The idea surprised her. She hadn't considered the possibility.

Amusement crinkled the corners of his eyes. "I'm fairly certain they'll let me into the loop," he said. "Me being a cop and all. I would have done so sooner, but my cell phone died, and I had to wait for Gareth to bring me the charger. Why don't you send Josh to get me when Luc leaves? I'll come over and make dinner, and I can fill you in then."

Her head was shaking before he finished. "You don't need to do that—dinner, I mean. We've asked enough of you."

A sandy brow shot up, then moved down to meet its partner. "Seriously?"

She couldn't hold his gaze. Not when he scowled that way. Not when her words she needed to speak were the polar opposite of what she wanted to say. "I meant what I said last night, Sean.

About no strings. You don't need to feel obligated to—"

"Grace."

She closed her mouth with a snap. Stared at the floor. Flinched at his impatient sigh.

"You really are the most impossible woman," he growled. His voice had dropped to a level curious ears wouldn't be able to hear. "Send Josh to get me when Luc leaves. I'll make dinner. I'll fill you in on what I find out about Barry. Then, after the kids go to bed, we talk."

His hand brushed back her hair, a gentle gesture so unexpected that she raised her gaze to his without thinking. Banked heat glowed in the green eyes.

"We talk," he repeated. "And we clear the air between us, because we can't keep this up. I won't keep this up. Understand?"

She hesitated, and then, because there really was no other response she could make, she nodded. He was right. There were words that needed to be said, decisions that needed to be made. Maybe by tonight, she would be strong enough to make them.

Sean leaned in to feather a kiss across her lips, startling her into going rigid.

"And that," he drawled, opening the door beside him, "is a part of what we'll talk about. Tell Luc I said hi."

The crunch of tires across gravel heralded the arrival of a vehicle just after lunchtime. Grace swept the last of the crumbs from the counter into the sink, then draped the dishcloth over the tap to dry. The kids looked up in unison from the kitchen table, where they'd hauled out their art supplies to make thank you cards for the nurses who had cared for their mother. It had been

Lilly's suggestion, and Grace still carried the lump in her throat from it.

"That'll be Mr. Tremaine," she said. "I'll go out and meet him."

"Do you want us to clear the table?" Josh asked.

"No, it's fine. We can have tea in the living room."

Wiping her hands on the seat of her jeans, she went to the door, opened it, and stepped out onto the porch. She closed the door behind her again, thankful for the warmth of the fall day that would let her and Luc remain outside for a few minutes. She had questions for him—things they needed to discuss— that the kids didn't need to hear. On the other side of the van, out of sight, a car door opened, then slammed. Grace smiled, descending the stairs to the grass and walking out to meet her friend. Despite the circumstances that had brought him here, it would be good to see a familiar face again. Very good.

Footsteps moved across the gravel. She reached the halfway point to the driveway as a man stepped out from behind the van. Her eyes widened. Her smile dropped into oblivion. The blood in her veins turned to ice.

Barry.

CHAPTER 34

Grace spun around in a race to the cottage. To safety. To the kids.

Their father was faster.

Heart pounding, she skidded to a stop as Barry faced her from the foot of the stairs, baseball bat swinging from one hand, blocking her way.

"Hello, Grace," he said. "Long time, no see."

Somewhere in the trees beyond the lawn, a blue jay scolded loudly and a red squirrel trilled an indignant response. Both sounds faded into the silence of the forest. The vastness between the cottage and civilization. Between them and help. Grace's stomach twisted. Heaved. She swallowed against the bile of sheer terror.

He'd found them. Barry had found them, and no one knew he was here, and now she was all that stood between him and Juli's children. *Her* children. Calm descended. She unclenched her hands, shifted her stance, stilled her mind. Her heart rate slowed. This was what she'd trained for, she thought. All those hours of practice, all that discipline, it had been for this moment. This fight.

She could do this.

She had to do this.

Barry advanced toward her.

Sean picked up his cell phone from the counter on the third ring. He glanced at the unfamiliar number on the display, then flicked the answer icon with his thumb. "Hello?"

"Sean, it's Luc Tremaine, your cottage neighbor. Is Grace with you?"

Sean frowned. "No. Why?"

"I tried to call her to tell her I'll be late, but she's not answering. And I think we might have a problem."

A chill snaked down Sean's spine. "What problem?"

"The cops have just cleared my condo. There was a break-in this morning while I was at the funeral home for Julianne, but there's nothing missing. At least, I thought there was nothing missing, but I've just realized I might be wrong. I keep a file for the cottage. There's a map in there that I photocopy for people who are driving out there for the first time, and—"

"The map is missing?" Sean interrupted.

"Yes. Barry's been seen a couple of times at the hospital, and it's possible he may have followed me home from there yesterday."

"How long ago? The break-in. How long ago was it?"

"Two hours, tops. Long enough to find the map and get out to—"

"He's here," Sean said hoarsely. "I heard a car go by five minutes ago."

"Oh, my God. Grace...the kids..."

Sean shoved aside the gut-deep terror wrenching at him. Crystal-clear thinking took over. The training of a cop. "I'm on my way to her," he said. "Call 911 and tell them what's happening. Give them directions. Give them my name and tell them I said it's a code 10-33. Have you got that?"

"Ten thirty-three," Luc repeated. The code for *officer needs assistance* that would guarantee the fastest possible arrival of the cavalry. "Got it. And Sean, for God's sake, be careful. He's—"

"Call," Sean snapped.

He dropped the phone on the counter, swiveled, and started for the sliding door. His crutch caught on the metal sill as he stepped through, and he stumbled. He stopped on the deck. Regained his balance. Closed his eyes. He couldn't screw this up. He drew a breath through his nostrils, exhaled through his mouth. Grace needed him. The kids needed him. Fingers clamped securely over the crutch handgrips, he started out again. Grim concentration marked every swing of his body between the crutches, every planting of their rubber tips on the deck, the stairs, the ground.

Hang in there, sweetheart. I'm coming.

From just inside the trees, Sean watched Barry Walsh circle Grace for the third time. She turned with him, just out of reach of the bat in his hands, her stance relaxed, watchful. Ready for his attack. An untrained opponent would have gone at her by now. Would have taken a swing and been disarmed. But Walsh was far from untrained and, within the force, had the reputation of never having lost a street fight. He would also know about Grace's martial arts experience. He wouldn't underestimate her.

Sean willed her not to underestimate him.

Walsh began a fourth circuit, then made a sudden feint to the left. Grace ignored it. Walsh scowled and the bat swung a little faster. Sean's lips curved in a tight smile. *So there, you bastard.*

A fifth circuit. Another ignored feint.

Sean ached to leave the shelter of the trees, to let Grace know he was there, but he didn't dare interrupt her focus. One crack in her vigilance and Walsh would be on her in a flash. She was good. She was very good, and much as it killed him to stand by helplessly, she was best left to finish what Walsh had started—her way. Sooner or later, he'd get impatient and take that swing at her, and then she'd have him. Of that, Sean had absolutely no doubt.

Strength and control emanated from her. He could feel the energy from here. She owned this, and he didn't think any woman had ever looked more beautiful.

Two more feints in quick succession. Walsh's scowl deepened. Darkened. He was getting edgy.

Go for it, you prick, Sean urged him. *I dare you.*

And then, the unthinkable. Movement from the cottage. The opening of a door. Josh stepping onto the porch, calling his aunt's name in a quavering, terrified voice. Distracting Grace for the split-second Walsh needed to swing the bat.

Sean burst from the trees with a yell. Grace's attention snapped back to her opponent, too late to stop the blow but maybe—maybe—soon enough to save her life. Bat and bone connected. Grace dropped without a sound. Sean yelled again.

"Walsh!"

Barry Walsh's head snapped up. He stared across the lawn. His gaze narrowed. "I know you," he said.

Sean slowed his pace, not daring to risk a fall. "Josh," he called. "Get back in the cottage and lock the door. Whatever happens, you stay inside, understand? The police are on their way."

Grace.

Tears streaming down his face, Josh nodded and stepped back toward the door. Walsh's voice stopped him.

"Hold up there, son. He doesn't give the orders, I do." He lifted the bat and rested it over one shoulder. Then he placed a booted foot on Grace's prone figure. "McKittrick, isn't it? You're famous after getting yourself shot up like that. How's the leg?"

Sean continued across the grass, trying not to look at Grace. He divided his focus between the man standing over her and the boy on the porch. "I meant what I said, Walsh. Backup's on the way. They'll be here any minute. Josh, inside."

"Josh, stay where you are," Walsh snapped. Then he snorted. "I just made the drive out here, McKittrick, remember? I know how long it'll take them, and I'll be long gone before then. Josh, get your sisters. Put your shoes and coats on, and come get in the van. Bring the keys."

"Don't do it—" Sean began.

"Would you just *shut up*?" Walsh scowled at him. "I came for my kids, and I'm taking them. I don't care if I have to break down every door in the place and drag them out screaming, so why don't we save them the additional trauma and let them do as I ask? Josh, your sisters."

Josh hesitated, and his father's furious gaze swung to him. "Did you hear me? Now!"

The boy visibly jumped, then scurried backward into the cottage, tripping over the doorsill. He disappeared from view. Walsh turned his attention back to Sean.

"You may as well stop there," he said. "You and I both know you don't stand a chance in hell."

"I just want to check on Grace."

Walsh prodded her in the back with his boot. "She's still breathing. That's good enough for now." He looked up. "I said stop."

Sean stopped. On the ground, Grace's eyes opened. Her gaze met his, glazed with pain but otherwise clear. Focused. Determined. With a monumental effort, Sean didn't react. He looked up at Walsh again. He had to keep him talking. Keep him distracted. He couldn't know that Grace was still conscious.

"You know you won't get far."

"I know I'll have a pretty good head start," Walsh shrugged and his eyes turned flat. Expressionless. "And I don't need to go far, anyway. Not for what I need to do."

Grace flinched at the words, and her brother-in-law looked down. Sean's blood ran cold. He started forward again, drawing Walsh's scowl back to him. Walsh hefted the baseball bat and nestled the end of it against Grace's head.

"What part of *stop* do you not under—"

In the blink of an eye, Grace grabbed his pant leg, gave a vicious pull, and toppled him to the ground. He landed with a grunt but even as she climbed to her feet, he rolled away and regained his, too. He still held the bat.

And Grace's left arm hung useless at her side.

Sean gauged the distance, dropped one of his crutches, hefted the other in both hands, and swung hard. He connected with the baseball bat. If he'd had both legs under him, it probably would have been enough to disarm the other man. Instead, the impact knocked the crutch from his grasp and him to the ground. Walsh kicked away his would-be weapon and only way of getting upright again, and then it was just him circling Grace once more.

A disabled Grace whose breath came in pained gasps.

They all knew there could be only one outcome this time.

Then the cottage door opened, and there came the unmistakable sound of a cartridge being chambered in a shotgun.

Through a haze of pain, Grace saw her brother-in-law step back. He looked over at the cottage, but she didn't think for an instant that his attention had left her. Even if it had, there was little she could do. Not with a broken arm. All she could do—all *they* could do, because Sean was just as much a part of this as any of them—was keep Barry distracted. Delay him until the police got here. Keep him from taking the kids and—

Grace left the thought unfinished. Focused instead on the boy standing on the porch. The boy pointing the shotgun at his father.

"Move away from them," Josh said, his voice cracking. Despite the tear stains on his face and the tremble of the weapon in his hands, his gaze was calm and determined. Too much so.

Grace drew a sharp breath.

A dozen feet away, Barry laughed at his son. "Are you kidding me? You don't know how to shoot, you idiot. And even if you did, you don't have the balls—"

The shotgun roared. The sound rolled out over the lake and bounced back in echo after fainter echo until it faded to nothing, leaving a stunned silence in its wake. Josh lowered the weapon from its aim at the sky. He pumped out the spent cartridge and leveled the gun again in Barry's direction.

"I mean it, Dad. Move away."

A single fresh tear tracked down his cheek. His finger tightened on the trigger. Grace's heart contracted. *Oh God, Josh...no.*

She looked at Barry. At his slack-jawed, disbelieving focus on his son.

Now.

Hugging her broken arm close, she gritted her teeth and buried the pain. Then she stepped past Sean and propelled herself off the ground into a spin, delivering the most vicious roundhouse kick she could summon to the back of Barry's head. He pitched forward onto his hands and knees on the grass, the baseball bat flying from his grip. Before he could recover, Grace landed, rebalanced, and caught him under the chin with a snap kick. He rolled onto his back, gave a single weak flop, and then lay still. Breathing hard, Grace stood over him, watching for him to move, wishing for the slightest twitch of a finger so she could deliver yet another blow.

He remained motionless.

She began to shake. Slowly she sank to the ground beside the man who had killed her sister. From a distance, she heard Sean's voice coaxing Josh to let go of the shotgun. She turned her head to find him on the porch beside her nephew, prying the weapon from the boy's fingers, laying it aside, pulling the boy down into a hug, rocking him gently. His gaze met hers over Josh's head.

"Are you okay?" he mouthed.

She made herself nod. His mouth curved into a faint, tight smile. Banked heat reached out from the green eyes to wrap her in its warmth, easing the shaking. The door behind him opened, and Sage and Lilly ventured onto the porch with Annabelle, each of them clutching one of the toddler's hands. Sean waved them over, settled Annabelle on his lap, and wrapped his free arm around both the other girls. His smile widened. He cleared his throat.

"Hey, Grace Daniels. You know I love you, right?"

Grace went still. Even her shivers stopped. "What?"

"I was going to tell you later," he said. "Then I decided now was better. I love you."

"Man owie," Annabelle patted his cast. She pointed to her unconscious father. "More owie."

The other three gazed between Grace and Sean with wide eyes, their mouths forming perfect o's.

"I—I—" Grace stammered.

"You love me, too," he coaxed.

"But you don't want kids."

Sage's bottom lip quivered, and Sean snugged her closer to his side.

"Turns out I do," he said comfortably. "But not just any kids. These ones. I want these ones."

For a long moment, Grace couldn't say anything past the lump in her throat. Josh, Lilliane, and Sage all watched her with wide, expectant eyes. Faint in the distance came the wail of a siren. She cleared her throat.

"Hey, Sean McKittrick," she said. "You know I love you, too, right?"

He grinned. "I suspected as much. But it's nice to know."

CHAPTER 35

Grace watched the ER doctor smooth the final coat of plaster on the cast encasing her arm. A tap came at the door, and it opened to admit a nurse followed closely by Sage, Lilly, Josh, and Sean. The nurse smiled.

"We were getting a little concerned," she said. "We thought we'd check on your progress."

Lilly came to stand beside Grace, Sage pressed close to her side.

"Another cast?" Lilly shook her head and sent an exasperated glance between Grace and Sean. "What are we going to do with you two?"

Sean chuckled. "Help us heal, I hope," he said. "We're all going to have to pitch in and give Aunt Grace a hand. No pun intended."

Josh joined his sisters. "Does it hurt?"

"A little, but they've given me something to help with the pain. I'll be fine." Grace lifted her good hand to her nephew's shoulder and tugged him close enough to kiss the top of his head. "As good as new. I promise."

"It's a clean break," the doctor said to Sean. "She'll be in the cast for about six weeks, give or take, but she can have her own doctor check it after five."

He peeled off his plaster-coated latex gloves, rolled away on his stool, and dropped them into the garbage bin by the counter.

"Keep it dry, and remember it won't be fully hardened for at least twenty-four to forty-eight hours, so no handstands or back flips." He gave the kids a wink, but none of them laughed. He raised an eyebrow. "I usually get at least a chuckle out of that one."

He did then, but from Sean rather than the kids.

"Grace holds a black belt in jujitsu and tae kwon do," Sean told him. "I don't think we realized you were joking."

Appearing somewhat nonplussed, the doctor muttered a farewell and left the room. Sean looked to the kids.

"You three want to go and help Uncle Gareth with Annabelle?" he asked. "Make sure she doesn't tear the place apart?"

"Sure." Josh gathered up his sisters, lingered long enough to give Grace a careful hug, and then the three of them followed the nurse from the room.

"Uncle Gareth?" Grace asked as the door closed behind them.

Sean gave her a lopsided grin. "I hope you don't mind. It seemed more appropriate that Mr. Connor under the circumstances."

Far from minding, Grace felt a curl of warmth at the idea. And at the reason behind it. But the *uncle* part wasn't what she'd been asking about.

"Of course I don't mind. I just wondered how your cousin managed to end up on Annabelle duty."

"I called him when you left in the ambulance. He arrived about twenty minutes ago. He and Gwyn are going to take the kids for us tonight. He'll leave us his car and take the van back to their place, and we can follow tomorrow when I've sobered up again from the drugs. He's booked us into a hotel for tonight. We'll cab it over when they release you."

Grace glanced at his leg. Today's fall had been the third for him. "How bad is it?"

"Sore, but surprisingly intact. They'll send the x-ray to my orthopedist to be sure, but it looks like nothing's moved."

Thank God.

Sean swung over to the exam table. He set his crutches aside and, with both hands, smoothed back the hair from her face. Then he pressed a kiss to her forehead. "You scared the hell out of me today, you know."

Her brain flashed back to the impact of the baseball bat against the forearm she'd thrown up in defense. The crack of the bone giving way. The knowledge that if Barry had connected with her skull as intended...

She gave Sean a wan smile. "I don't mind admitting I scared the hell out of me, too."

Sean rested his forehead against hers. "I'm not surprised. I have to tell you, though, the way you took him down? Those kicks? I don't think I've ever seen anything more magnificent in my life. You saved their lives, Grace."

"Do you think he really would have done it?" Tears squeezed between her eyelids. Even now, her brain couldn't quite wrap itself around the idea. "His own kids?"

"I know he would have," Sean said gruffly. "I've seen it happen before."

"What happens to him now?"

"He'll be charged with your sister's murder, and I'm guessing the Crown will add four counts of attempted kidnapping with intent. I'll find out more after his arraignment."

"And until then?"

"He'll be held in custody until his trial." Sean's arms tightened around her. "And then, with luck, for the rest of his life. At the very least, he won't be eligible for parole for at least twenty-five years, so you and the kids are safe, sweetheart. You can breathe again."

Silence settled between them. Out in the corridor, something rolled by, and shoes squeaked against tile. Grace nestled into Sean's shoulder. Barry might be out of the way—figuratively as well as literally—but one more pressing matter still stood between her and breathing.

"Can I ask you something?"

"The answer is yes."

"Yes, I can ask?"

"Yes to your question."

"But you don't know what it is."

"You want to know if I meant what I said at the cottage," he replied comfortably. "About loving you. The answer is yes. The other answers are no, yes, and no. No, I don't think it's because of the circumstances or any inflated sense of honor or responsibility. Yes, I meant what I said about wanting the kids. And no, I don't need time to think it over. I already have."

Grace pulled back. She wanted to believe him—with all her heart and soul, she wanted to believe him—but so much had happened. So many emotions had ridden so high for so long...

She took a deep breath and braced herself.

"When?" she asked. "When have you had time to think about it, Sean? About any of it? We've known each other for a week. We haven't had time for—"

He put a single finger across her lips. His bottle-green eyes glowed with intensity. Absolute certainty. Bottomless love. Grace inhaled a soft breath.

"From the time Luc called me today until the time you took that bastard down," he said, his voice quiet, "I lived a hundred thousand lifetimes, Grace Daniels. I saw what my world would be like without you, without those kids, and I died a little inside. I died a lot. I love you. I love *them*. And I want nothing more than to spend every waking moment of my life showing you just how much. So yes, I meant it. Every single word. Understand?"

A hundred different emotions swamped her. Relief. Gratitude. Contentment. Overwhelming love. Sheer, unadulterated joy. She slid her good arm around Sean's back, clinging to him. Lifted her face. His head descended, his lips touched hers...

Another tap came at the door.

Sean drew back with a muttered curse as the nurse poked her head through the opening, her expression apologetic. "I'm sorry, but I gave you as long as I could. We need the plaster room for another patient."

Grace felt impatience thrum through Sean. Then he gave her a wry smile and nodded to the nurse. "Of course. We're coming now."

He shifted back onto his crutches. "Are you okay to walk?" he asked.

Grace snorted as she slid off the exam table. "Asked the man on crutches."

Sean looked from his own cast to hers, then followed her through the door the nurse held open for them. "We do make a fine pair, don't we? Talk about the halt and the lame."

Grace skidded to a stop and turned horrified eyes on him, the reality of their situation sinking in. Him on crutches, her in an arm cast, and four kids...

"How in heaven's name will we manage?" she asked.

Sean grinned and planted a kiss on her lips. She blinked at him.

"What was that for?"

He kissed her again. "You said *we*. As in you and me. How will we manage."

"Oh. I guess I did, didn't I?"

"Does that mean yes?"

"Yes, what?"

"Yes, you'll marry me?"

"I—" Grace paused. "Wait. Is that a proposal?"

"I suppose it is—unless you want me to wait until I can go down on one knee and ask properly."

She hesitated. Thought about it. Smiled. "The answers are yes, no, and no," she said. "Yes, I would be honored to marry you. No, I don't want you to go down on one knee."

"And the other no?"

"I don't need time to think over, either." She stood on tiptoe, balanced carefully against his chest, and placed her lips beside his ear. "I love you, Sean McKittrick. Now, let's go say goodbye to our kids and then check out that hotel, shall we?"

"Why, Grace Daniels, you can't possibly be suggesting..." Sean looked down in such shock that Grace laughed.

"Am I suggesting we figure out how the heck we'll get it on with both of us half-encased in plaster? Absolutely. You have a lot of dreams to answer for, you know." She started down the corridor toward the waiting room, and their waiting kids.

Sean caught up to her just before the double doors. "Dreams?"

"Mmm-hmm." She slanted a sideways glance at him. "Shockingly creative ones, I might add."

He grinned, a wicked gleam entering his eyes. "Do tell."

"Oh, I will," she promised, pushing through the doors. "In great detail."

Then the kids were there, and Annabelle was delivering kisses-better, and Sean's cousin was hugging her, and the comfortable chaos of family—their family, hers and Sean's—closed around them.

And as her good arm pulled in as many people as it would hold, Grace felt the brush of her sister's presence, saw her smile, heard her words.

"Together always," Julianne said.

"Together always," Grace whispered to her family. "I promise."

Sean's hand settled onto her shoulder and squeezed.

OTHER BOOKS BY LINDA POITEVIN

The Ever After Series
Gwynneth Ever After
Forever After (novella, e-book only)

The Grigori Legacy
Sins of the Angels (Grigori Legacy #1)
Sins of the Son (Grigori Legacy #2)
Sins of the Lost (Grigori Legacy #3)

About the Author

Linda Poitevin is the author of both contemporary romance and dark urban fantasy (respectively referred to by her spouse as her light and dark sides). In her other-than-writing life, she walks a giant dog and is minion to the world's cutest kitten. She's also a wife, mom, friend, coffee snob, gardener, and avid food preserver (you know, just in case that whole Zombie Apocalypse thing really happens).

She loves to hear from readers and can be contacted through her website at *www.lindapoitevin.com*.